The New Shell Guides

The Channel Islands

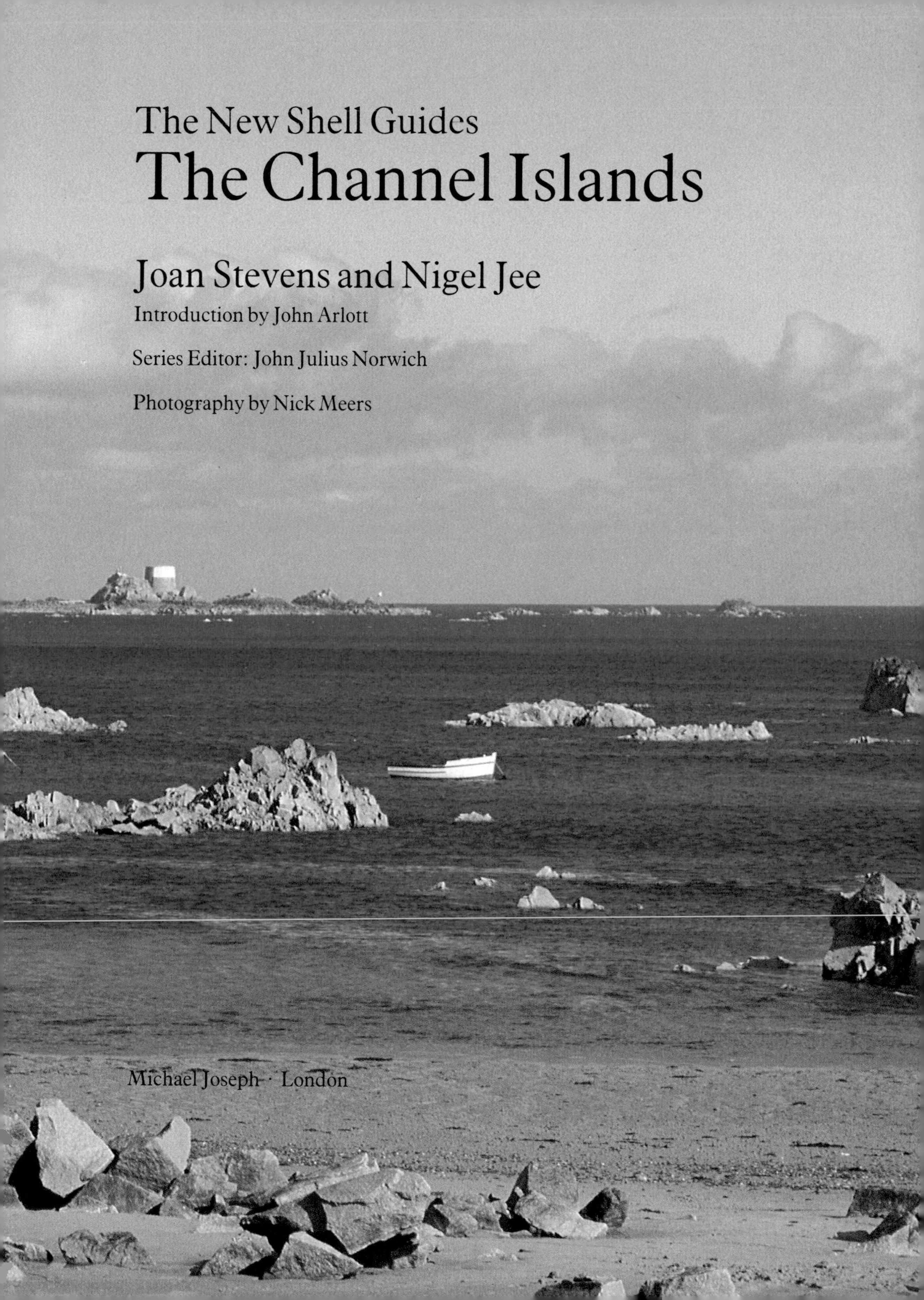

The New Shell Guides
The Channel Islands

Joan Stevens and Nigel Jee

Introduction by John Arlott

Series Editor: John Julius Norwich

Photography by Nick Meers

Michael Joseph · London

First published in Great Britain by
Michael Joseph Limited, 27 Wrights Lane,
London W8 5TZ 1987

This book was designed and produced by
Swallow Editions Limited, Swallow House,
11-21 Northdown Street, London N1 9BN

British Library Cataloguing in Publication Data:

Stevens, Joan
    The new Shell guide to the Channel Islands.
    1. Channel Islands — Description and travel — Guide-books
    I. Title   II. Jee, Nigel
    914.23′404858   DA670.C4

Cased edition: ISBN 0 7181 2760 9
Paperback edition: ISBN 0 7181 2765 X

Editor: Raymond Kaye
Cartographer: M L Design
Production: Hugh Allan

Filmset by SX Composing Limited, Rayleigh, England
Printed and bound by Kyodo-Shing Loong Printing, Singapore

The name Shell and the Shell emblem are registered trademarks

Shell UK Ltd would point out that the contributors views are
not necessarily those of this company.

The information contained in this book is believed correct at
the time of printing. While every care has been taken to ensure
that the information is accurate, the publishers and Shell can
accept no responsibility for any errors or omissions or for
changes in the details given.

A list of Shell publications
can be obtained by writing to:

Department UOMK/60
Shell UK Oil
PO Box No. 148
Shell-Mex House
Strand
London WC2R 0DX

*Front jacket photograph: Mont Orgueil Castle, Jersey
(see p. 57)
Back jacket photograph: A breuvoir (drinking trough) near
Red Houses, Jersey
Title-page: Icho Tower, St Clement's Bay, Jersey
(see p. 53)*

Contents

John Julius Norwich was born in 1929. He read French and Russian at New College, Oxford, and in 1952 joined the Foreign Office where he served until 1964. Since then he has published two books on the medieval Norman Kingdom in Sicily, *The Normans in the South* and *The Kingdom in the Sun*; two historical travel books, *Mount Athos* (with Reresby Sitwell) and *Sahara*; an anthology of poetry and prose, *Christmas Crackers*; and two volumes on the history of Venice, *Venice, The Rise to Empire* and *Venice, The Greatness and the Fall*, now published in one volume as *A History of Venice*. He was also general editor of *Great Architecture of the World* and, more recently, author of *The Architecture of Southern England*.

In addition, he writes and presents historical documentaries for BBC television and frequently broadcasts on BBC radio. He is chairman of the Venice in Peril Fund, a Trustee of the Civic Trust, and a member of the Executive and Properties Committee of the National Trust.

Joan Stevens (neé Collas), daughter of an army officer whose family came to Jersey in the fifteenth century, spent many years as the wife of an administrator in Africa. As her passion for the history of Jersey developed through her publications, she became a foremost authority on the subject. Her fluency in the French language was an enormous help in her historical work, for which she was awarded an MBE and FSA.

Nigel Jee's association with the Channel Islands began in 1952 when he was appointed biology master at Elizabeth College, Guernsey, where he taught for twenty years. He has a deep love of both the history and natural history of the Islands, and in the conservation of their unique natural and man-made environment. He was a founder member and later chairman of the National Trust of Guernsey; he is a past president of La Société Guernesiaise and editor of their annual *Transactions*. He is a member of the States of Guernsey and at present chairs the committees concerned with agriculture and island planning.

John Arlott was born in 1914 in Basingstoke and now lives in Alderney. He has written, co-authored or edited around eighty books and booklets since 1943. About three-quarters of these books are about cricket, with which his unmistakable Hampshire voice, so familiar to radio listeners, is synonymous. However, his career in wine has been nearly as long and prolific as that in cricket. As well as his regular column for the *Guardian* newspaper, he has contributed articles to a wide range if magazines.

Colin Partridge studied architecture at his home town of Cheltenham. After working in London, he moved to Guernsey in 1972 to develop his interest in military architecture. He is a member of the Fortress Study Group and a founder member of the Alderney Fortifications Centre.

Nick Meers was born in Gloucestershire in 1955 and gained a diploma from Guildford School of Photography in 1978. He brings to the New Shell Guides experience gained from landscape and wildlife assignments ranging from Canada's National Park to the Cayman Islands, from Ireland to Israel, from Wisconsin to West Africa.

Editorial Note

Each entry in the two Gazetteers has a map reference immediately after the heading. For example: Bonne Nuit Bay has the reference (2/4A). The figure 2 is the map number (see pp. 176-188) and 4A is the grid reference; 4 is the across and A the down reference.

Places printed in CAPITAL LETTERS within the text of an entry have separate entries under their own names in their respective Gazetteers.

Gazetteer entries are listed alphabetically. 'The', 'Le', 'La' and 'Les', if part of the name, follow the main element, i.e. Corbière, La (alphabetized under C) and Hospital, The (alphabetized under H). However, names beginning with L', such as L'Ancresse Bay, are alphabetized under L.

Statements about buildings, gardens etc. being open to the public, and at what times, are based on the latest information available at the time of going to press and are, of course, subject to alteration. It is prudent to apply locally for the most up-to-date details.

La Hougue Bie, Grouville, Jersey – a favourite place of the late Joan Stevens *(see p. 52)*

Acknowledgments

Guernsey Section

First I must record my gratitude to my co-author Joan Stevens, whose sudden death immediately after she had completed the Jersey section of this book was a tragic loss to her numerous friends in the Channel Islands and beyond.

I am most grateful to Roger and Margaret Long, to whom all my questions regarding Jersey were directed after Joan's death. Their forbearance and help were greatly appreciated. Finally I must thank my daughter-in-law, Maggie Jee, for deciphering and typing my manuscript.

Nigel Jee

Jersey Section

I would like to record my thanks to many of my colleagues and friends who have assisted me in compiling this work. In particular I would mention Mr P. Bisson, Mrs F. Le Sueur, Mr R. Mayne, Mr J. McCormack, Mr P. J. Romeril, and my co-author Mr N. Jee who has been subjected to many telephone calls. Most of all I thank my daughter Collette who has given me constant support, particularly with the cartography.

Joan Stevens

Introduction

JOHN ARLOTT

The people of mainland Britain generally know little about the Channel Islands – probably because school syllabuses virtually never include them. Although the islands are British, they are not part of the United Kingdom; and – by their own will – they are only Associate Members of the EEC. Lying within the Gulf of St Malo, geographically speaking, of course, they are French; and every island is within sight of France. Although they have never actually been French, France – where they are known as Les Îles Anglo-Normandes – has coveted them. They passed to the English crown when William Duke of Normandy made himself King of England in 1066, and they have been outstandingly loyal to that crown ever since. Victor Hugo, who lived many years in Jersey and Guernsey, described them as 'pieces of France fallen into the sea and gathered in by England'.

The Islands are divided into two Bailiwicks, each headed by a Bailiff. The Bailiwick of Guernsey is formed by two groups: the more northerly comprises Alderney (independent until 1948), with the lighthouse rocks of the Casquets and the unpopulated Burhou and Ortac; the more southerly, Guernsey itself, Sark (still a seigneurie with many unique rights of its own), Herm, Jethou and a few odd islets. The Jersey Bailiwick comprises that island and the islets of the Minquiers Reef and the Ecréhous. Spread across an arc of about 30 square miles of the English Channel, they cover an area of 75 square miles and have a population of about 130,000. By comparison the Isle of Wight is twice the area – 147 square miles – with a population of 122,900.

How they work

The islands owe their ultimate loyalty to the Duke of Normandy, who is also the monarch of England, in a line of contact running down from the Throne, through the Privy Council, the Home Secretary, the Lieutenant-Governors (the Monarch's representative in each Bailiwick) to the Bailiffs, who are chief magistrates and presidents of the States of their Bailiwicks. Since the middle of the 19th century the islands have advanced from the semi-feudal to the democratic. They are ruled by their own non-party-political parliaments called States, or, in Sark, the Court of Chief Pleas (which can be overruled by the Seigneur, but he, in turn, by the Guernsey States). Foreign policy and international relations, however, are handled by the British Foreign Office.

Until relatively recently the Norman-French patois of each island was the language of the people. A number of notices are still printed in standard French, but English is now the accepted language of business and – except in Sark and among some of the country people of Jersey and Guernsey – of general social life.

The law

Channel Islands law, completely unlike English, is based on the Norman. Each Bailiwick has a Court of Appeal; a Royal Court (founded by King John) which is

Petit Portelet Bay, Gorey, Jersey (see p. 62)

competent to try any offence except treason; and the Lower Courts, run by local magistrates or Jurats. There is also a court in Alderney and a Seneschal's Court in Sark. The two Bailiwicks administer their laws differently: Jersey through an Attorney-General and a Solicitor-General; Guernsey through a Procureur and a Comptroller; all are appointed by the Crown except the Crown Solicitor, nominated by the Attorney-General. The two legal systems are so different that a lawyer or advocate of one Bailiwick may not practise in the other.

One unique, and relatively uniform, item of Channel Islands law is the historic Clameur de Haro, originally an appeal to the legendary Rollo, first Duke of Normandy, by which an aggrieved citizen may call out a traditional formula at the scene of the offence, which must stop immediately. *(See p. 46.)*

The difference

The most common error of those who do not know the Channel Islands is mentally to lump them together. In fact, although attack from outside has always welded them into unity, they are highly individual, sharply and conspicuously different. Simply to hear an islander refer to the Muratti Vase (the inter-island soccer competition) as the 'internationals' is to recognize the distinction they feel. The situation probably was best set in perspective by Edith Carey when she wrote of the true Channel Islander: 'To the world in general he asserts himself an Englishman, but in the presence of the English he boasts of being a Jerseyman or a Guernseyman.'

At close quarters, these communities are so distinct that even the Norman-French patois of each island is different. Even identically spelled personal names come out differently. A declining number of people in Jersey and Guernsey still speak the patois; a greater proportion of those in Sark; none in Alderney, or Herm, for different reasons that will emerge. The respective patois are preserved and recorded by the Société Jersiaise and the Société Guernesiaise who also, like the Alderney Society on that island, maintain libraries and museums of immense value to historians, archaeologists and naturalists, and of interest to any visitor.

History

The islands have a long history, again quite unlike England's. Palaeolithic occupation is evidenced by such relics as human teeth and the other remains include the bones of the great auk and the woolly mammoth, now in the Jersey Museum. In about 6500 BC the melting of the great ice cap created the Channel Islands, separating them from the land mass of Europe. About 2000 BC settlers or emissaries from Iberia buried their royalty in the dolmens and erected the menhirs, to be found on several of the islands.

The waves of invasion from the east, which continued for about 800 years, began about 300 BC, when the Gallic Ugnelli from the opposite west coast of France – then known as Armorica – settled the islands. Then came the Romans, and Antoninus, in his itinerary of about AD 300, listed Caesarea, Sarnia and Riduna, generally accepted as Jersey, Guernsey and Alderney.

The Roman influence was mainly mercantile; but soon came the Saxon, Frankish and Frisian raiders who pillaged the entire coast and deposed the Roman ruler of Armorica. The Viking, Rollo, acquired Normandy from Charles the Simple of France in 911, became its chieftain and a Christian, instituted a feudal system and created the Clameur de Haro. Soon afterwards his son, William Longsword, added

The Albert Marina, St Peter Port, Guernsey (see p. 152)

the Channel Islands to his duchy. In 1035 his descendant, William II of Normandy, succeeded to the dukedom and, in 1066, conquered England; hence the comment that England is the oldest surviving possession of the Channel Islands. When France conquered Normandy (1204) the Channel Islands remained loyal to King John who, in return, granted them their first constitution and increased liberties.

They were to pay dearly for those privileges for on several occasions invading French forces captured and, if only briefly, held the islands; and from 1461 Jersey was occupied by the French, until the English fleet recaptured it in 1468. In 1483 Edward IV obtained from Pope Sixtus IV a Bull decreeing that, in the event of war, the islands should be treated as neutral. They were, however, so harassed by freebooters and privateers that Sixtus ordered the plundering to stop under penalty of excommunication.

There came a long period of peace. Sir Walter Raleigh became Governor of Jersey (1600-3). He introduced the growing of tobacco so successfully that it unbalanced the royal customs revenue and in 1628 its cultivation on the islands was forbidden.

With the outbreak of the English Civil War in 1642, Jersey was Royalist, Guernsey for Parliament, though Castle Cornet in Guernsey held out for Charles I. Again in 1781 the French invaded Jersey, where Major Pierson rallied a force to repulse them, was killed, and became an historic island hero.

Over many years, the islands provided haven for refugees such as the Huguenots and, later, the aristocrats and other dissidents from the French Revolution. Soon, however, the old familiar pattern recurred. From Napoleon Bonaparte – perhaps deterred by the Martello defences – to Napoleon III, against whom the Victorian forts were built, the French threat continued. The First World War was fought at a distance from the islands, though many of the island men died in battle.

There was a period of quiet until the Second World War. In 1940, Winston Churchill offered the French common citizenship if they fought on, and in anticipation of their agreement, he sent troops and armaments to the Channel Islands. Within a day of their arrival, on 16 June, France surrendered. The British Government told the islands they were to be demilitarized and offered to evacuate the population.

Many of the recent settlers who retained ties with mainland Britain accepted the offer; and many children were sent away. A large proportion of the old island people stayed on, and saw the Occupation through, for rather longer than they anticipated. Virtually the entire population of Alderney left, however, warned that the Germans proposed to make it a strategic strongpoint. In fact it became virtually one vast gun emplacement, a concentration camp, and a place of horror.

Demilitarization spared the islands from attack after the initial machine-gunning. The Germans moved in on 30 June 1940; the few Jews, and the potentially rebellious, were instantly transported to Germany or beyond. Otherwise the Germans behaved correctly at first towards the inhabitants. Then more and more Channel Island loyalists and suspected loyalists were imprisoned or transported. Meanwhile many islanders acted in various ways in support of the Allies. Harsher deportation measures followed. All suffered tight surveillance and privations. Much is left of the German installations; gunpoints, bunkers, underground hospitals make grim contributions to the landscape, especially in Alderney. The islanders remained loyal throughout their hardships until, on 8 May, the German officers in the islands reported to the Bailiffs that the war was over; 9 May is now celebrated as Liberation Day, and a public holiday, in all the islands except Alderney. There, despite its being retaken by British troops on 16 May 1945, the first islanders did not return until the following December, to a battered, plundered, disorganized island. They had little to celebrate with a public holiday.

The war done, the islanders set about repairing their territory and their economy. Tourism had been a growing source of revenue since the mid-19th century; indeed, it was as holiday resorts that mainland Britain first genuinely recognized and appreciated the islands. The tourist trade grew steadily with the improvement of travel services. Sadly, the rising cost of transport and other problems caused a steady decline in the export of the fine granite quarried in the islands. Tomato growing began in about 1890 and increased steadily until recently, when transport charges and astute competition from other, government-subsidized, European countries – especially Holland – adversely affected that trade. In the same sector, early potatoes and flowers still contribute to revenue, and latterly growers have continued to exploit the islands' early growing season, compared with the British mainland, by introducing back-up crops of courgettes and calabrese (Jersey) and peppers (Guernsey).

The newest, and toweringly important, economic growth sector is in finance. The Jersey and, secondly, Guernsey finance industries began their growth phase in about 1960. It has proved a big stimulus to the islands' economy. At first, only the big United Kingdom banks were represented there. The last 25 years, however, have seen a steady increase in the number of foreign banks and deposit-taking institutions registered in Jersey and Guernsey. The principal banks voluntarily report to the Bank of England for statistical purposes. The responsibilities for banking, however, rest with the States of Guernsey and Jersey, who grant annual licenses to operate to financial houses which, after inspection, they approve. The 'clean image' of the Channel Islands has been indicated as an important factor in this growth. The value to the islands of the finance industry is exemplified by the fact that, by 1985, there were 4500 employees of the big bank and trust companies. In Jersey during 1985 deposits more than quadrupled and the island is said to challenge Zurich as an internatonal banking centre. In Guernsey, total deposits also rose over the same period.

This growth has contributed vastly to tax revenue as well as providing employment for so many local people. Both Jersey and Guernsey in recent years have acquired many wealthy tax-paying new residents, who find the islands attractive from this point of view. Immigration controls in Jersey make it difficult even for a wealthy person to move there now. The control of new residents into Guernsey is less stringent but is growing tighter. This investment aspect of life in the two main islands offers by far the strongest hope for a healthy economic future.

The islands

The islands are, indeed, so different – even their flora and fauna differ – as to demand separate treatment. They have, however, some common attributes. Long before history began they were formed – and for years their houses were built – of stone, generally the local granite.

One of the special 1948 issues of postage stamps bore a picture of an old cart full, apparently, of rubbish. It was in fact a *vraic* cart, and its use reflected the importance to all the islands of *vraic* (seaweed), the traditional and valuable manure used there on the crops for centuries.

The three larger islands – Jersey, Guernsey and Alderney – all produce their own traditional woollen sweater, as well as other knitwear.

There occurs throughout the islands, too, an unusually great rise and fall of tides, which influences much of the marine life there: and this should also be read as a

Sunset over Jethou and Herm with Brecqhou in the foreground, viewed from the Pilcher Monument, Sark

caution to visitors. The variation may be as much as 40 ft, which is twice that found on most British coasts.

These are islands of small farms and old mellow farmhouses, their character carefully preserved. In each of the three chief islands there is a single main urban centre.

The Bailiwick of Jersey

Jersey is the most southerly of the three larger islands, lying almost 14 miles due west of Carteret, the largest at a little less than 29,000 acres, and the most populated (approaching 80,000 inhabitants) of all the Channel Islands. It is also the warmest of them, facing the sun as it slopes from its northern cliffs down to the southern beaches. It is, too, undoubtedly the wealthiest of them, and its high standard of living is matched by its cost. Its fertile soil, which used to maintain the islanders in basic food during their relative isolation, now provides early potatoes and other vegetables, and the rich dairy produce of the highly economical Jersey cattle. The modern influx of wealthy settlers means that the traveller arriving by air cannot fail to be impressed by the number of handsome houses in fine grounds.

The island has been well laid out and, despite a certain opulence in its buildings and intensive cultivation, it has more open land than Guernsey. The strikingly large stretch of sand at St Ouen's Bay – well known for surfing – is backed by the best of that open country *(overleaf)*. Also, the great tidal range means that the complete ebb exposes some 12 square miles of rocks, pools and beaches on the south-east coast.

Jersey is well serviced, and in recent years has attracted a growing number of holidaymakers and tourists from countries other than Britain. Although St Helier is not so impressive as St Peter Port, it has many amenities and visitors. The sea front is pleasing, the harbour area serviceable, there are pedestrian shopping precincts, well-stocked markets, and a pleasing town centre in Royal Square.

The best-known natives probably were the 'Jersey Lily', Lillie Langtry (1853-1929) and John Everett Millais (1829-96); but important for his work on the island scene was the artist Edmund Blampied, who portrayed its people and work.

Jersey has two dependencies. **Les Minquiers** – to the fishermen The Minkies – about 9 miles to the south, are a series of reefs which, exposed at low tide, have about the same area as Jersey itself. Only one of them, Maîtresse Île, is inhabited, and that only in summer. The **Ecréhous** are about 5 miles east-north-east and a mile nearer to Jersey than to France. Three of the islets, Maître Île, Marmoutier and Blanche Île, have usable buildings. Marmoutier has a scattered 'street' of old, mostly ruined cottages and a Customs House, manned (rarely) by Jersey. Maître Île has the ruins of a medieval priory.

The Bailiwick of Guernsey

Guernsey – 'Green Island' – is second in size of the islands (25 square miles) and roughly triangular in shape. The Bailiwick of Guernsey includes the islands of Alderney, Sark, Herm and Jethou. Its attraction as a holiday resort is heightened by its mild climate, due in part to the influence of the Gulf Stream. It has an impressive main town in St Peter Port, with its eye-catching skyline, and the finest port, harbour and marina facilities in the Channel Islands. It has, too, a busy sea front and a generous covered market. Its biggest problem is over-population, partly the result of favourable taxation scales: the figure in 1986 was about 55,000. Its narrow roads, built from fear of Napoleonic invasion, are crowded and parking is a problem.

*Daffodil bulbs in a field
near Grouville, Jersey*

*Glass houses near Albecq, Guernsey: market gardening
is an important industry*

The arriving air traveller is at once struck by the number of glasshouses, for Guernsey's modern economy has been based on market gardening and its famous breed of cattle, strongly reinforced latterly by tourism and finance. Unlike many other islands, Guernsey has never been ruled for any length of time by any single family.

Guernsey has many attractive bays and the characteristic water lanes, some imposing cliffs, many with caves, notably Le Grand Creux (70 ft deep) in Fermain Bay. Inland it is a place of tidy small farms, some still with tethered cattle, small groups of old houses, and the typical red granite churches.

The island's most famous resident probably was Victor Hugo who, banished from France in 1852 for opposing Louis Napoleon, eventually settled in Guernsey where he lived until 1870. His house, in Hauteville, is preserved as he left it and well maintained; it may be visited.

St Peter Port faces Herm and Sark, to which boats are available. **Lihou**, reached by a 600 yd causeway from L'Erée, is about 50 acres in size. It has the ruins of the 12th-century Priory of Our Lady of Lihou and a modern house.

The remarkable island of **Sark** lies 7½ miles east of Guernsey; it is about 3 miles north–south and a little over a mile at its widest. It consists of two islands, Great and Little Sark, connected by La Coupée – an isthmus both perilously narrow and vertiginously high, 300 ft above the sea. The island is, in effect, a plateau rising to 360 ft. Its two harbours, Creux, said to be the smallest in the world, and the new La Maseline, opened in 1949, are connected with the tableland by rock tunnels. Its population of about 600 is increased vastly during the holiday season by day trippers, arriving by one of the boat services from Guernsey.

Prehistoric dolmen builders occupied Sark. In 568 St Magloire founded the monastery the Vikings destroyed 250 years afterwards. The French captured Sark,

Overleaf: St Ouen's Bay, Jersey – the surfers paradise

occupied it, made it a prison colony, and abandoned it before Philip de Carteret of Jersey took it. In 1565 Queen Elizabeth I granted him a charter as Seigneur of Sark on condition that he manned the island defences. The charter was sold several times until it came to a Mrs Collins of Guernsey, whose descendants own it at present.

Over the years, Seigneurial edicts have banned motor vehicles (except farm tractors) and transistor radios, divorce (because no laws exist to decree it) and only the Seigneur may own a bitch. There is no income tax, VAT, wealth tax or death duties. Sark has no town as such but the roads, including The Avenue which leads to Le Manoir, original residence of the Seigneur, contain church, school, two banks and a few shops. There are hotels and pubs. Sark is a beautiful, quiet place, with its great cliffs, sunny beaches, and valleys full of flowers.

The island of **Herm,** 3 miles east of Guernsey, is 1½ miles by ½ mile, and 500 acres in extent. There was a Neolithic burial ground here. Christianity reached it about the 5th century – probably by way of Sark. The existing chapel of St Tugual dates from the 11th century. Herm was a game preserve of the Governors of Guernsey; granite was quarried there, and exported. Guernsey bought Herm from Britain after the Second World War and leased it to Major Peter Wood. He developed it most competently as a centre of tourism, and also a farm with a large herd of Guernsey cattle.

Convenient for holidaymakers from Guernsey, Herm is extremely popular as a day trip. Its small village provides a shop, post office, tavern, grocery, gift shop and restaurants. This well-wooded island also bans cars and transistor radios.

Jethou has been called the most beautiful of the Channel Islands, despite a grim reputation for smuggling, and for housing the gallows for Guernsey. It is a 20-acre hill with two copses which are a riot of flowers in spring, and charming beaches.

Alderney, the most northerly of the Channel Islands, is also the nearest to France, lying 8 miles west of the Cherbourg peninsula, 22 miles north-east of Guernsey, and 90 miles south of Southampton. It is third of the islands in size, but much smaller than Jersey or Guernsey. Lozenge-shaped, it is about 3½ miles long, 1¼ miles wide, covers 1962 acres and has a population of some 2200. The currents of the Swinge, between Burhou and the north-west side, and the Raz, between France and the south-east side, render these areas too perilous for small vessels and they are reckoned impossible for swimmers. Access to Alderney is generally by air, or there is a fortnightly roll-on/roll-off ship from Torquay, Devon. There is evidence of prehistoric and Roman occupation. For centuries, even after it became part of the Duchy of Normandy, and subsequently a possession of the English crown, Alderney was harried by pirates.

Two events established the distinction between Alderney and the other islands. In the mid-19th century the building of the great jetty and the 15 new forts and batteries necessitated the importation of quarry workers, builders and soldiers who, from 1847 to 1864, outnumbered the islanders by about ten to one. Then, as we have seen, during the Second World War the island was evacuated. Thus there is now no cohesion of island people, no patois. It remains ringed by forts now devoted to many – unwarlike – ends.

The intensely moving Hammond Memorial at Saye overlooks the site of a German slave labour camp. It carries memorial plaques to the slave workers of the Second World War who died on the island, engraved in Polish, Hebrew, Russian, English, French and Spanish.

St Anne Church, Alderney (see p. 102)

Alderney's mainly 19th-century chief town, St Anne, contains some three-quarters of the population. The parish church of St Anne, built in 1850, is said to be the finest church in the Channel Islands.

Les Casquets are a group of 30-ft high rocks on which so many ships were wrecked that since 1710 there has been a lighthouse there. They lie 7 miles west of Alderney.

Tiny **Burhou Island,** about 1 mile north-west of Alderney, is a well-known bird sanctuary. Its birdwatchers' hut can be rented, except during the sea birds' breeding season, for a nominal amount, on application to the States of Alderney.

The German Occupation of
the Channel Islands

COLIN PARTRIDGE

The German Occupation during the Second World War was the most traumatic event in the history of the Channel Islands. As Hitler's armies swept into France in May 1940, the fate of the islands was sealed.

The British Government's announcement of demilitarization came too late to prevent civilian loss of life in the German air raids on St Helier and St Peter Port. However, before the first enemy forces landed in Guernsey on 30 June, 6600 people from Jersey, 17,000 people from Guernsey and all but a handful of Alderney's population of just over 1000 had taken the painful decision to evacuate to England.

The headquarters of the German Commander of the British Channel Islands was established in Jersey in September 1940. Each island also had its own commandant. Effective local civilian administration in the two Bailiwicks was permitted to continue by the Germans through the Supreme Council of the States of Jersey and the Controlling Committee of the States of Guernsey, both of which had been set up in anticipation of the need for emergency government.

Life soon became a rigorous routine for the islanders. A succession of orders had seen the confiscation of private vehicles and radios in the first weeks of occupation; food rationing soon followed, together with the requisitioning of land, and this inevitably supported a black market. The Germans made attempts to control local food production and farming, but these proved ineffective in the long term and local output gradually declined. Many shops soon found it impossible to trade normally as goods became scarce and a form of barter flourished.

Domestic fuel became increasingly scarce and the general standard of living fell rapidly after September 1944, when sea communication with the Continent was eventually cut after the Allied breakout from Normandy. But for the arrival of the Red Cross ship *Vega*, which made five voyages to the Channel Islands between December 1944 and May 1945, the civilian population would have faced starvation.

The early years
For the first year of occupation, a succession of different German army units served as the garrison force and defences were set up only at tactically important positions. The airfields in the three larger islands remained in use, although Alderney's was soon to be closed down and obstructed, while the main line of communication with the Continent was maintained by sea through the ports of Granville and St Malo and, to a lesser extent, through Cherbourg.

Before invading Russia in June 1941, Hitler sent a number of artillery batteries and the strengthened 319 Infantry Division to the Channel Islands. In the months following, a series of orders from the German Armed Forces High Command decreed that the Channel Islands were to be permanently fortified, and each arm of the Wehrmacht was given specific orders defining its role in this plan. With America's entry into the war in December 1941, fresh impetus was given to the programme for building permanent fortifications with the arrival of the paramilitary Organisation Todt.

The Tower at Les Landes, Jersey (see p. 24)

For Hitler, the primary purpose in occupying the Channel Islands grew into a desire to incorporate them into the so-called Atlantic Wall. But the degree to which these defences were to be developed in the space of just two and a half years of intensive building explains why senior officers in Normandy bitterly opposed the commitment of vital resources to these offshore islands in 1944.

From early 1942, restrictions on the movements of civilians in the larger islands reflected the increasing demand for land for defensive works. The Fortress Engineer Staff surveyed the selected sites and determined the pattern of infantry defences in accordance with tactical requirements. Several hundred standardized designs were developed for coastal defence works as the war progressed and the Channel Islands possess many examples of these.

The principal islands were divided into coastal defence sectors with mutually supporting strongpoints. These not only comprised the offensive positions, but also the many passive supporting installations. They were surrounded by firing trenches, fixed flamethrowers, mines and barbed-wire entanglements. Many of these strongpoints were located in fortified positions of historical significance.

The beaches were invariably obstructed by steel and concrete obstacles, and continuous concrete anti-tank walls were planned to prevent armoured vehicles moving inland, although not all of these were completed. Extensive tunnelling in Jersey, Guernsey and Alderney afforded protection for mobile reserves, ammunition, fuel, power supply and hospitals.

Defence against aerial attack was assured by a large concentration of anti-aircraft guns of various calibres manned by Luftwaffe personnel, with a total of 31 batteries in Jersey, 34 in Guernsey and 21 in Alderney. Of these, six batteries, each of six 8.8 cm guns, were sited in Jersey and Guernsey, with four batteries in Alderney. Air force and navy radar installations provided advance warning of Allied aerial and naval activity, but were seldom effectively used for gun-laying purposes.

The coastal batteries

The main strategic value of the Channel Islands rested on the power of the medium and heavy coastal artillery batteries. Being the most westerly island, Guernsey was selected as the site for the heaviest battery, of four 30.5 cm guns, which together with the planned heavy batteries at Cap de la Hague in the north and Paimpol in the south were intended to seal off the Bay of St Malo and provide a protected corridor for German coastal shipping.

Of the fifteen coastal artillery batteries emplaced in Guernsey by the end of 1944, three were manned by the German Navy, five by 319 Infantry Division and the remainder by 1265 Army Coastal Artillery Regiment. There was a total of sixteen batteries in Jersey, five in Alderney and one in Sark. Captured German documents show that these batteries were regularly engaged in action, their fire being directed by the command posts receiving information from the prominent direction-finding towers that ring the larger islands.

Jersey

In Jersey, one of the finest of these towers can be seen at Les Landes. On the open ground nearby are the concrete emplacements for the four 15.5 cm guns of Battery 'Moltke'. To the south stretches the wide expanse of St Ouen's Bay. The casemates of a number of strongpoints can still be seen at intervals along an almost continuous

Coastal defence gun, La Corbière, Jersey

concrete anti-tank wall, the best of these being a 4.7 cm anti-tank gun bunker at La Carrière and a position for a 10.5 cm coast defence gun at La Corbière. These two sites are opened to the public at limited times during the summer months by the enterprising local branch of the Channel Islands Occupation Society. Also at La Corbière, a second direction-finding tower has been converted for use by the Jersey harbour authority with the addition of a glazed observation platform. The battery of four 22 cm guns at La Moye protected the left flank of St Ouen's Bay and here can still be seen a unique direction-finding post, originally camouflaged as a house.

At Noirmont Point, strategically lying between St Brelade's Bay and the larger St Aubin's Bay to the east, are to be found the extensive remains of Battery 'Lothringen'. This battery has seen much clearance and restoration work by the industrious members of the Occupation Society, and the impressive underground battery command post with its armoured observation dome, as well as a third naval direction-finding tower sited in a forward position on the cliff edge, are also open to the public at specified times. The numerous supporting installations and the unusual elevated gun emplacements can all be explored on this headland, which has been acquired by the States of Jersey in commemoration of those islanders who gave their lives in the Second World War.

Inland, at L'Aleval in St Peter's Parish, are to be found the bunkers comprising the headquarters of the German command in Jersey. The Fortress Commander's bunker at the Strawberry Farm is extremely well preserved, with much of its original equipment and fittings intact, and is open to the public. The bunkers of the Artillery Commander and the Infantry Regimental Commander lie on private ground nearby. The wooded valleys of St Peter and St Lawrence, which run down to St Aubin's Bay, were the sites for much of the tunnelling activity in Jersey, the most impressive being that at Meadow Bank which was developed into a military hospital and now forms one of the island's leading tourist attractions. The extensive underground corridors contain an operating theatre, wards and staff quarters, most still retaining their original equipment, while the unfinished sections of the tunnels give a stark impression of the conditions under which the workers laboured.

Equally impressive is the Bunker Museum, adjoining the Jersey Motor Museum in the centre of St Peter's, which houses a comprehensive collection of material covering all aspects of the German Occupation of Jersey. Exhibitions of interest are also to be found in the museum at La Hougue Bie near Grouville and in Elizabeth Castle. At the former, the interiors of two rooms of a command bunker have been reconstructed and display material from the Société Jersiaise and Cabot collections; at the latter many of the German works added to the earlier castle are accessible to the public, including two 10.5 cm casemates, still with their guns. The Island Fortress Occupation Museum at the Weighbridge in St Helier displays German militaria of a wider interest and has an audio-visual theatre showing films about the Occupation.

Guernsey

The distinctive direction-finding towers are also a feature of Guernsey's coastal landscape. The tower at Chouet stands perilously close to the edge of the quarry, and that at Fort Saumarez has been constructed on an earlier round tower. The direction-finding tower at Pleinmont, similar to the one at Chouet, has been leased by the Guernsey branch of the Occupation Society; this too has been restored and is open to the public on specified days during the summer.

Adjoining the car park at L'Angle is the command post of Battery 'Dollmann' with its flat roof over the rangefinder platform – the only installation of this type in the Channel Islands. On the headland immediately to the east stands the unique, stepped naval direction-finding post, reminiscent of the bridge structure of a warship. The crudely constructed tower at La Prévôté, further to the east, appears squat and ineffectual by contrast. The only other observation post of interest was the ingeniously converted mill tower at Hougue du Moulin, Vale, where three concrete platforms were added and the original wooden cap replaced; partial demolition of this addition has regrettably been carried out since the war.

The wide, sandy beaches of Guernsey's northern and western shores show abundant evidence of the German wartime defences, the concrete anti-tank walls at L'Ancresse and Vazon being particularly impressive. The casemates along these beaches are virtually all intact and can be inspected at close quarters, while the intervening strongpoints still show the extent to which the Channel Islands' defences were developed. At Fort Hommet, two pairs of north- and south-facing 10.5 cm gun casemates can be seen, the former still displaying applied camouflage treatment and surrounded by numerous bunkers and field positions. Near the slipway in the centre of Rocquaine Bay, a short section of concrete anti-tank wall is flanked at each end by 4.7 cm anti-tank gun casemates with a central bunker originally mounting an armoured steel dome which has been cut out of the concrete in one of the postwar scrap drives.

Of Guernsey's inland sites, the central command complex at La Corbinerie in St Martin's comprised the headquarters bunkers for 319 Infantry Division, the Artillery Commander and the island signals network. At St Jacques in St Peter Port, the

Fort Grey Maritime Museum, Rocquaine Bay, Guernsey (see p. 141)

headquarters of the Naval Commander for the Channel Islands and his signals staff were housed in two large bunkers linked by a short tunnel, which, although still accessible, have a small group of houses built over them.

The largest coastal artillery battery in the Channel Islands was sited on high ground in St Saviour's. The four turreted 30.5 cm guns of Battery 'Mirus' were manned by naval personnel and mounted in open emplacements with adjoining underground magazines and crews' quarters. One of these gun positions, although devoid of its main armament, is accessible to the public through the grounds of the Tropical Vinery at Les Rouvets, while the three massive reserve ammunition bunkers stand beside the road at La Houguette and Courtil Michele and in the Rue du Lorier. The concrete base for the battery radar stands on the north side of the Rue de la Croix Crève Coeur adjacent to the command post and personnel shelter. At La Varde on L'Ancresse Common the open emplacements and personnel shelters of one of the island's six 8.8 cm anti-aircraft batteries can be inspected.

Guernsey too has its underground hospital at La Vassalerie in St Andrew's Parish. This is the largest German installation remaining in the Channel Islands and took over three and a half years to complete, being in use only for a short period after June 1944. It is now open to the public during the summer months.

The German Occupation Museum at Les Houards, near Le Bourg, contains a most impressive collection of military equipment, small arms and larger calibre weapons. An extension houses reconstructed settings, giving equal emphasis to civilian life during the Occupation, and also contains an audio-visual facility. Exhibitions of Occupation interest can also be seen at Castle Cornet, where the German additions to this majestic castle can be visited.

Battery 'Mirus', La Houguette, Guernsey (see p. 27)

At Fort George, overlooking St Peter Port, the military cemetery contains the only German war graves remaining in the Channel Islands. Here lie the remains of 111 German personnel who died during the Occupation. At the Foulon Cemetery in St Peter Port there are 21 graves of British seamen whose bodies were washed ashore in October 1943 after the naval action in which HMS *Charybdis* and *Limbourne* were sunk. The annual service of remembrance is faithfully observed by the Guernsey people, whose spirit of passive defiance is exemplified by the 'V' for victory sign still preserved on the wall of number 4 Brock Terrace in the Grange.

Sark

Sark had a relatively peaceful Occupation, the most outstanding events being the two British Commando raids. The repercussions of the first raid in October 1942 extended far beyond the island's shores, and led to the shackling of British prisoners of war as a reprisal for the tying of hands of the German prisoners taken in Sark. The island also escaped the construction of major defence works and mounted only one coastal artillery battery of three 8.8 cm guns in the last months of the war. Today, the most prominent feature is the concrete lining to the tunnel leading to Creux Harbour, and La Coupée, joining Great and Little Sark, which was widened by German prisoners of war after the Liberation. The Seigneurie garden has a small gun park which contains a 3.7 cm anti-tank gun.

Alderney and the darker side of Occupation

Alderney occupied just as important a position as Jersey and Guernsey in the Channel Islands defence plan, although considerably smaller in size. The four concrete emplacements for the 15 cm guns of Battery 'Annes' on the Giffoine are clearly visible from the air and can be explored on the ground, together with the battery command post and supporting installations. The four concrete casemates for the 10.5 cm guns of Battery 'Marcks' stand menacingly above Roselle Point and were also manned by navy personnel for the protection of the harbour entrance.

At Mannez Garenne can be seen one of the best-preserved 8.8 cm anti-aircraft batteries in the Channel Islands. Standing within the battery perimeter and dominating the skyline is the massive coastal artillery fire directory tower, with its three observation platforms. Immediately to the south, the sands of Longy Bay are ringed by a concrete anti-tank wall flanked by casemates for anti-tank guns, while the fort on Raz Island has two casemates built into the old masonry for 10.5 cm guns. In common with their policy of utilizing sites of historic military value, the Germans added concrete works to most of Alderney's magnificent Victorian forts and batteries, turning them into infantry and artillery strongpoints. Fort Grosnez and Fort Albert are especially interesting in this respect.

Bibette Head is well worth a visit to gain an impression of a typical field defence system. Here the rifle and communication trenches remain on the headland overlooking the harbour approaches, linked with machine-gun and mortar pits. A west-facing 10.5 cm casemate is connected by a tunnel to a bunker mounting the only remaining armoured steel cupola in Alderney. In a field beside the road at Saye Farm, several steel beach obstacles lie rusting in the grass.

At Les Rochers, the Fortress Commander's bunker can be visited by arrangement with the Alderney Fortifications Centre, whose members offer expert guided tours of the island's sites of military interest during the summer months. Close by, on the south side of Longis Road, is the substantial hospital bunker intended for use as a field dressing station.

A prominent feature of the townscape of St Anne is the German water tower at Les Mouriaux, built on top of a well-preserved signals bunker. The Alderney Society Museum, housed in the old town school in the High Street, contains displays of German military equipment and, perhaps most poignantly, objects associated with the darker side of Alderney's wartime history: the camps built by the Organisation Todt for the workers brought to the island to build the fortifications. The sites of the four camps were at Saye Bay, the Haize, Platte Saline and near Telegraph Tower, the last-named being the most notorious. 'Sylt' camp was taken over in 1943 by an SS construction battalion and run as a concentration camp. The pillars to the gates of the inner camp compound, together with some of the hut bases and two of the peculiar, pointed concrete sentry posts on the camp perimeter, remain as sombre testimony to the brutal acts committed here. Those who died and were buried in the workers' cemetery on Longis Common have not been forgotten. The Hammond Memorial, raised by an island family in the 1960s, commemorates all those foreign workers who died in Alderney and forms the focal point of the moving annual service of remembrance that takes place in May.

The return of freedom

Liberation finally came to the Channel Islands on 9 May 1945 – nearly a year after the Normandy landings – with the unconditional surrender of the German forces. The last months of the war had been the most arduous and difficult for the islanders who had stayed. For those who returned from evacuation and the deportations of September 1942, the discovery that the islands had been turned into the fortified outposts of the Atlantic Wall came as a great shock. The numerous defence works that survive are a permanent memorial to those five years of occupation.

The Green Lanes of Guernsey

NIGEL JEE

Before 1810 the roads of Guernsey were a labyrinth of narrow, winding lanes, muddy in winter and dusty in summer. Most were local tracks connecting the farmsteads with the parish church, with the mill, and with the nearest beach for collecting seaweed for use on the land. There were no direct roads from one part of the island to another, and a journey to town from the remoter country districts was a major undertaking.

In 1810 Guernsey's popular Lieutenant-Governor, General John Doyle, began a programme of road improvement of which details will be found under 'The Military Roads of Guernsey' *(see p. 136)*. Although intended for military purposes, Doyle's roads opened up the countryside and enabled tourism, commerce and the export of stone and produce to develop. Even today, when Guernsey's 25 square miles contain 31,000 motor vehicles, they still form the basis of the island's main road system.

Since the arrival of the car early in the present century, not only the main roads but most of the country lanes have been surfaced with tarmacadam and given over to motor traffic. Nevertheless, either because they are too narrow or too little used to warrant the expense, a number of old roads have escaped the widening and surfacing of the 20th century. The map *(overleaf)* shows over 50 of these 'green lanes'. Some are wide enough for a horse and cart, others barely wide enough for a pedestrian. Many are extremely attractive. With some ingenuity a limitless number of walks can be devised, making use of the green lanes, through beautiful scenery far from the crowds that are attracted to the beaches.

Among the green lanes indicated on the map is the footpath between Saumarez Park and Cobo, originally created by the 4th Lord de Saumarez and recently re-opened by the States of Guernsey as the 'Heritage Walk'. It is described in the gazetteer under Saumarez Park. The other lanes indicated on the map are of considerable antiquity.

Several of the green lanes radiate from the ancient parish churches. St Saviour's Parish has two such lanes, with traces of a third. One, from the south side of the churchyard, is a paved track leading down through the trees to join the main road at Sous l'Eglise. Beside the steps leading down from the churchyard to the path are a set of rude stone seats which formed the feudal court of Fief Jean Gaillard. Here the officials of the lord of the manor collected the feudal dues and tried minor offenders. Beside the road at the bottom of Sous l'Eglise is a pleasant *abreuvoir* or drinking place for cattle and horses.

Another lane begins as a grassy path across the churchyard to the west of the church, crosses the main road and continues for a short distance between high banks, before crossing a narrow road and passing the front of an old house, La Vielle Sous l'Eglise, with a strange bottle-shaped chimney. The green lane continues for a quarter of a mile down a secluded valley, Le Beauvallet, with the remains of a millpond on the left and a large field, formed quite recently by removing the hedges between several small fields, on the right. The lane finally joins La Rue du Moulin at

A green lane, near the Talbot Valley, Castel

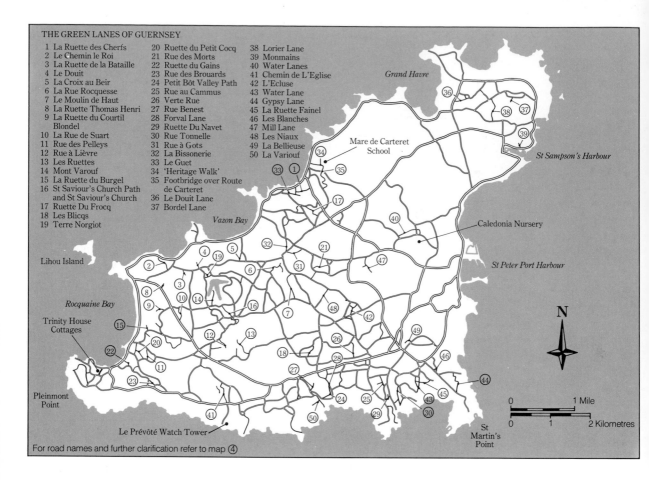

THE GREEN LANES OF GUERNSEY

1 La Ruette des Cherfs
2 Le Chemin le Roi
3 La Ruette de la Bataille
4 Le Douit
5 La Croix au Beir
6 La Rue Rocquesse
7 Le Moulin de Haut
8 La Ruette Thomas Henri
9 La Ruette du Courtil Blondel
10 La Rue de Suart
11 Rue des Pelleys
12 Rue à Lièvre
13 Les Ruettes
14 Mont Varouf
15 La Ruette du Burgel
16 St Saviour's Church Path and St Saviour's Church
17 Ruette Du Frocq
18 Les Blicqs
19 Terre Norgiot
20 Ruette du Petit Cocq
21 Rue des Morts
22 Ruette du Gains
23 Rue des Brouards
24 Petit Bôt Valley Path
25 Rue au Cammus
26 Verte Rue
27 Rue Benest
28 Forval Lane
29 Ruette Du Navet
30 Rue Tonnelle
31 Rue à Gots
32 La Bissonerie
33 Le Guet
34 'Heritage Walk'
35 Footbridge over Route de Carteret
36 Le Douit Lane
37 Bordel Lane
38 Lorier Lane
39 Monmains
40 Water Lanes
41 Chemin de L'Eglise
42 L'Ecluse
43 Water Lane
44 Gypsy Lane
45 La Ruette Fainel
46 Les Blanches
47 Mill Lane
48 Les Niaux
49 La Bellieuse
50 La Variouf

For road names and further clarification refer to map ④

the point where it skirts the end of the central and longest of the three tongues of St Saviour's Reservoir. The name of the road refers to Le Moulin de Beauvallet, whose ruins can just be made out beside the road opposite the tip of the reservoir.

If you pass the ruined mill and continue westwards along La Rue du Moulin, the next turning on the right leads into a cart track which runs along a spur, Le Mont Varouf, between two arms of the reservoir. Before the dam was built and the three valleys flooded, the track continued to Perelle. Now that it no longer goes anywhere except the shore of the reservoir, it is a secluded lane used only for gaining access to the surrounding fields and for walking dogs.

Returning to La Rue du Moulin and continuing a few yards further west, you come to a short section of green lane, sunk between high hedges and still being deepened by horses' hoofs, which cuts off a corner in the metalled lane leading directly towards St Saviour's Church.

In St Peter's Parish a section of church path survives, still known as Le Chemin de l'Eglise. Starting from Les Buttes, the ancient archery ground immediately to the east of the church, a lane leads south to connect by a short section of green lane with La Rue des Prés. After just over a quarter of a mile a green lane opens on the right. It dives across a miniature valley and then crosses a metalled road and continues towards the coast. This section is Le Chemin de l'Eglise; it connected one of the two sections of the south coast that lie in St Peter's with the parish church. The green lane eventually gives way to a narrow metalled lane which continues towards the coast. As it approaches the cliff it runs along the shoulder of a hanging valley and ends in a car park at the Prévôté. Brooding over the scene is an observation tower of German concrete, built on the site of a Napoleonic watch house.

In the Castel Parish the old settlement of King's Mills has a number of green lanes radiating from it. The parish church is over a mile away and there is no obvious church path except for the present main road between the two, which was widened and straightened by Doyle. There is, however, a lane called La Rue des Morts, whose name suggests that coffins were carried that way to the church. Travel west for a quarter of a mile along the main road from the church and La Rue des Morts begins as a turning to the left by a television mast. Starting as a narrow metalled road, it soon becomes a green lane which continues between fields and greenhouses to join a lane to the west of Les Pelleys. From here another green lane, just wide enough for a pedestrian or a donkey, descends the hillside into the Talbot Valley. Beside the path at its junction with the Talbot Valley Road is a stone marking the entrance to the Ron Short Walk. This is a footpath through National Trust property which climbs to the shoulder of the valley and affords some splendid rural views before descending through woodland to the Talbot Valley Road.

Two green lanes, La Rue à Gots and La Bissonerie, were left as backwaters when Doyle's military road from St Peter Port to Vazon was cut through the fields from Les Eturs to the bottom of La Houguette Road. La Rue à Gots leaves Les Eturs and drops down the hillside towards King's Mills, cutting off a corner now formed by the Houguette Crossroad. At its bottom end it joins another of Doyle's roads from Camp du Roi to King's Mills. A few yards to the west, and the opposite side of the road, is the entrance to La Bissonerie. It is a delightful lane, shaded by elms and skirting a series of meadows which run down to La Grande Mare. Once a cart road between King's Mills and Cobo, La Bissonerie is saved from modern traffic by a bottleneck at one end and a granite pillar at the other. At its northern end it continues as La Rue de la Hougue, from which a footpath just wide enough for a single pedestrian climbs a gorsy hillside to the brink of a quarry where once was the chapel of St Germain.

One of the most delightful of the green lanes, with extensive views over King's Mills and the west coast, is La Rue Rocquesse. It is reached from a short lane marked 'Single Track Road', which cuts off the corner between King's Mills Road and the Talbot Valley. Half way along this lane a cart track leaves to the south; there is just room to leave a car at the beginning of the track if nobody else has had the same idea. The track soon forks and the right-hand branch, La Rue Rocquesse, climbs the hillside behind King's Mills. This escarpment was once a sea cliff, but is now stranded well inland, the low-lying area known as La Grande Mare having subsequently developed between the cliff and a pebble ridge which was formed at Vazon Bay.

The cart track climbs between field hedges with oak and sweet chestnut to the top of the escarpment, where the hedgebanks between the fields are treeless but full in season of primroses, sheep's-bit and violets. Spread out below are La Grande Mare, Vazon and the headland of Fort Hommet. The track eventually joins a metalled lane, La Rue des Grantez. Turning left, you continue to climb the hill, passing a bramble patch with parts of a German fortification visible within it. This is the site of the former windmill of Les Grantez. The lane continues for half a mile along the edge of the southern plateau of Guernsey and ends in a T-junction with La Rue des Boulains.

The left-hand turning will take you down a steep hill between high banks. La Rue des Boulains forms the border between the parishes of St Saviour and the Castel, and the hedges bordering it are probably among the oldest in the island.

At the bottom of the hill another left turn will bring you into La Rue du Moulin de Haut. Some traffic may be encountered in this winding lane, though a notice proclaims that it is unsuitable for motor vehicles. The lane follows the miniature Fauxquets Valley, with a hanging oak wood on one side and a meadow on the other. After bending to the right it passes Le Moulin de Haut – the upper of the three water mills from which King's Mills derives its name – before joining the Talbot Valley Road. The millstream flows beside the road from here back to King's Mills.

One of the glories of Guernsey is its south coast, whose magnificent cliffs are followed by a continuous path from end to end. Several of the valleys running down to the bays of the south coast contain green lanes that connect with the cliff path and afford endless scope for devising circular walks.

Two wooded valleys run down to Petit Bôt, containing between them a network of footpaths. One, Forval Lane, leads down from the Forest Road into the eastern of the two valleys. It can be reached either from Le Chêne traffic lights, or from Les Pièces, a little to the east. Between the tall banks of Forval Lane there runs both a footpath and a stream. These 'water lanes' are a delightful feature of the south coast valleys, and there is even one on the northern outskirts of St Peter Port, just to the north of Collings Road and the Caledonia Nursery. The edges of the stream in Forval Lane are encrusted with a luxuriant growth of liverworts, with golden saxifrage and Cornish moneywort in places.

At its lower end Forval Lane joins the road in the eastern valley, or another footpath can be taken which traverses the spur between the two valleys before dropping down to the stream in the western valley, eventually joining the road from Le Bourg to Petit Bôt.

Opposite the Manor Hotel, which faces you as you climb towards Le Bourg, is a narrow lane which climbs the shoulder of the valley towards the south-west. Soon the lane rounds a hairpin bend but a footpath continues through woodland to connect with the cliff path overlooking Petit Bôt. Alternatively, the road can be followed round the hairpin bend to the delightful hamlet of Le Variouf, whose cottages cling to the hillside beside a twisting lane.

Guernsey's best-known water lane runs from La Ville Amphrey to Moulin Huet in St Martin's Parish. Like Forval Lane it is sunk between high banks that leave just enough room for the stream and a narrow path. There is a convenient car park above Moulin Huet, from which a footpath continues down to the bay. The entrance to the Water Lane is among the trees near the top of this path, to the north of the car park.

The Water Lane climbs steeply at first, levelling off as it approaches La Ville Amphrey, a group of old houses clustered round a granite well with a cattle trough, from which the stream issues. From here a metalled road continues up the hill towards the old windmill at Les Camps du Moulin, now sadly surrounded by housing estates. A more peaceful walk is to follow a path beside a farmyard to the east of the 'wishing well'. This is the beginning of another green lane, La Ruette Fainel, which emerges opposite the front door of Le Vallon, a large house in the Gothic style, once the seat of the Carey family. The public path reaches the road through the front gate of Le Vallon. Turn right outside the gate and then right again and a path leads down the side of the Vallon estate to join the cliff path back to Moulin Huet.

Channel Island Cattle

JOAN STEVENS AND NIGEL JEE

Jersey cattle, La Ferme Morel, Jersey (see p. 81)

The two Channel Island breeds of cattle are known throughout the world: indeed, in many places the words Jersey and Guernsey may convey nothing other than the two dairy breeds. Both breeds are renowned for their rich milk and for the docility of the cows, though not of the bulls.

The Jersey is a fine-boned animal, small in comparison with the Guernsey and most other breeds, with large limpid dark eyes and black eyelashes that would be the envy of any film actress. She has a short 'dished' face, concave between the eyes, her nose is black and her ears are fringed with black hair. In the past her coat could vary from pale cream to a near-black colour known as mulberry, but now the most usual shade is a soft biscuit colour. This may be broken by white, often with white ankle socks; the luxuriant tail switch is also often white. When groomed to appear at a parish or island show the Jersey really is a creature of quality, yet she has not always been so: the present near-perfection of form is the result of careful breeding over the last hundred years. The bulls are a darker colour than the cows and of a considerably less docile disposition. Considering her diminutive size and her modest intake of food the Jersey cow produces an extremely high yield of milk with a butterfat content of well over five per cent.

The Guernsey is larger than the Jersey, but still much smaller than the black and white Friesians now so common elsewhere. A century ago her coat could be of

A Guernsey cow, Castel, Guernsey

various colours but now it is always fawn, but varying in shade from dark red to a pale sandy colour, with a pattern of white markings that often includes a white star on the forehead. The face is longer and straighter than the Jersey's and the nose is flesh-coloured. The milk, especially when the cows are out to grass in the summer, is of a characteristic rich yellow colour.

All the cattle of Jersey are of that breed; those of Guernsey, Alderney, Sark and Herm are all Guernseys. The only exception is that in Guernsey some cows are inseminated with imported beef semen because the resulting cross-bred steers and heifers fatten for beef more quickly than pure-bred Guernseys. However, great care is taken to ensure that all the breeding stock remain pure Guernseys.

During the 18th century thousands of Channel Island cattle were exported to England, often under the name of 'Alderneys', perhaps because Alderney was the last port of call before the ship arrived at Poole or Southampton. The small, deer-like animals were much in demand to adorn country estates, and to provide cream for the dairy. As the Channel Island herds began to improve, laws were passed in Jersey and Guernsey banning the importation of live cattle into the islands, first from the Continent, then from the United Kingdom, and finally even between Jersey and the Guernsey Bailiwick. This was partly to protect the island herds from the cattle diseases that were rife on the Continent, but it also had the effect of maintaining the purity of the Jersey and Guernsey breeds. The Jersey breed has been isolated since 1789 and the Guernsey since 1819. The two breeds that are now so well known are the result of selective breeding since that time.

Because of the guaranteed purity of the breeds, and their freedom from such diseases as brucellosis and bovine tuberculosis, the Channel Islands continue to attach great importance to the ban on the importation of cattle. This is one of the points that has caused the greatest anxiety in connection with the Common Market, in which theoretically there should be no barriers to the movement of animals.

Until the Second World War there was a flourishing export trade in Channel Island-bred cattle. Both breeds have proved to be highly adaptable, and many went to the former British colonies and to the dominions. There are large herds of Jerseys in the United States and New Zealand in particular, and of Guernseys in Canada, Kenya, South Africa and Australia. Since the war the export trade has dwindled, largely because of the high cost of shipment, though there is still some export of cattle from Jersey.

Until quite recently all the island cattle were tethered, and a few herds are still managed in this way. Each cow is attached by a chain around her horns to a peg driven into the ground, which has to be moved three or four times a day. In the summer the cows are milked in the field, where they spend the night. In the winter they are led in a bunch along the lanes to their stalls where they are milked and spend the night. In Jersey it is still common in winter to see the animals wearing coats.

Tethering makes efficient use of the limited land, for the grass can start to grow immediately behind the line of cows as they move across the field. However, moving the pegs and leading the animals individually to drink is costly in labour, and today most herds run loose behind an electric fence, or even spend their lives in a covered yard and have the grass brought to them. The horns, no longer needed as a means of attachment, are removed to avoid injury.

Cattle shows are an integral part of island life and competition for the many silver cups is keen. With the tendency towards larger and fewer farms it is becoming more difficult to give the animals the individual attention they used to receive, and entries are not quite as numerous as in former years. Nevertheless, as an opportunity of seeing the two breeds at their best, and of hearing the Norman-French language of the islands at the same time, the summer shows of Jersey, Guernsey and Sark are unsurpassed.

Food and Drink

JOHN ARLOTT

In a restaurant, a visitor to the Channel Islands is invariably presented with an English-type menu; it is generally near-French, sometimes fairly authentic Italian, occasionally, in Jersey, ethnic German, Chinese or Indian. That does not mean that there is no Channel Islands cuisine – it is the subject of, for example, Amanda Closs's *Tastes of the Channel Islands* (1983) – but catering establishments find it simpler to serve food to which people are accustomed. The islands' cookery is the product of their situation, of their Norman origins, and the basic foods available over centuries when their nearest neighbour, France, was often at war or at best unfriendly and Britain was too remote by the transport available to contribute to their larders.

In 1981, however, the Hotel l'Horizon, at St Brelade's Bay in Jersey, which has a considerable culinary reputation, attracted many enthusiasts for a Channel Islands dinner. This was the menu:

Des Ormers de Jèrri
(Jersey ormers)

D'la Soupe d'Andgulle
(Conger eel soup)

Des Pais au Fou
(Jersey bean crock)

Un d'mie Honmard fraid des Iles
(Half lobster)

D'la Sauce Mayonnaise
(Mayonnaise sauce)

Des Nouvelles Patates au Persi
(Parsleyed new potatoes)

D'la Salade
(Salad)

Des Bourdelots a tout au Nier Beurre
(Pastry-wrapped apples with black butter)

Un Assortiment d'Fromages
(Assorted cheeses)

Da Celeri
(Celery)

Le Café
(Coffee)

Des Petits Fours
(Petits Fours)

Several items are obvious. Of the others, the ormer – from the French *oreille de mer* – is the most famous islands dish. Related to, but smaller than, the Pacific abalone, it is scarce from much 'ormering', and is being driven south by falling temperatures. In the islands it is extracted from its mother-of-pearl-like shell, scrubbed, pummelled, floured, fried and then casseroled with pork or bacon, carrots and herbs, until tender, when the taste and texture is like that of liver. Conger eel soup is made from the head of the conger eel boiled in milk with marigold flowers.

The bean crock, or bean jar – said to be the origin of baked beans – is the great 'universal' of Channel Islands cookery; and it must have almost as many variants as it has cooks. Basically it is dried beans, soaked overnight and then casseroled with pig's trotter, belly pork or shin beef, onions and seasoning. It has, of course, two different forms: the Guernsey, which calls specifically for haricot beans, carrots, thick stock and herbs; and the Jersey, which requires five different kinds of beans.

Black butter, which used to be made in great all-night parties, consists of cider which is simmered and into which, when it has reduced, peeled and cored apples are tipped, boiled to a pulp; finally sugar and spices are added and the 'butter' is allowed slowly to cool.

Although the splendid dairy products from Jersey and Guernsey cows (the Alderney is now extinct in the Channel Islands) have long been available, they are too rich to produce such piquant cheeses as those of nearby Normandy. The islands, however, produce a profusion of plain, fruit, dough and lard cakes, buns, biscuits and bread as well as sweet and savoury puddings. There are, too, the traditional Easter sweets, the *fiottes* (balls of flour, sugar and eggs cooked in milk), sweet biscuits, first boiled and then baked, and 'wonders' – a kind of Jersey doughnut made in the shape of a figure eight.

Like all country economies, too, that of the Channel Islands included many soups: cress, cabbage, oyster, tomato (of course), and Sark pottage (mackerel, gooseberries, cabbage, ham, onions, flour and milk).

Obviously seafood was – and is – a staple. The more unusual items are cockles served hot, baked mullet, oyster soup, pickled mackerel and, an old Channel Islands favourite, octopus served hot with bean jar. It has been suggested that Victor Hugo's vivid descriptions of octopus in *Les Travailleurs de la Mer*, as taken up and plagiarized by subsequent writers, created its general connotation of horror.

A severe epidemic in 1904 means that oysters are not as readily available as they once were. Lobsters, crab (especially spider crabs in Guernsey) prawns and shrimps are island favourites. Bream, garfish, monkfish, cod, mackerel, John Dory and bass are all available from local waters. Many of the best restaurants in the islands specialize in fish; and there can be no more splendid display than that on the fish slabs in St Peter Port market.

So far as drinking is concerned, tea has long been an island preoccupation. The traditional 'milk-a-punch' was made on Milk-a-Punch Sunday (the first Sunday in May) when – and still in Alderney – milk could be taken from any cow or eggs from any roost and the publican would add the rum; now it is simpler for the pubs to supply the drink complete – and free.

For centuries fishermen and others sailing out of the islands brought wine home from France without payment of duty: and, of course, smuggling was by no means unknown. Cider was produced on a considerable scale in the islands as early as the 16th century; and in 1681 John Poingdestre recorded that 'there were not enough casks in the islands for much above half that was made.' As the hold of the Customs tightened, an increasing quantity, too, was exported. The quality of Jersey and Guernsey cider was similar but Jersey's bulk was greater: to such an extent, indeed, that in the last century one quarter of that island's arable land was given over to apples. By the 1890s as much as 35,000 sixty-gallon hogsheads were being exported each year. Now, little is produced, apart from a small quantity made by farmers for their own use, and a single commercial exception. Some, though, is imported from France.

Wine is generally imported at the favourable local rate of duty; much of it out of British bond. There has been a considerable production in Jersey and Guernsey of dessert grapes but virtually none for wine: again with a single exception.

The exception in the case of both drinks is Robert Blayney of La Mare Vineyards, St Mary, Jersey. From his 12 acres of orchard and vines (the latter planted only in 1972) he produces each year, by traditional methods and in his own presshouses, some 5000 bottles of cider and an average 12,000 bottles of his two wines: Clos de

Vines in April, La Mare Vineyards, Jersey

Seyval and Clos de la Mare. Clos de Seyval, a medium-dry fullish white wine, is made from Seyval grapes; the Clos de la Mare from the Reichensteiner grape blended with a small proportion of the aromatic Scheurebe. La Mare is a family undertaking which also produces a wine mustard and a cider mustard. The vineyard, centred on an ancient farmhouse, is proving successful as an attraction for tourists.

THE BAILIWICK
OF JERSEY

'Britannia', The Lamplighter public house, St Helier

Previous page: Île aux Guerdains, Portelet Bay (see p. 62)

The Bailiwick of Jersey Gazetteer

Almorah Crescent (2/4B) This striking crescent named after a town in India, where the wife of the builder had been born, is probably Jersey's most distinguished piece of Regency-style architecture, though built in 1845. It was a joint effort by a group of artisans, an interesting enterprise. The interior décor suggests a later date than the exterior, a characteristic of other local houses of the period. Conservationists are most concerned about its upkeep, for it is the detailing of its balconies which give it such prestige. Its situation above the town, where it is visible from almost every angle, make it the 'Acropolis' of ST HELIER.

Battle of Flowers, The *see* Victoria Avenue

Battle of Jersey, The *see* Royal Square

Bonne Nuit Bay (2/4A) This most attractive and popular bay lies on the north coast in ST JOHN'S PARISH. First called Male Nocte ('Bad Night') it is recorded from 1160 as Bonne Nuit. The change in name may have been in an effort to placate evil spirits, or as a prayer for protection. In the middle of the bay is a rock, Le Cheval Guillaume, which used to be a favourite resort on Midsummer's Night – St John the Baptist's Day. It was thought that to row round the rock was a protection from bad fortune: probably a very ancient custom.

In medieval times the little bay was dominated by a priory dedicated to Ste Marie, and the headland of Frémont Point supplied the monks with their fuel as far back as 1160. The priory was suppressed in 1415 and its site is not known precisely.

The bay later became a favourite haunt for smugglers, as well as for fishermen, and is now a popular resort for sailing and bathing. The fort at the east end, La Crête, built in 1835, is part of the ring of coastal defences that surround Jersey; there was also a boulevard, a guardhouse, a powder magazine and a barracks, though no

Bonne Nuit Bay

La Corbière lighthouse from L'Oeillère

enemy attack ever took place here. The pier dates from 1872.

In summer the hills around the bay are ablaze with heather, honeysuckle and many other wild flowers.

Bouley Bay (2/5A) A haven with the deepest water round the island's shores, Bouley Bay was seriously considered for developing as the main harbour in the mid-19th century.

The idea of a harbour here is not new; in the Extente (list of royal revenues) of 1274 the bay was already called Portus de Boley, and in 1685 it was again being considered as a harbour, but the surrounding steep hills probably ruled it out as impracticable. The existing pier was built in 1827, as testified by an inscribed stone with the initials of the builder, Abraham de la Mare. On the hillside, hidden among the bracken, is a stone trough dated 1834 with the initials of those neighbours who had the right to use it for washing their clothes. Some of the woods on the slopes belong to the National Trust, and delightful walks can be taken all around the coast here. The steep and tortuous hill is used for an annual hill climb event which attracts large crowds.

CLAMEUR DE HARO

Every book on Jersey will speak of the picturesque custom of Le Clameur de Haro. If a person feels that he is sustaining damage to his real property, he can, in the presence of witnesses, call out:

> *Haro, Haro,*
> *à l'aide mon Prince,*
> *on me fait tort.*
>
> (Rollo, Rollo, my Prince,
> come to my aid,
> I am being wronged.)

This must be done on the site of the alleged wrong and the malefactor must stop instantly until the case has been investigated by the Royal Court. Heavy fines will follow if the Clameur should have been wrongfully raised.

It is a custom of great antiquity and is a direct appeal to the Duke of Normandy, embodied now in Her Majesty the Queen. It was raised in Normandy at the Conqueror's funeral, and has been raised in Jersey in quite recent times. *(See also* Guernsey Customs, Celebrations and Ceremonies *on p. 125.)*

Corbière, La (2/1C) The name means a haunt of crows or ravens, birds of ill omen, and certainly the reef has been disastrous for many ships. It was first mentioned in 1309, and a legend tells that in 1414 a Spanish ship was wrecked here, and the area was covered with casks of wine, the perquisite by right of the Seigneur. In 1495 it is said that five more Spanish ships were wrecked; their crews were treated with such cruelty that a sandstorm that followed was thought to be divine vengeance – for the blown sand covered and spoiled an area of arable land. The tale of wrecks continued through the years and in 1859 the *Express* was lost at La Rosière, a cove beside Corbière Point, with loss of life.

It was not until 1873, however, that the decision was taken to build a lighthouse. This was designed by Imrie Bell, a noted engineer, and constructed in concrete, an innovation at the time. It is 35 ft high and the light, now electric, must have saved many lives. But there is another danger lurking here, for the incoming tide is treacherous, and as late as 1946 the assistant lighthouse keeper lost his own life in attempting to save that of a visitor trapped by the waves.

An old quarry here now contains a desalination plant to treat sea water. This is in theory a most excellent idea for supplementing the island's water supply – were it not so costly to run; consequently it is used only in times of shortage.

La Corbière was the terminus of the now defunct Western Railway, and beside what was the platform can be seen a large granite stone over 12 ft by 6 ft. It is probably a prehistoric capstone but its name, La Table des Marthes, is curious. This may be a form of 'martyr' and indicate sacrificial rites, or it may just refer to the game of knucklebones, *marthes* – a children's game in what was, until this century, a remote and desolate spot.

Cotte de St Brelade, La (2/2C) Old Stone Age Man lived here before Jersey was an island. Raised beaches, that is to say places where water-worn boulders and pebbles indicate a higher sea level than at present, are found around the island at 26 ft, 60 ft and 98 ft above the present-day mean tide level. And between these eras the sea fell far below it.

The earliest phase in the story of La Cotte is 130,000 years ago. Axes of the Acheulian period have been found and in 1910 a highly important discovery was made, that of 13 teeth of Neanderthal man, the only actual human remains to be found. Many animal bones have been

---

THE CONSTITUTION OF JERSEY

Jersey is a dependency or apanage of the Crown, but not of Parliament: a 'peculiar of the Crown' as it was called by Philip Falle (1656-1742), the earliest Jersey historian. This is because the Channel Islands were part of Normandy in the days before 1204 when Normandy and England were under one ruler, and have never subsequently been incorporated into the United Kingdom.

The island is governed by a legislative assembly known as the States, which originated as an offshoot of the local judicial body, the Royal Court. To this day the Bailiff (who is a lawyer), appointed by the Crown, takes the chair in both, as President in the former and as Chief Magistrate in the latter. The Royal Court consists of the Bailiff and twelve Jurats, lay magistrates chosen by an electoral college. The States are composed of three elements or *états*. Today these are: 12 Senators elected by an all-island franchise; the 12 Constables (somewhat akin in their functions to an English mayor) each representing a parish; and 29 elected Deputies, each representing a parish or electoral district within a parish. All these elected members serve without emolument. Also present in the States, with a voice but no vote, are the Law Officers of the Crown – the Attorney-General and Solicitor-General – and the Dean, the head of the Established (Anglican) Church in the island, who today is usually also the Rector of ST HELIER'S PARISH. Before the constitutional reform of 1948 there were fewer Deputies and no Senators, but the Jurats, then elected on a limited island-wide franchise, served in the States as well as in the Court, and the Rectors of the 12 parishes were also members.

The Channel Islands are self-governing communities which are not represented in the Westminster Parliament and are responsible for their own fiscal affairs. This independence, especially in regard to taxation, is the outcome of the recognition by successive sovereigns over the centuries of the islands' loyalty to the Crown. Thus the States of Jersey can and do control the island's internal (but not international) affairs, though new laws must be ratified by Her Majesty in Council. There is also an immemorial right of appeal to the Privy Council in civil judicial cases, though now very seldom used. A Court of Appeal to hear ordinary civil and criminal appeals from the Royal Court was established in 1961.

Jersey's position in relation to the European Economic Community is complex. She is not a member of the Community but is within the Common External Tariff. It was not economically possible for the island to remain isolated when Great Britain joined the EEC, and Jersey fully recognizes the great advantages it receives from the close and ancient links with the United Kingdom.

unearthed, including rhinoceros and elephant skulls. As time went on the cave became filled with bones and debris, and man seems to have abandoned the site around 75,000 years ago.

Excavation in the cave has taken place intermittently since 1910, but notably since the Second World War, firstly by a very skilled amateur archaeologist, the late Reverend Christian Burdo SJ, and then by the late Dr C. McBurney, who year by year brought over his Cambridge students, including HRH Prince Charles, to continue the work and to unravel all the mysteries it presented.

The site and its finds are of international importance. The finds, particularly the bones, are kept in carefully controlled conditions by the Société Jersiaise, the local archaeological society. The site has now been sealed off, partly because it is a dangerous place for the unwary, and partly to preserve further evidence for future generations.

Devil's Hole (2/3A) This is a natural tunnel through the rocks on Jersey's north coast, leading to a circular opening, approached down steep paths. It can be visited by climbing down, but it is unwise to try to approach it by sea. It is a stirring sight with a rough sea and incoming tide.

The real name is Le Creux de Vis, 'screwhole', corrupted into 'devil'. In 1851 a French vessel, *La Joséphine*, was wrecked here and four of the crew were rescued by a nearby farmer. It has been suggested that her figurehead was somewhat like the Devil, and with a body and limbs added, it became the effigy of the Devil shown at the spot for years.

Ecréhous, Les (2/6A) A reef of rocks east-north-east of Jersey consisting of three islets. On one, the Maître Île, there was a chapel and a small priory dedicated to Ste Marie, already mentioned in 1203. Here the priest in charge had the duty of keeping a light burning to warn sailors of the dangerous rocks, as recorded in 1309. Only the lower part of the walls of the chapel remain, but it is enough to form a reasonable assessment of what the building was. Contiguous to it are the remains of 19th-century fishermen's huts almost as derelict. The priest's house must have been on the site of one of them.

On the main island, Marmoutier, are several minute houses, built for fishermen, and now used as holiday homes for some fortunate families. There is even a Customs House with the Jersey arms carved upon it. The islets are immensely popular with sailing vessels both from Jersey and from France. (If you come from the Continent beware of letting your dog loose, for Les Ecréhous are governed by the same anti-rabies restriction as Jersey itself.)

The third islet is the Blanche Île, accessible over a sandbank at low tide, and even boasting a freshwater well.

Over the years two men, Philippe Pinel from 1848, and in more recent years Alphonse Le Gastelois, have chosen to maroon themselves over there. Those who stay there, even for a night or two, find an un-eerie charm in the solitude and peacefulness of the surroundings, with the waves and sea birds for company – but in winter conditions the islet is a real hermitage.

See also Minquiers, Les

Elizabeth Castle (2/4C) The earliest evidence of man here is the great hump of rock in which is a cave, the reputed home of St Helier, hermit, missionary and patron saint, who gave his name to Jersey's capital and its parish. According to legend he was murdered there by pirates in AD 555. He was among the earliest Christian missionaries to come to Jersey. A small oratory was built over the cave in the 12th century.

It was not until 1594 that a beginning was made to fortify the islet, when it was seen that MONT ORGUEIL CASTLE on the east coast was out of date as the main defensive point. Queen Elizabeth's military engineer, Paul Ivy, was sent over to design a fortress, and the upper part on the west was completed by 1600 when Sir Walter Raleigh arrived as Governor. The house in which he lived remained the Governor's official residence until the 18th century, when it was found to be increasingly inconvenient to be cut off by the tide for half the time. This very fact contributes not a little to the romantic atmosphere of the castle and makes it a site of exceptional historical interest.

When Charles II came to Jersey as Prince of Wales in 1646, fleeing from England and then from the Scilly Isles, and as King in 1649 (proclaimed and accepted by Jersey though by no other part of his kingdom) Elizabeth Castle is where he stayed. The local diarist Jean Chevalier kept a day-to-day record of the period so that we know every detail of Charles's movements. It was here that he made the original grant of land to Sir George Carteret, to be named New Jersey (though the present American state of that name is not the first land given); it was here that he performed the ceremony of Touching for the King's Evil, when he was the acknowledged king;

Elizabeth Castle

and it was here that Clarendon, the most loyal of his followers, wrote his *History of the Rebellion*. As Prince and as King he was accompanied by a large and motley crowd of courtiers and followers, all penniless, whose presence put a great strain on a small town not then geared to tourism. It was in recognition of the safety and hospitality and loyalty he received that Charles gave to Jersey its splendid ceremonial mace.

Elizabeth Castle held out for a long time for Charles against the Parliamentary forces, but it was finally surrendered in 1651 when a bomb from the Jersey mainland fell on to the old abbey church, where ammunition was stored in the crypt. Thus an early medieval church disappeared, as well as the last shreds of Royalist resistance. Forts, moats, gates and look-out were added, many bearing arms or initials that proclaim their date. In the mid-18th century the fine granite barracks were built to designs by J. H. Bastide.

The long breakwater dates from 1872, when it was designed to be the western arm of a greatly enlarged St Helier's Harbour, but the fury of the south-west gales destroyed that particular effort, leaving the one arm complete. Before and during the First World War the castle was garrisoned. A picket house used to stand where there is now a slipway (departure point for the amphibious Dukws that take visitors to the castle), and this was where troops returning from shore leave were kept if they were not in a state to make the journey back to base.

The whole complex was handed to the States of Jersey in 1922, though during the German Occupation it again saw military service, bristling with guns (two are still there), and a garrison of 100 men.

Much work is now being done to interpret the site for visitors, and very full information is available. Even the fives court is being repaired and will be used by enthusiastic players. In 1985 Elizabeth Castle had 116,000 visitors (it is open to the public from March to October).

Fishermen's Chapel, The *see* St Brelade's Church

Fort Regent (2/4C) The fort is built atop the great hill, La Montagne de la Ville, which protects the town from the east. The hill was used by the townspeople in medieval times for grazing their animals, and for cutting furze for fuel, and later it was used as a place for promenading and admiring the views, which are spectacular. On the eastern side there was a pre-Reformation chapel, la Chapelle des Pas, so named from a supposed footprint of the Virgin to whom it was dedicated, but it was removed for military reasons when in about 1804 the hill was converted into a defensive point. Completed in 1814 and named after the Prince Regent, later George IV, the fort never had to be put to the use for which it was designed, though troops were stationed there until well after the First World War. The designer was General John Hambly Humfrey and it was a magnificent fortress of its time; the ashlar granite work of the retaining walls should be noticed.

The decision to fortify this potentially strong position was first taken after the Battle of Jersey (*see* Royal Square). During levelling work in 1785 a dolmen was uncovered. This was dismantled and presented to the then Governor, General Seymour Conway, whose archaeological interests were well known. The dolmen was taken to England, floated up the Thames to the general's home, Park Place, Henley, and re-erected in his garden, where it still stands today.

When it was no longer used to garrison troops the fort gradually became forlorn and derelict. In 1958 the States of Jersey bought it from the War Department, and decided to convert it into a leisure centre and conference hall. A benefactor, Sir John Wardlaw Milne, left money for this purpose feeling rightly there was so little for visitors to do in bad weather. With inflation the original bequest could not measure up to the costs, but the States continue to offer a wide variety of entertainments there; the swimming pool, though not beautiful on the skyline, is much enjoyed by both residents and visitors.

Glass Church, The *see* St Matthew's Church

Gorey (2/6B) The village, and between 1873 and 1929 a railway station, take their name from the district. This appeared in 1180 as Gorroic, a name that has seen many changes in spelling over the years. The present little harbour was built early in the 19th century, mainly for the use of the oyster fishing industry which prospered until about 1850, when it gradually disappeared owing to over-dredging. In 1834 alone it is reported that 305,000 bushels of oysters were exported, and restaurants supplied them free to their customers. Later in the century shipbuilding yards occupied the shoreline, where now a sea wall and promenade delight the tourist.

In 1833, to provide English services for the fishermen and packing women, a church was built on the hill. Rows of single-storey cottages in the village were also built to accommodate them. The use of the word 'village' is rare in Jersey, where settlement patterns have been different from England, but it has always been given to Gorey.

In the summer the little harbour is a busy sight, with privately owned yachts jostling for space with vessels from the opposite coast of France, which can be seen very clearly in good weather.

Gorey Castle *see* Mont Orgueil Castle

Green Island *see* Motte, La

Grève de Lecq (2/2A) This is a bay on Jersey's north coast, steeped in history. The high conical hill on its east is an Iron Age fortification. The mill, now an inn, was first mentioned in 1551, but is probably far older than that. There are frequent references in documents to its maintenance, and provision of its millstones, as well as to rules governing the miller and, most important, the free flow of the water feeding it. The mill straddles the stream dividing the parishes of ST OUEN and ST MARY, a stream that gushes out onto the beach, to the delight of children making sandcastles there.

A tarmacadamed car park, which is full to overflowing in summer, surrounds the Jersey Round Tower built in 1780; overlooking this are the Barracks, now National Trust property and open to the public in the summer, built around 1810. Other barracks were built to accommodate garrison troops at BONNE NUIT BAY, ROZEL BAY and in ST PETER'S PARISH – the last-named being the biggest of them. But the Grève de Lecq Barracks are the sole survivor; there is a block for officers, four barrack rooms, with all the ancillary buildings of stables, stores, ablution blocks, magazine and prison cells, all constructed in fine dressed granite.

The pier, of which only a section remains, was built in 1872. As it started to disintegrate large blocks of stone were strewn on the beach, threatening it for bathers. However, all this has now been cleared, and it remains one of the most popular of beaches. The cave at Val Rouget to the east can be explored at low tide, but the greatest care should be taken not to be caught by the incoming tide. The beautiful scented tree lupin, white or pale yellow, used to abound on the sandhills around the bay, but modern buildings and the landscaping of the surroundings have greatly reduced them.

Grosnez Castle

Grosnez Castle (2/1A) On the north-west promontory of the island stand the ruins of a medieval castle. Little is known of its history, but it was already described as being in ruins, *Grosnes Castrum diritum*, on Popinjay's map of 1540. It seems probable that it was intended more as a refuge in times of attack, especially as it had no well, than as an active military installation in its own right. It may either have been deliberately destroyed during the French occupation of 1461-8, or it may have been damaged during du Guesclin's attack in 1373, when two castles are mentioned: one is certainly MONT ORGUEIL, and the second is not known for sure. A gully to the north-west is called Le Creux aux Français, and may support this theory. Carved corbels that decorated the Gothic arch fell into the dry moat long ago, and they are now exhibited at LA HOUGUE BIE. The decorations incised upon them deserve close inspection.

Slightly to the south may be seen a German concrete coastal tower, a fine piece of military architecture of its period, and it was to the west of Grosnez Castle that many German guns were dumped after the Occupation.

Halfway down the cliff on the north there is a lighthouse, from where the views are spectacular on a clear day; it is very necessary to shipping, as these are dangerous waters. In the summer the headland is ablaze with heather, dwarf gorse and many other flowers. Slightly inland there is a race course. Races are run here with great enthusiasm several times a year.

Grouville Church (2/5C) This church, like its neighbour to the north, is dedicated to St Martin of Tours but it is styled St Martin de Grouville, while the other is St Martin le Vieux.

The nave appears to be the oldest part, with the tower dating from the 12th or 13th century. The crossing under the tower has a quadripartite vault, and the roof, unusually for Jersey, is unvaulted; the present wooden roof dates only from *c.* 1866.

Over the years there have been changes of floor level, of up to 2 ft. This may partly explain a most curious carved head, with its forehead pierced, set in a recess and now at floor level in the south-east corner of the church. Its purpose is unsure but may have been an aumbry.

In the 15th century the crossing and chancel were altered and the tracery of the fine east window is of that date.

The font, of which the plinth is modern, is most interesting: it is 15th century and has a bowl within a bowl, all carved out of the same piece of granite. This was to catch drops of holy water falling from the child's head into the sanctified water, and it is very rare. It was made for ST HELIER'S CHURCH and was thrown out at the Reformation. The Calvinist regime would not allow its re-use and it was subsequently moved to LA HOUGUE BIE but was given to Grouville Church when that property was acquired by the Société Jersiaise. Unusually for Jersey, the church has two piscinae and there is a carved bowl, medieval in origin, of mica lamprophyre stone, with a complex device in raised design and the IHS monogram. The bell is dated 1768, and was refounded in 1881.

At the west end of the nave is the standard of the 1914 Jersey Overseas Contingent; militiamen did not have to serve outside the island, but these volunteered for such service.

The church silver is displayed in a treasury and includes several locally made items – wine cups, a platter of 1688, a ewer of 1781 and a baptismal dish of 1782.

In the churchyard there is a memorial to seven grenadiers of the 83rd Regiment, killed during de Rullecourt's landing, which culminated in the Battle of Jersey (see Royal Square). In recent years the unsightly Roman cement, put there in 1788, which clad the steeple of this and other churches, has been removed, exposing the warm colouring of the native granite, an enormous improvement. The north wall of the church has retained some fragments of medieval plaster, a rare survival of what may have covered all the churches in the Middle Ages.

Grouville Parish (2/5C) Grouville Parish boasts one of the finest bays on the island, the Royal Bay of Grouville, which stretches from La Rocque Point to Gorey Harbour.

On the land adjoining the beach is one of the most picturesque of links golf courses in Britain. The Royal Jersey Golf Club was founded in 1878 and granted its Royal Charter by Queen Victoria. Its greatest player was Harry Vardon to whom a memorial stone has been placed on the 12th fairway. The Club has produced many international players and its present professional, Tommy Horton, was a Ryder Cup player and former captain of the Professional Golfers' Association.

Within the bay are a number of forts and Martello towers built as defences during the Napoleonic Wars; the two principal ones offshore are Seymour and Icho towers, which can be reached at low tide on foot.

In 1984 a plaque was placed by the steps of La Rocque to commemorate the landing of a French force of 700 soldiers on 6 January 1781. They marched to St Helier where they were finally defeated in the Royal Square.

Harbour, The see St Helier's Harbour

Havre des Pas (3/3C) For most people this name will evoke a picture of the Swimming Pool. With the island's rise and fall of the tide (the second greatest in the world), swimming pools are more important in Jersey than elsewhere.

Among more modern villas in the area, largely now hotels and guesthouses, may be noticed some older houses with exceptionally good wrought-iron balconies.

Shipbuilding yards ringed a greater part of Jersey's south coast in the late 18th century and through the 19th; preserved at Havre de Pas is that of Francis Allix whose last vessel, the *Florida*, was launched there in 1877. A commemorative plaque records the details.

The hill above Havre des Pas, Le Mont de la Ville, now crowned by FORT REGENT, held the Neolithic dolmen that was presented to the Governor of the time and removed to England. On the eastern slope of Le Mont de La Ville there was a pre-Reformation chapel, demolished in 1814, dedicated to Our Lady of the Footprints (les Pas). It thus gave its name to the haven in the lee of the promontory where the Fort d'Auvergne Hotel now stands.

Hospital, The (3/1A) Jersey's General Hospital in ST HELIER is at present being greatly enlarged. The main central building was erected in 1859 after a fire. A series of vicissitudes had dogged the hospital over the years.

The first hospital, so called, was more of a poorhouse and orphanage and was started in 1765; but in 1779 it was requisitioned as a barracks, and most of it was destroyed by exploding gunpowder in 1783. The legitimate inmates returned in 1793, but were again evicted in 1799 for foreign troops to be stationed there. Only in 1801 did it return to its intended use.

It was not until the mid-19th century that the differing claims of paupers, orphans, lunatics and the sick were recognized as demanding segregation.

Hougue Bie, La (2/5B) There is a great deal of history centred in this one spot. The origin of he word Hougue, common all over the Channel Islands, is *haugr*, Old Norse for a mound or hill. A legend tells the story of one Paynel, Seigneur of Hambie in Normandy, who came to rid Jersey of a dragon that lurked in St Lawrence's marsh. This association with Hambie is taken to account for the Bie in the name. *(See p. 8.)*

The great burial mound, or tumulus, which can be seen from afar, covers a Neolithic tomb. It is one of the finest in Western Europe, dating from at least 3000 BC. It was not discovered, although suspected by archaeologists, until 1924. As often happened, the early missionaries built a chapel upon the mound, doubtless already venerated as a place of worship. The chapel to the west is dedicated to Notre Dame de la Clarté, our Lady of Light, or of the Dawn; that to the east, known as the Jerusalem Chapel, is thought to be late 15th century. It is likely, however, that Dean Mabon, who is credited with building the chapel, adapted an existing structure, for no division can be found in the masonry. He it was who added the crypt to the east, forming it, as he said, as a replica of the Holy Sepulchre in Jerusalem, which he visited in about 1510. Here he organized pseudo-miracles, which deceived pilgrims to the site. In the Jerusalem Chapel there are wall paintings, of archangels, of 15th-century date. The date on the scroll one of the angels is holding refers to some later work.

In 1759 General James d'Auvergne bought the property, and around the chapels he built an elaborate tower, for years known as Prince's Tower, after his nephew and heir who was Prince of Bouillon. Within the tower he contrived a kitchen and various rooms. When in 1919 the local archaeological society acquired the site, the tower, already in a dangerous condition, was demolished, uncovering the medieval chapels.

During the German Occupation the site was heavily fortified – for each succeeding generation has found the mound an excellent observation point.– and the bunker in the grounds now houses a military museum of the Occupation. There are also archaeological, geological and agricultural displays, making this, with its park-like setting, a place that caters for all tastes.

Icho Tower (2/6C) This is a minute islet over a mile to the south of Jersey, and accessible on foot only at the lowest tides (see title-page).

It has a Martello tower built in 1811, and must have been a lonely posting for men on guard there. However, the site is far older, for there is evidence of a cross here as early as 1563: presumably it had been there long before that, for

such a date is after the Reformation, when no one would have put one up. It was stated in 1685 to be an iron cross, hence the islet's alternative name of La Croix de Fer.

Herons may often be seen here in winter, and occasionally grey seals visit the rock.

Île au Guerdain see Portelet

L'Étacq (2/1A) This name is of Old Norse derivation (*stakkr*, a pile, stump or stack) and so must date from the 9th or 10th century, when the Vikings roamed these waters. The rock mass with a flat platform upon it used to have a Martello tower, but it was blown up during the German Occupation.

L'Île Agois (2/2A) The Île Agois, almost certainly taking its name from the Goes family, is a minuscule island in Crabbé Bay. Within living memory a plank bridge connected it with the mainland and sheep were taken over to graze. It slopes steeply to the north-west, is only approachable at low tide and is covered in blackthorn. It belongs to the National Trust for Jersey. Excavation was undertaken in 1974, when the archaeologists camped on the island and worked in most arduous conditions. Their work showed this was a 7th- or 8th-century eremetic site or settlement, a type of very early monastery. Some 18 Roman coins of the 3rd century AD have been found in its inhospitable soil.

JERSEY WILDLIFE PRESERVATION TRUST

Founded 20 years ago by Gerald Durrell, the famous writer and naturalist, this trust exists to do all in its power to preserve endangered species of wildlife, and during the time that it has been established, and with HRH Princess Anne as Patron, it has achieved notable success. Its headquarters are situated at Les Augrès (2/5A) in Trinity, a splendid property with beautiful traditional round arches and other features of Jersey vernacular architecture. The Zoological Gardens the Trust maintains are enhanced by the surroundings, and imaginative tree planting and landscaping have made it a delightful place.

Ownership of this beautiful property has passed through several families down the centuries, and the visitor may notice many initialled stones of the Payn, Dumaresq and Perchard families.

A snowy owl at the Zoological Gardens

Above: The indoor market, St Helier
Opposite: One of the original hexagonal letterboxes

Longueville Manor (2/5B) As you drive eastwards out of ST HELIER you will pass an ancient
manor house, now a prestigious hotel, and its
round-arched entrance on the roadside. Though
much altered in modern times there are substantial traces of a 14th-century house. It is
known that there was a manorial chapel dedicated
to St Thomas à Becket and the small road along-
side is still called La Rue St Thomas. The
colombier (dovecot) was already recorded in 1299
and was rebuilt in 1692; it now belongs to the
National Trust. *(See p. 56)*.

The name Longueville, which occurs here and in
two vingtaines (parish subdivisions) in Grouville,
probably stems from Longueville in Normandy.

Markets, The (3/2B) Every visitor should make a
tour of ST HELIER's markets. In the main market
there are mostly vegetables and fruit, and there is
a separate fish market near by. This latter has in
recent years been rebuilt and modernized, presumably making it more hygienic but at the same
time losing some of its character. Here a wide
range of fish can be seen and bought. What

attracts the visitor most are perhaps the varieties
of shellfish, in particular the ormer, *oreille de mer*,
a rare delicacy, and quite delicious if well pre-
pared. Another rather unusual fish is the conger
eel, from which conger soup is made, a local
speciality.

Until around 1800 the market was in the ROYAL
SQUARE, le Vier Marchi, but congestion made it
unsuitable and an open market was built on the
site of the present one; the central space was
surrounded by roofed colonnades, but this in
turn became too congested, and the present fine
market was built in 1882. There is an elaborate
central fountain made by Abraham Viel, with
goldfish, encircling cherubs and foliage, all to the
great interest of visitors who may be seen taking
photographs of it, and the entrancement of
children. Outside the recently opened Post
Office, within the market, is one of the original
hexagonal letterboxes, one of four installed as an
experiment by Anthony Trollope, the novelist,
then Post Office Surveyor. Made in 1851, they
were the first in the British Isles.

The well-stocked stalls, with banks of flowers,
stacks of brightly coloured fruits and mountains
of fine vegetables, make a gay and cheerful sight
at all seasons.

Minquiers, Les This reef lies east of Jersey and to the south of LES ECRÉHOUS. Both reefs were the subject of a case taken to the International Court at The Hague in 1953. It was ruled that both groups belonged to Jersey, that is to say to Britain, and not to France, who was claiming them. The case was of more importance in international law than the size of the reefs might suggest, for Great Britain had lost more than one case and was not anxious to lose another.

Over the years much granite has been quarried from the islets: so much so that on one occasion the fishermen dropped the quarrymen's tools into the sea, as they feared the islands, and thus their fishing base, would quite disappear.

This has always been a valuable fishing ground and fishermen built themselves small stone houses on Les Minquiers (usually pronounced 'Minkies'); these are now mainly used by islanders who have boats, and enjoy the fishing and the tranquillity. At low tide the area uncovered is greater than that of Jersey, and it is said that to watch an incoming spring tide at sunset is one of life's greater experiences.

Such a remote and unspoiled area is clearly a good place for observing wild life habitats, and many sea birds may be seen, and even, on occasion, a nightingale. In archaeological times (Les Minquiers were a Bronze and Iron Age site) the grey seal frequented the islets. The main plant cover now is tree mallow and sea beet, or sea spinach.

Clearly this is a dangerous reef, and in 1840 the *Polka* was wrecked there on 16 September. Then on 24 September the *Superb*, wishing to see the scene of the first tragedy, suffered the same fate.

Mont Mado (2/4A) The visitor to Jersey will often hear reference to Mont Mado granite, the best building stone of all, used for as long as there are records. Huge quarries in the north of ST JOHN'S PARISH resulted, but these are now levelled and grassed over, after serving as rubbish tips for some time and now one would never know that they had ever been there.

The quality of the stone was such that it was widely used for the cornerstones of buildings, and the surrounds of doors and windows. In 1650 it was said that the quarry was exhausted, as all the good stone had been extracted, but it was not so, and Mont Mado stone was used for another three centuries after that.

The colombier (dovecot), Longueville Manor (see p. 55)

THE JERSEY MILITIA

The earliest reference to a defensive army, taken to be the germ of the Jersey Militia, is in 1336, when 'all men capable of bearing arms' were ordered to be organized for defence.

Over the years this evolved into a force to be reckoned with. No militiaman was obliged to serve outside Jersey except for the direct personal safety of the monarch. Although details naturally changed over the years, in general all able men between 16 and 60 had to serve, and without pay. The militiamen mounted guard along the coasts, manned the towers, attended drill, and kept fire beacons in readiness in case of attack.

There were, for many years, four regiments, plus an artillery unit; the five arsenals were built in 1843 for drilling and storage of equipment. Most of these have now been converted into housing.

It was in 1830 that the King's ADC, Colonel (later Sir) John Le Couteur, had a conversation with William IV and asked if the prefix 'Royal' might be added to the militia name, to which His Majesty replied 'Royal? Oh, certainly!', and this was announced to coincide with the jubilee of the Battle of Jersey (1781). Several parish churches have militia colours, now very fragile, in safe keeping.

The militia was mobilized in July 1914, and in March 1915 a large voluntary contingent left for overseas service. A total of 862 Jerseymen fell, the number serving being 6292. In the Second World War the militia again served, absorbed into a battalion of the Hampshire Regiment.

In 1946 the Royal Jersey Militia was finally disbanded after 600 years of faithful service, a proud record.

Mont Orgueil Castle (2/6B) When floodlit during the summer it seems that a fairy castle has risen into the sky above the tiny harbour of GOREY. There is likely to have been a defended strongpoint here since the New Stone Age, but the castle dates from when King John (Good King John to Jersey) lost Normandy. It is first mentioned by name, or by inference, when the king granted to Philippe d'Aubigny 'the custody of Jersey with our Castle'. From then on alterations were made to strengthen Mont Orgueil Castle, also known as Gorey Castle or le Vieux Château, and to bring it up to the most modern standards of each succeeding generation. The most serious threat was when it became apparent that cannon mounted on the hill opposite, le Mont St Nicolas, could bombard it – a much greater danger than bows and arrows had ever presented. So within Mont Orgueil Castle changes and additions of many dates can be seen,

such as the old 13th-century keep; the 15th-century Harliston Tower, named after the Governor of the time, Sir Richard Harliston; and the Somerset Tower, which is Elizabethan.

A formidable fortress to storm, Mont Orgueil has withstood many assaults, but capitulated only between 1461 and 1468, when Pierre de Brezé, Comte de Maulevrier, took it, and then probably through collusion: Margaret of Anjou, wife of Henry IV, was anxious to gain an outpost for the Red Rose party and may have been implicated. Before that, in 1294, 1338 and 1373, to name but a few instances, raiders from the French coast opposite unsuccessfully tried to conquer it. Included among these was Bertrand du Guesclin, the most famous soldier of his time, and even he failed.

However, by the end of the 16th century it seemed as if the castle was doomed, as it could no longer withstand modern forms of attack. At various stages, notably in 1515 and 1531, reports were made on its condition and they were not complimentary; and repairs as well as increased armaments and stores were ordered. When Queen Elizabeth's engineer, Paul Ivy, gave his advice, it was to replace Mont Orgueil by an entirely new fortress, ELIZABETH CASTLE. The prevailing idea was to 'slight', that is to demolish it, but Sir Walter Raleigh, Governor from 1600 to 1604, saved it from this ignominy saying, 'It is a stately fort of great capacity . . . it were a pity to cast it down.'

During the Civil War Lady de Carteret held out at Mont Orgueil while her husband, Sir Philippe, defended Elizabeth Castle, until the final capitulation of the island to Parliament in 1651. The castle was the island prison until 1679, and various householders living on the Royal Fief (domain) in the parishes of ST MARTIN, ST SAVIOUR and Grouville had the duty of acting as *halberdiers* to conduct prisoners from the Castle to the Royal Court in town for trial. During the Commonwealth it was used as a state prison for many well-known Royalist supporters.

In 1793 England declared war on France in support of the French royalists and G. R. Balleine, a local historian of note, has written 'By keeping the Chouan risings blazing in Normandy he [Philippe d'Auvergne] gave the Republican army at St Malo so much to do in its rear that it had no time to attempt invasion.' He was referring to that colourful character Philippe d'Auvergne (later adopted as heir to the Duke of

Overleaf: Mont Orgueil Castle with Gorey Harbour

Bouillon), who was a naval officer. In 1794 he was given the task of defending the Channel Islands and obstructing the enemy's coastal trade, and of obtaining information on the enemy's activities. He was also charged to assist the numerous French insurgents and French refugees in the island. Mont Orgueil was his headquarters, and his secret service, *La Correspondance*, was vital.

The 18th and 19th centuries saw little if any military activity in the Castle, which became much run down. It had a moment of glory on 3 September 1846 when Queen Victoria drove there in the course of her visit, the first ever official visit by a reigning monarch, and Her Majesty, who was then quite young, climbed to the Grand Battery. It is interesting to note that she was accompanied by Earl Spencer, who signed the visitor's book on her behalf.

Mont Orgueil Castle was transferred by the Crown to the States of Jersey in 1907, and that body, through its Public Works Committee, is responsible for its maintenance. Archaeological digs have been undertaken on various occasions and show that there is still much to learn about this outstanding monument, which sees about 129,000 visitors each year. It is open to the public from the end of March to October.

Motte, La (2/5C) Eighteen cist graves of about 1000 BC have been discovered on the very small islet of La Motte, or Green Island as it is also called, separated from the shore by 100 yd of rock, uncovered at half tide. These were in grave danger of disappearing through erosion by the sea. Some were removed and re-erected with great care, and can now be seen in the grounds of LA HOUGÜE BIE.

Wild gladiolus (*G. communis L.*) can be seen growing here: such isolated and undeveloped spots often are the most rewarding to the botanist.

Mourier Valley (2/3A) This somewhat remote valley in the north of Jersey used to buzz with activity when its stream powered three water-mills: le Vieux Moulin, le Moulin à papier and le Moulin du Mourier. The paper referred to was made from rags and bones. The last-mentioned mill was recorded as the property of the King in 1309, when one of the royal tenants had the duty of bringing timber and millstones from any place between Cherbourg and Mont St Michel.

There is now a small reservoir operated by the Jersey New Waterworks Company, who pump its water to other points.

THE MUSEUM OF LA SOCIÉTÉ JERSIAISE

Jersey's main museum occupies a fine merchant's house in ST HELIER (3/2B), built in about 1810 by Philippe Nicolle, a merchant and shipbuilder; the present lower courtyard was his building yard. It later came into the possession of Jurat Josué Falle, who, in 1893, gave the usufruct of this house to La Société Jersiaise. This society, founded in 1873 for study and research on all matters pertaining to Jersey, had outgrown various premises as its activities widened and it began to accept objects for display. A large library is stocked with most books and newspapers concerning Jersey. Its activities are too varied to be described here, but they embrace geology, archaeology, all branches of history, and of natural history. Well over 30,000 visitors a year come to see this interesting museum.

The house is itself an historical exhibit of the early 19th century; the stairs, architraves, grates and panelled shutters are all of the period. The adjacent building put up in 1973 houses a lecture room and library. Plans for future expansion will include the display of the highly important artifacts from LA COTTE DE ST BRELADE.

The art gallery shows a selection of paintings by local artists, or of local scenes.

Being remote, the valley is a good place for studying wild flowers, and particularly sea birds. The inrush of the rising tide in the gully to the west is quite frightening in its speed.

'Le Mourier' may derive from an extinct family name, or it may refer to blackberries, *les mûres*, and it is indeed an ideal place for picking them.

Noirmont (2/3C) *Quand Nièrmont met san bonnet, Ch'est signe de plyie* ('It is a sign of rain when Noirmont dons its cap') – this is the Jersey French saying indicating the dark clouds that gather there before a south-west gale. In old documents it is called *Niger mons*, the Black Hill, suggesting that it was often cloud-laden.

A Bronze Age burial mound, La Hougue de Vinde, of about 2000 BC, is situated to the south of the promontory. A large part of this headland, on the fief de Noirmont, belonged to the abbey of St Michel in Normandy, but it reverted to the Crown with the suppression of alien priories in 1413, for there was a small priory here. The exact site, and that of its chapel, are unknown. The Crown, in the person of Charles I, donated it to Sir George Carteret: 'on account', as the Patent says, 'of the good and faithful service bravely performed by him against the Turks'. Turks, in this instance, refers to the Sallee Moors, and the service performed was the freeing of slaves. Sir George's descendants later sold it, since when, with the Manor House, it has changed hands several times. The first manor was built in 1695, and replaced in about 1830, but it has been much altered and modernized in recent years.

When harbour extensions were being discussed in the mid-19th century some people favoured St Catherine's and some Noirmont for a deep-water berth, but the former was chosen (*see* St Catherine's Breakwater). A Martello tower, La Tour de Vinde, was constructed at the southern tip of the promontory between 1810 and 1814; and the Germans, who recognized a strategic point when they saw one, constructed an armoured observation dome and naval direction-finding tower there. This is cared for by the Jersey Occupation Society, which does so much to preserve these military relics of a recent age.

A large area of the promontory was bought by the Jersey States to remain an open area, as a war memorial, and efforts to take it over for any purpose are fiercely resisted by the public.

German armoured observation dome and naval direction-finding tower, Noirmont Point (see p. 25)

Such a wide open space is bound to be the resort of many species of bird, insect and flower, among them the Dartford Warbler. The one-time Seigneur, living in the Manor House, was a keen naturalist, hence many of the pre-Second World War recordings.

Pinacle, Le (2/1A) A natural rock on the west coast at Les Landes, so like a menhir that it automatically became a centre of worship. Evidence has been found at its foot of five different periods when man has occupied this windswept neck of land. Neolithic man was here, followed by Bronze Age and then Iron Age settlers, and finally during the latter period came the Gaulish invasions. Veneration for this awe-inspiring rock must have played a vital part in its story. A coin of the Emperor Commodus brings the picture up to about AD 200, probably associated with the remains of a *fana* or heathen shrine identified there.

Intrepid people sometimes climb to the summit of Le Pinacle, or the Pinnacle, rock, and some have fancied they can see faces carved on the rough granite of its sides. A place of such antiquity, where generation upon generation has come and worshipped, is bound to be full of

mystery, but to those who are not archaeologists the main glory here is the wild flowers in May. There is a blaze of colour from creeping broom, dwarf gorse, thrift, bird's foot trefoil, daisies and bluebells. The approach across Les Landes still has a variety of flowers, but these are suffering from the increase of cars and motorbikes that now drive over them.

Portelet (2/2C) In the middle of the pretty little Portelet Bay in the south of Jersey is the **Île aux Guerdains**, taking its name from the Guerdain family *(see pp. 42-3)*. On it is a Martello tower, built in 1808; it is nice to know that coal was sent out there and 'barrack utensils' sufficient for one sergeant and 12 men. Their quarters must have been somewhat cramped.

This island is often – erroneously – called Janvrin's Tomb. Philippe Janvrin, captain of the *Esther*, had to observe quarantine for plague, and remain on board in Belcroute Bay. He had lately come from plague-stricken Nantes, and he died on board in 1721. Because of fear of contamination his body could not be brought ashore so he was buried on this tiny island. The memorial stone erected by his widow has disappeared, probably when the tower was built, less than a hundred years after his death.

The inrush of the tide as it encircles Île aux Guerdains is treacherous, and in 1915 eight young Jesuit students (there was a Jesuit training college where the Hotel de France now stands) drowned there, an event that deeply shocked the island. One island family has a tradition of a reluctant young man being caught by an ardent admirer as the tide met round the island.

A house, now an inn, bearing the date 1606, with the initials of Thomas Le Goupil *dit* Guerdain and his wife Marie Benest, is a good example of a vernacular building of the period. It is unusual, however, in being so near the sea, for builders then did not wish their houses to be seen from the sea for fear of attack.

Prison, The Jersey has had several prisons. The first we know of was in MONT ORGUEIL CASTLE, where conditions for criminals were, as was the custom, inhumane. During the English Civil War the castle also served as a state prison for offenders against, in turn, the Royalists or the Parliamentarians. The owners of certain houses in the three easternmost parishes had the duty of escorting prisoners to ST HELIER for trial, armed with halberds; thus they were called *halberdiers*, and their houses *Maisons halberdiers*. The duty

appertained to the house, and therefore to whoever was the owner at the time. The great inconvenience of taking prisoners such a long distance for their trial ended in the 1680s, when a new prison was built at the western perimeter of St Helier, straddling the only road leading in from the country.

In 1811 this prison was in turn superseded by a very fine granite building designed by Captain Victor Prott and costing £19,000 – a stupendous sum at that period. Over the years it had to be enlarged, as the population grew. During the German Occupation many islanders spent time there, either as hostages or for petty offences against regulations.

In its turn this prison was demolished (the stonework of the fine granite façade was saved to be incorporated, it is hoped, in some prestigious building) and the site was used for hospital enlargement. A new, and yet larger, prison was built on a fine coastal site at Le Moye (2/1C) and came into use in 1975.

Queen's Valley (2/6B) This is a most beautiful valley and almost the only one left unspoiled, with just one very minor road traversing it. Its alternative name is La Vallée des Moulins, the Valley of the Mills, and indeed there were three watermills in its length: Le Moulin de Haut, Le Blanc Moulin and Le Moulin de Bas. These royal mills were recorded as early as 1274.

In 1855 Victor Hugo, then in exile in Jersey, extolled the serenity of the valley in a poem. George Eliot was in Jersey in 1857 and wrote rapturously of the verdant countryside, and referred to 'the exquisite vale of the Queen's farm'.

In February 1986 the States of Jersey voted in favour of flooding Queen's Valley for the construction of a reservoir. The local water company had long wanted to build a large new reservoir here, which would flood the valley to a great depth, but would insure against water shortage in dry years. This plan has been opposed by conservationists on the grounds that a natural, unspoiled piece of countryside with historical associations would be lost for ever, and the National Trust would be deprived of land bequeathed to it in perpetuity.

Royal Square, The (3/2B) This attractive paved area, an oasis of quiet in the middle of bustling ST HELIER, has seen much of Jersey's history

The gilded lead statue of George II, Royal Square, St Helier (see p. 64)

RAILWAYS IN JERSEY

From the time when the value of railways was recognized in England, far-seeing Jerseymen tried to introduce them to the island. But it was not until 1870 that ST HELIER was connected with ST AUBIN by a single line of standard gauge track, provided with a crossing point at Millbrook, halfway along the route. This Western Railway was extended to LA CORBIÈRE, with a 3 ft 6 in gauge, in 1884. In 1872 a line was laid from St Helier eastwards to GOREY. Both companies, the Eastern and the Western, had a remarkable record for punctuality and safety, the trains ran at approximately half-hour intervals, and the fares were counted in pence. When a high spring tide threw giant waves over the sea wall along St Aubin's Bay the school train could be much delayed, to the delight of the children whose lateness had to be excused.

However, the railway lines served mainly the south and east coasts and did not help those living inland and in the north. Once bus companies, covering all parts, sprang up the day of the railway passed. In 1936 the Western line could no longer face the competition and closed; its Eastern rival had closed in 1927 for the same reasons.

The stations and halts are still well remembered, and a few of the station houses survive. Not architecturally beautiful, they are nevertheless reminders of a period that has gone. Perhaps their significance to the island scene was recognized when one, Grouville station, was listed as an important building for preservation. The platform and line are clearly seen in the garden of what is now an attractive little house.

enacted. For centuries it was the market place, le Vier Marchi, until a new market was built in 1880. Before that the area was surrounded by produce stalls on Saturdays, and farmers' wives would bring in their butter, eggs, poultry and vegetables, and exchange them for things they could not produce at home. Where the Natwest Bank now stands was an open area, the Cornmarket, La Halle à Blé. Curiously, the first floor, now a club, was then the town house of Susanne Dumaresq, Lady of La Haule, and John Wesley preached from here in 1787. Butchers and fishmongers, as well as many other trades and crafts, were accommodated.

On various occasions, notably in 1646, Royalist-held ELIZABETH CASTLE bombarded the square, at that moment under Parliamentary rule; Jean Chevalier, who lived at the east end of the square, has left vivid accounts of the scene in his diary.

There is a small picket house, purchased by the States from the British Government in 1934. On it there is a large sundial erected in 1825. It does not face quite due south because at that period Jersey time differed from Greenwich by 8 minutes.

There used to be an iron cage in which prisoners waiting to be taken into court for trial were placed. It stood at the east end, but was no longer necessary when a town prison was built in the 17th century (*see* The Prison).

The gilded lead statue represents George II and it was unveiled with great ceremony and pomp in 1751. It is the work of John Cheere, brother of the more famous Sir Henry, and it was at this point that the Vier Marchi was renamed The Royal Square. It is at the foot of this statue that all royal proclamations are read.

The most momentous event to have taken place here was the Battle of Jersey on the morning of 6 January 1781, when Philippe Charles Félix Macquart, Baron de Rullecourt, a soldier of fortune, arrived from La Rocque where he had landed secretly with 600 French troops. The Lieutenant-Governor, roused from sleep, was made to believe the force was far larger, and to save lives he capitulated. But others, both in the British garrison and the Jersey Militia, were made of sterner stuff. Captain Mulcaster (after whom a street is named), serving at Elizabeth Castle, refused to surrender, saying he did not understand French. Meanwhile Major Francis Peirson, stationed out at St Peter, rushed all available troops to town, and met the invaders in the Royal Square. The battle was short and decisive. Rullecourt was killed, but so also was the brave young major, perhaps Jersey's most popular hero, and to whom an undying debt is recognized. A granite slab marks the approximate place where he fell. Although a mere skirmish by modern standards, had the French been successful, as well they might, the French king would have followed up the victory immediately, and England would have found it hard to reconquer this, her most ancient dominion.

On the south of the square are the governmental buildings, the States, the Royal Court and the Public Library. There was an official building on the site at least as early as 1329, and Chevalier in the 17th century wrote that it was single-storeyed, thatched and unimpressive. A new Court House or *Cohue* was built in 1647 in MONT MADO granite with French slates. Carved arms of the Sovereign, the Governor and the bailiff were made by a mason from St Malo. A little over a century later the Court House was again rebuilt in

1764. The existing range of buildings was completed in 1866. The Royal Court room has some interesting paintings. There is one of George III, looking very young, by Philippe Jean, a local artist best known as a miniaturist; one of Field Marshal Seymour Conway by Gainsborough; and a copy of the American painter John Copley's famous 'Death of Major Peirson', the original of which hangs in the Tate Gallery, London. There are other portraits of island dignitaries, including the Bailiff, the late Sir William Vernon, by J. H. Lander, and one of Lord Coutanche (Bailiff during the German Occupation) by Sir James

Gunn. Recent additions have been a 1978 portrait of HM The Queen by Ken Howard, and a portrait by Norman Hepple of the States Chamber with the Bailiff reading the loyal address.

The States Chamber accommodates the people's representatives and here all deliberations take place. Above the Bailiff's chair hangs a banner with the three leopards passant, arms of England, whose use was permitted to Jersey.

The Public Library was started in 1736 by Philippe Falle, the island's first historian, and was housed in a brick building in Library Place. Falle's initials with the date can be seen on the

---

REFUGEES, SETTLERS AND EMIGRANTS

Jersey has for centuries welcomed refugees, religious and political. The first to arrive on a large scale were French Huguenots after the Reformation; the flow was intensified after the Massacre of St Bartholomew in 1572. Jersey had accepted Protestantism very readily and welcomed these unfortunate refugees – and in particular their clergy, to fill vacancies among the 12 rectorships, where a French-speaking minister was essential. After the Edict of Nantes in 1598, some of the Huguenots returned to France, but many stayed, or went on to other countries. Another wave of these refugees poured over after the Revocation of the Edict in 1685 and this time they stayed for the most part and became integrated into island life. Among them were many craftsmen and Jersey silver, so valuable today, can be largely attributed to Huguenot silversmiths. At the time of the French Revolution, from 1789 onwards, fresh waves of homeless persecuted French families flocked over, though being largely Roman Catholic, they were not so readily absorbed into island life. After Waterloo many half-pay British army and navy officers brought their families to Jersey to benefit from the low prices, mild climate and congenial social life, and to their arrival we can attribute the fine terraces built to the north of St Helier.

These influxes had been assimilated gradually and their advent was mainly beneficial. Up to the First World War, and between the wars, many new residents arrived and tourism boomed. Since the Second World War the incoming tide has become a tidal wave. If there had been no controls on settlers there would not now be an open field left, nor a house available that a local family or young couple could afford to buy. Control is mostly exercised through the availability of housing and the number of wealthy residents permitted to buy houses is strictly controlled, but in spite of this the population soars.

From the start of the new potato industry, around 1870, seasonal farm workers have come to the island in great numbers, until recently from Brittany, but

now mostly from Portugal and Madeira. (Many Portuguese babies are now Jersey-born, and so have citizen's rights.)

The overall effect of Jersey's prosperity has now become rather overwhelming for what was a small, basically rural community. It has brought great pressure on essential services and on leisure facilities, and, perhaps most of all, on water. On the other hand it must be remembered that without the revenue generated by the attractiveness of Jersey, the island would not be able to provide its population, indigenous, settlers or visitors, with the wonderful medical and educational facilities now offered.

To set against this pattern of immigration of refugees and settlers, there was in the 19th century in particular widespread emigration, mainly to Canada and Australia, where a glance at telephone directories will show a considerable number of Jersey names – in some cases those of families that have died out in their homeland. These people, usually young couples, left to find better opportunities in countries that beckoned to newcomers. It was not unknown for a couple to take some of their children and leave the older ones in the care of the grandparents. The population of Jersey had exploded in the middle of the 19th century, and there was no future for members of large families in such a small community.

And so this microcosm called Jersey has seen a shift of population over the centuries, accepting the newcomer, and losing its younger sons, until now some parishes, notably St Brelade, have about 80 per cent non-native parishioners.

The clock cannot be turned back. Changes have occurred over many centuries, and throughout Jersey has managed to retain its essential character, to absorb and nurture the new, and to graft it on to the old. The speed and intensity of modern change is such that it will tax to the utmost the skill of the Jerseyman to remain a Jerseyman, but we suspect that he will succeed.

Rozel Bay

cistern heads. The building, which now houses a States Department, has a notable staircase and other detailing of the period. By 1886, however, the library had far outgrown its premises and the books were moved over to a fine new domed building of dignity and character. Again the library is under heavy pressure for space and there are plans to move it once more.

Set into the wall near the Public Library entrance is a commemorative plaque to Wace, the 12th-century poet who was Jersey born, as he himself tells us.

The letters Vega 1945 are cut in the paving near by; the large V was cut during the Occupation without the Germans noticing it. In 1985, to commemorate the 40th anniversary of the Liberation, an explanatory legend was inserted round these figures.

The chestnut trees that give such pleasure in spring and summer were planted in 1894. At all times there are people, young and old, strolling or sitting in the Royal Square, enjoying its serenity.

Rozel Bay (2/6A) Now a luxury restaurant, Le Couperon de Rozel was a small barracks for garrison troops, built in about 1810 and similar to that at GRÈVE DE LECQ. The little pier was built in 1829 and often sheltered some of the GOREY oyster fishing boats.

The promontory to the east, Le Couperon, has a Neolithic passage grave or long cist, 27 ft long, dating from 2500 BC. The stone at the end,

scooped out with what is known as a porthole, is probably ritualistic and originally divided the tomb in two, and the whole is likely to have been covered by an earth mound. Beside it there is a late 17th-century guardhouse built by 1689.

Above the bay, and on the TRINITY PARISH side of this very green valley, is part of a great earth rampart, a promontory fort known as Le Castel de Rozel, dating from the Iron Age. Place names in the area suggest it was originally far longer and stronger than it now is. Gaulish and early Roman coins have been found buried in it, all within the last century BC, so it must have provided a defensive position against early invaders, and may perhaps have been later occupied by refugees from Gaul, who hid thousands of their coins there.

Jersey's first lifeboat was launched at Rozel in 1830. This was done with great ceremony and with high hopes of the good it would perform for the benefit of mankind, as indeed it has.

La Chaire in the bay was for some time the home of Samuel Curtis (1799-1860), the well-known botanist, with his widowed daughter Mrs Fothergill. Here they created a notable garden with many semitropical plants. The best known are the two (one pink and one white) magnolias, *Magnolia campbellii*; they must have been planted after his death as the species was first seen in Britain in 1868. These magnificent trees are

St Aubin's Fort, St Aubin (see p. 68)

usually at their best around 15-18 March and should certainly be seen by everyone who has the opportunity to do so.

Rozel Bay rather suffers from being too popular, with the inevitable cry for more parking space. It would be indeed sad if part of this lush and verdant valley had to disappear beneath a coat of tarmacadam for parking.

Rozel Manor (2/6A) The attractive name Rozel, which as Roselle has become popular as a girl's name, is a form of *roseau*, a reed. As a place name in Jersey it stems from Norman times, when a Seigneur from Rozel in Normandy had land in Jersey. The Seigneur of Rozel has the privilege of being the Sovereign's butler and of acting as such during royal visits to Jersey. One Raoul Lemprière bought the estate from a previous owner, de Barentin, in about 1360 and his descendants held it for five generations. After vicissitudes of sale and marriage, it came back into the Lemprière family in the 18th century, and remains with the descendants of this line still.

The early manor stood near the chapel and has quite disappeared, though we know something of it and of the daily life of a seigneur of the time from the account of the trial of Renaud Lemprière during the Norman invasion of 1461-8.

The present manor house was built in 1770 by Charles Lemprière, and in 1820 it was greatly enlarged and covered with hard unyielding Roman cement. Inside, though the décor of the main salon is of this century, the entrance and stairs are very fine 18th-century work.

The chapel at Rozel Manor is medieval and its setting is idyllic. The heavily carved choir stalls date from about 1600 and represent saints with their symbolic attributes. The pews, of the end of the last century, were made from wood cut on the estate. After the Reformation this chapel was demoted to some ordinary use, but was restored in about 1859 by the then Seigneur, when the wide west door was inserted. By any standards this is a large building for a private chapel. The dedication is in doubt but is probably to St Mary (not St Anne, as some books state).

The gardens were already well known in the 1460s and have remained outstanding, running down this sheltered well-watered valley. In spring the magnolias, rhododendrons and azaleas are a joy to behold. The manor and grounds are not normally open to the public.

St Aubin (2/3B) It is most curious to find a village named after a saint, with no trace of a church or chapel dedicated to him. He is Aubin, Bishop of Angers, who died *c*. 550, a known protector against pirates and so a most appropriate dedication for this area. It has been suggested that he may have had a chapel on the islet known as St Aubin's Fort, all traces of which could have disappeared under later defensive works.

St Aubin is referred to in documents as a town, *une ville*. The story that it was once the capital of the island is quite erroneous, but it was, the commercial centre, particularly in the late 17th century when prosperous merchants built themselves fine houses along the Bulwarks and in the High Street, La Rue du Crocquet, which took its name from a rock that disappeared when the road and railway were constructed. During the English Civil War prize ships were brought in, their contents judged by a court, and sold by auction – a source of considerable wealth to the captors.

In 1715 the principal inhabitants petitioned the Bishop of Winchester to permit them to build a chapel of ease, pointing out the arduous journey up and down steep hills they had to make to attend services at ST BRELADE'S CHURCH. In 1735 the foundation stone was laid, but services were not held there until 1749, a considerable delay since the original petition. The building of this chapel, the only post-Reformation church in Jersey until recent times, was a good example of cooperation and self-help. Various parishioners contributed according to their means, some giving items of silver and some contributing their time and labour in building or in cartage of materials.

After 140 years this chapel was deemed to be unsafe and the present fine church was built in 1892. It contains a notable stained-glass window made by William Morris's firm. It was given in memory of Augusta de Gruchy, wife of William Lawrence de Gruchy, a Jerseyman. She was a writer and a poet and there is reason to think she knew many of the members of the glittering pre-Raphaelite set when she and her husband were living near Edward Burne-Jones at Highgate. Certainly she admired his work.

The Bulwarks beside the harbour were built by and at the request of merchants in 1790; they thus gained some land from the sea, creating long narrow gardens to each house. The north pier was added in 1817. (In 1683 Dumaresq wrote: 'The conveniency of the pier has occasioned a small town to be built consisting of about four score houses.')

However, it was not until 1841 that a road connected St Aubin with ST HELIER. Before that you went by boat or, at low tide, across the sands, and even when horse omnibuses made their appearance they had to respect the tide. It must indeed have been laborious to get from La Haule, just north of St Aubin, to the tip of the pier, so near and yet so far, for you had to start up La Haule Hill, go down the High Street, and again up behind the merchants' houses to Bulwarks Hill.

The architecture of these tall houses is interesting. It follows the vernacular pattern of the Jersey countryside but because of the restricted space and the steepness of the hill, the houses had to rise to four or five storeys, instead of the customary two. Consequently the steep stairs are particularly fine and impressive; the merchants, often shipbuilders or shipowners, were able to call on the skills of their carpenters to make them.

St Aubin's Fort (2/3C) Accessible at low tide, St Aubin's Fort lies to the south-east of the little town of ST AUBIN. It measures 300 by 200 yds, but its position in relation to the land is strategic.

The lower part of the existing tower, built of random granite, dates from around 1542. Edward Seymour, Lord Protector of the young Edward VI, was then Governor, and he and the local authorities became increasingly aware that Jersey urgently needed better defences. It did, however, prove very difficult to extract the necessary money from the reluctant islanders, who were constantly being asked to pay for this or that. When rumours of the Spanish Armada reached Jersey there was widespread anxiety, and in 1588 repairs were carried out and a battery was added. Constant threats of invasion produced a series of orders for repairing and garrisoning the fort.

During the English Civil War a Parliamentary Governor, Major Lydcott, was in command of the island for three months, during which time the tower was surrounded by bulwarks and further cannon installed. But soon the Royalists regained the upper hand and remained so for eight years.

On 12 May 1646 the young Prince Charles, later Charles II, visited the fort during his brief stay. Much repair work followed during the ensuing years, but after the Parliamentary capture of the island in 1651 the fort had to surrender. A pier was added around 1680, 'a peece for eternity' it was called.

In 1730 there was further anxiety about defence and John Henry Bastide, a military engineer, came over to supervise work. Then in 1838 the engineer Colonel John Oldfield found the fort again inadequate for defence and the work carried out then can be detected in the changes in the masonry of the tower and elsewhere. At that time a 30-man garrison was contemplated, to work six guns. The provision of fresh drinking water had

Merchants tall houses, St Aubin

always been a problem and a tank to contain 4476 gallons was installed. However, the fort was never used in war and in this century it has been rented to individuals for summer holidays. It was subsequently acquired by the States and is now used for youth activities. During the Occupation it was once more used by troops and heavily fortified, stressing how soldiers in every century have recognized its important geographical and strategical position.

In calm weather St Aubin's Fort seems to lie along the horizon like a battleship at anchor: and perhaps that is what it is.

St Brelade's Church (2/2C) Beware of guide-books that tell you this church was built in 1111 – a highly suspect date of doubtful origin, though it may well commemorate a date of some significance to the church, but now unknown. In fact there was a parish church here well before 1066. The dedication is almost certainly to St Branwallader, a companion of St Sampson, whose name appears with a variety of spellings from 1055 onwards.

The oldest part is the 11th- or 12th-century chancel, followed by the tower and nave, perhaps a century later, and a north transept of the 13th century. The south transept, probably 15th century, is a rebuild of an earlier one, and now serves as the south porch. The west porch is mainly 15th century, and the north aisle was constructed in 1537, with the staircase turret slightly later. Many window surrounds are probably 16th century, often with later tracery, and all with modern glass. A bell for the tower, the replacement of a far older one, was cast in ST HELIER in 1754 by Maître Jacques Pitel, but the existing bell dates from 1883.

As in many of the other Jersey parish churches the pointed barrel-vaulted roof covers the nave in three bays and the chancel in two. Such roofs were, it is surmised, a 13th-century addition to existing walls: they would have been less vulnerable than wood or thatch to fire and the sword. On the west wall note an extremely ancient gargoyle.

The very early unornamented piscina can be dated between 1275 and 1300 when this style was in use. It is a double one, allowing the priest to wash his hands and the communion vessels separately. The font, of stone from the French Chausey islands, was found on a hillside in 1845, hidden by gorse, and it was then reinstated. It had doubtless been put out at the Reformation. There

Opposite: St Brelade's Church
Below: Beau Port with St Brelade's Bay beyond

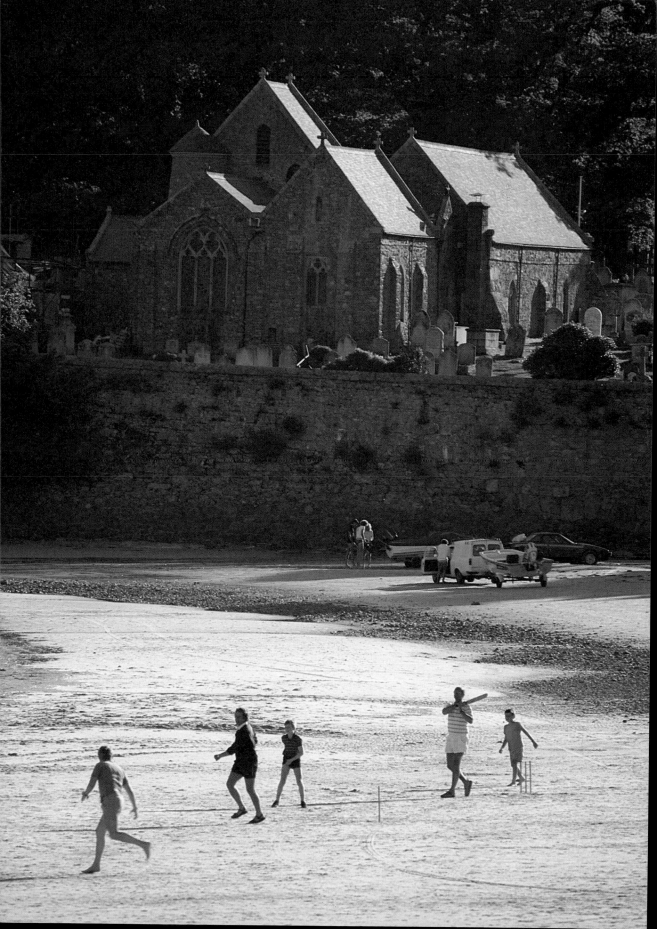

is a holy water stoup in the north wall of the west porch, and a sundial on the south porch dated 1837.

An enlargement to the medieval church was made in 1537, giving a north aisle, and this must be the date of the round-headed arch, with rare rope moulding, at its west end.

A big restoration took place early in this century under the auspices of the then rector. Like other island churches it had a *galerie des fumeurs*, a smokers' gallery, so that those addicted could smoke in peace during the sermon; this was removed in 1843.

From the south-east corner of the churchyard there is a short flight of steps leading down to the beach. This is traditionally said to be the *perquage*, a sanctuary path by which criminals could flee the island under the protection of the church and so escape trial by the courts.

The churchyard is now very full and the closeness to the sea and the serenity of the setting has always made St Brelade a preferred church for burials. Many local families can be found among the memorials, such as Marett, Pipon, Robin and Le Couteur. Two splendid ancient oaks shade the path to the west door, adding their dignity, and feeling of continuity, to the atmosphere. The north-east entrance to the churchyard was designed by Colonel John Le Couteur in 1850; was it he, such a keen cultivator of camellias, who planted them along the churchyard wall? The lychgate at the west entrance was given by Lady Trent, widow of Jesse Boot, first Baron Trent, in 1933.

The Fisherman's Chapel,

La Chapelle ès Pêcheurs is situated very close to the church; this is not unusual in Jersey. The stained glass, like that in the parish church, is by H. T. Bosdet (1857-1934), a local craftsman, and depicts the life of St Brendan, once believed to be the patron saint. No dedication is known for the chapel, though St Mary is likely in view of the painting on the east wall. Recent archaeological study shows that the chapel is all of one build and is late 12th century. This does not preclude the existence of a previous chapel on the site.

After the Reformation the chapel was used for various secular purposes, being at various times a bell foundry, military post and armaments store.

In quite recent years the chapel has had a great deal spent on it and much work has been done on the wall paintings. They had suffered considerably from neglect as well as the action of salt-laden

air. These 14th- and 15th-century paintings are of scenes from both the Old and New Testaments. The east wall shows the Annunciation with, in customary medieval manner, the donor and his family kneeling in prayer. It may record the de Sottevast family who seem to have had connections with the church. These are by far the most extensive of Jersey's wall paintings, and their survival is a miracle. The possibility of a family connection fits in with the archaeological evidence and the nailed wooden coffins, of 15th- or early 16th-century date, found under the floor, together with the feeling that the building was a mortuary chapel for a wealthy family.

Remnants of JERSEY MILITIA colours – the two flags of the South West Regiment of Royal Jersey Militia – remain. Other colours, from the Newfoundland Fencibles, were returned to them in 1922.

St Brelade's Parish (2/2B) St Brelade's parish stretches over the south-west part of the island and most of it lies within le Fief de la Reine. It covers the south part of St Ouen's Bay and stretches round the south coast almost to Beaumont. The sandy part above St Ouen's Bay, Les Quennevais, takes its name from *chenvière* or hemp (*Cannabis sativa*), grown here for ropes, a vital crop in a seafaring community. Legends say the area was covered with sand as divine judgment on wreckers, but the force of the south-west gales can easily explain it. The whole area, with Les Blanches Banques adjacent, is rich in dwarf wild flowers, the most spectacular being the burnet rose, *Rosa pimpinellofolia*, and the spotted rock rose on the more southerly cliffs. The dunes here are recognized as being of great scientific importance, incorporating evidence covering at least 3000 years. There are archaeological remains, including three scattered menhirs of before 1500 BC.

Above Petit Port is La Sergenté, the Beehive Hut, a Neolithic tomb of perhaps 3500 BC. La Marquanderie Hill leads up from St Brelade's Bay to the Quennevais area, and just to the east of the hill is a field where a hoard of 12,000 Armorican (Brittany) coins was found. They are made of an alloy of copper, tin and silver and can be dated to around 50 BC. This was an extremely important discovery, of the greatest interest to numismatists.

The area around La Moye Point, with the new prison inland from it, contained quarries, no longer used, which produced the granite for the Thames embankment.

Among several distinguished parishioners was Jean Martel (1694-1754), famous for the brandy made at Cognac.

La Moye Golf Club has its course here. It was founded in 1902 by George Boomer, father of the famous golfer Aubrey Boomer.

St Catherine's Breakwater (2/6B) The long arm of this breakwater in St Catherine's Bay now serves yachtsmen, swimmers and fishermen. Its original purpose was, however, defensive, an answer to the threat of new French coastal installations, at Cherbourg in particular. The British Government decided on two naval stations, or 'harbours of refuge' as they preferred to call them, in Jersey and in Alderney. This one was begun in 1847 and hundreds of labourers were brought over for the work.

The second arm, which was to have started at Archirondel, never progressed very far. Years of indecision ensued. Finally, and not very surprisingly, work was abandoned in 1852, mainly because relations with Napoleon III's France had improved (to the fury of Victor Hugo, in his Channel Island exile!). But it was also realized that the harbour would in fact be badly sited for protecting either merchantmen or men o' war.

St Clement's Church and Priory (2/5C) The dedication here is probably to Clement I, the third Pope. Before 1025 the estate of Pierreville, named from a lame monk, Pierre, belonged to Mont St Michel Abbey. It became the Priory of St Clement, and was situated to the south-west of the church. It should perhaps be explained that though there were at least six priories in Jersey in medieval times, they were very small and humble institutions. They seem to have comprised merely a small chapel, with a priest's house adjoining, and apart from saying Mass and other services they existed largely for the purpose of collecting the revenues due to their parent abbeys in Normandy. It is not surprising that Henry V, then at war with France, decided to suppress all alien priories in the Channel Islands and in England. Tithes due to the Norman abbeys were at the same time confiscated by the Crown.

As to the church, Duke William (later William I of England), gave half its revenues to the nunnery of Montvilliers, though the advowson belonged to St Sauveur le Vicomte.

The present nave, tower and transepts, the oldest parts, are probably 12th century, and two small narrow windows (one of them of recent construction or reconstruction) can be seen in the north wall. That the roof has been raised can be clearly made out in the gable lines at the junction of nave and chancel; and it is highly likely that the existing stone roof, replacing wood or thatch, was added in the early 13th century. The chancel appears to be slightly later. There is a very fine east window with original tracery, probably 15th century.

The magnificent 15th-century Chausey granite font (whose design inspired the carving on the oak lectern made in 1985) was, like others, thrown out at the Reformation and found centuries later buried to the north of the church. St Clement is alone in having two carved piscinae, one to the south of the main altar and the other in the north chapel, both 14th century.

This church is rich in 15th-century wall paintings. St Michael conquering the dragon appears on the north wall of the nave and is in good condition after recent restoration. In the south transept appears the legend of 'Les Trois Rois vifs et les Trois Rois morts', the Three Living and the Three Dead Kings, a scene depicted in many English and French churches, and in the Castel church in Guernsey. This is a moral tale indicating the frailty of human life. Fragments of two other scenes, probably Ste Marguerite and Ste Barbara, survive in the north transept, and careful restoration work on them is planned.

The church plate is well displayed in a special case in the north transept. It includes four items of Jersey silver, wine cups dated 1594, 1624 and 1659 respectively, and a baptismal dish of 1702. Under Calvinist influence, when fonts had been thrown out, baptism was performed from large shallow bowls. There are two copper collecting pots, of the unique Jersey pattern, dated 1738.

Built into a pillar in the chancel arch is a stone seat for the benefit of the sick or elderly before pews were provided, hence the expression 'the weakest go to the wall'.

In the churchyard, and leaning against the south wall, is one of the island's oldest dated memorial stones. It bears two dates, 1596 and 1606, and heraldry recalling the Seigneurs of SAMARÈS MANOR. There is a splendid yew tree there, a reminder of the time when its wood was needed for making bows and when archery practice on *les buttes* took place very near the churches, as is attested by several place names. The bell, Normandy work, dates from 1828.

The churchyard slopes upwards towards the north and is most attractive, with a central path leading to a magnificent funerary monument to the Labey family, now in sad disrepair.

St Clement's Parish (2/5C) This is the smallest of Jersey's 12 parishes, but the 1981 census showed a population of over 7000. The coastline from Le Dicq almost to La Rocque is rock-strewn for the most part, and the fast-flowing tide presents a fascinating and ever-changing picture. During equinoctial gales there is often flooding, and erosion where there is no sea wall, so residents may have to watch parts of their gardens crumbling into the sea.

The passage grave, Mont Ubé, takes its name from the hill on which it stands, a corruption of Mont Tubel, the hill of the Le Tubelin family. Dating from around 2800 BC, the dolmen is surrounded by woods belonging to the National Trust. It was discovered in 1848 and many enthusiasts have had a hand in excavating it. Most unfortunately at some time its capstones were used as building material, and the tomb itself served as a pigsty in the 19th century. Like other dolmens it was originally covered by a mound of earth.

La Dame Blanche, a menhir 11 ft high, is probably 3000 years old. Standing in a cultivated field, it was sadly damaged a few years ago. On that same property there was a medieval chapel dedicated to St John the Evangelist, and fragments of moulded stone were still there in recent

La Dame Blanche, St Clement's Parish

years. The chapel is known to have been active in 1495, but by 1540 it was in ruins.

A tall granite outcrop, called Rocqueberg, now stands within a modern garden. This was the centre of a witchcraft movement in the 17th century. Some natural marks on the rock were taken to be the Devil's imprint. Le Hocq Tower, built in 1788, is a good example of a Jersey round tower, picturesquely sited on a bluff; it is now used for youth activities.

Nicolle Tower, now owned by the Landmark Trust, which lets it as holiday accommodation, stands near the Mont Ubé dolmen. Starting as a signal station in 1792, it was probably then just a single cell dwelling for a coastguard. In 1821 it had a hexagonal addition made to the west, and finally it was heightened and given 'Gothick' windows. It continued to be used as a lookout during the German Occupation, as it may have been since medieval times.

St Clement's most famous one-time resident was Victor Hugo. Fleeing from Napoleon III he sought exile in Jersey from 1852 to 1855. He lived with his family at Marine Terrace, now demolished, until his support for articles in the *proscrits'* newspaper *L'Homme*, defamatory to Queen Victoria, caused his expulsion. He then went to Guernsey and stayed there for 15 years. During his time in Jersey he wrote two volumes of poetry, *Les Châtiments* and *Les Contemplations*.

St Helier and its Parish (2/4B; 3) The parish of St Helier's consists of much more than just the town, for it extends northwards into rural areas with prosperous farms and serene valleys.

In early medieval times the area now covered by the town was a marsh, le Marais de St Helier. A dolmen, as yet not excavated, lies under the Gas Works buildings (3/3A), evidence of a change in land levels. To the west, on land that was sand dunes until the building of the sea wall, are two Neolithic sites, a gallery grave, and a cist within a stone circle, dating from about 2200-2500 BC.

There was already a market in St Helier by 1299, and from this grew, very gradually, the capital of the island. The parish took its name from the 6th-century St Helier, whom it venerated. The town wall, la Muraille de la Ville, of which some fragments can be traced, was already quoted as being built 'long since' in 1607, to hold back the encroaching sand.

Visitors will note that many street names in the central area are bilingual: Vine Street, La Rue des Vignes, had a vine growing there in living memory; King Street, La Rue de Derrière, was a back street behind more important houses; Hill Street was La Rue des Trois Pigeons, referring to an inn of that name. Halkett Place preserves the name of a Lieutenant-Governor; Beresford Street and Conway Street of two Governors. Burrard Street recognizes the fact that Sir Hugh Burrard gave the land over which it passes; Mulcaster Street recalls a hero of the Battle of Jersey (*see* Royal Square). Don Street and Don Road recall a much-loved Lieutenant-Governor whose name appears in many places. Dumaresq Street, Hue Street, Le Geyt Street, and others all take their names from families connected with them. But for Broad Street, La Rue d'Egypte, no convincing explanation has been found.

The Parade Gardens (3/1A) are laid out on land levelled for militia parades, and amid the lawns is a striking statue and monument, again to General Don; in the same park there is a French Resistance monument in the form of a cross of Lorraine. Near by is the Cenotaph (3/1B) erected in 1923 to honour 862 islanders who fell in the First World War; the names of all who lost their lives in the Second World War have been added, a total of 463. A lovely peaceful area is the Howard Davis Park (3/3C), given in memory of Howard Davis, killed in the First World War, by his father T. B. Davis, a great benefactor of the island. It is well tended, fills a real public need, and is sometimes used for large ceremonies and Royal occasions. Near the entrance is a statue of George V.

Street sign, St Helier

Another smaller garden at West Park, now named the Victoria Park (3/1A), contains a statue of Queen Victoria of 1890. It was moved from another site and placed here in 1971. There are in all 50 acres of parkland in St Helier.

Apart from the ST HELIER'S CHURCH (3/2B) many other churches and chapels were built in the 19th century. St Mark's (3/2A) was consecrated in 1846, and seen by Queen Victoria on her visit that year; St James's (3/3B), now sadly empty, in 1829; All Saints (3/1A) in 1835; St Paul's (3/2B) in 1891 and St Simon's (3/2A) in 1866. The last-named was designed by G. F. Bodley. Roman Catholics and Methodists, as well as many other denominations, have their meeting places for worship, the most spectacular being the Grove Place Methodist Church (3/2B) of 1847; besides its services, this is the venue for splendid renderings of religious music, such as the Messiah, by local amateur choirs – the acoustics are particularly good. The Roman Catholic cathedral, 1883, originally French-speaking, is an arresting landmark in New Street, tall and striking. The Halkett Place Evangelical Church (3/2B) of 1855 is under threat of closure.

The Town Hall (3/1B), which should really be called La Salle Paroissiale, was built in 1870, and looks like it: the architectural style is ponderous, with a French flavour of its period.

The Opera House (3/1B) by contrast is delightful. First built in 1900, it was burned down in 1921 and then reconstructed. Some of the later internal décor could with advantage be removed, as the cosy Edwardian atmosphere of most of it is entirely suitable for the type of play or concert performed there by both visiting and local amateur artists.

The visitor should prowl round St Helier on foot. Though no really old buildings have survived, and some of the modern architecture is not to everyone's taste, he will be rewarded by the sight of splendid mid-19th century terraces in Rouge Bouillon (3/1A) and Queen's Road (3/1A), as well as the 1828 Royal Crescent (3/3B) and happy little 'Gothick' extravaganzas here and there. The Victorians, here as elsewhere, were wealthy, ambitious and fearless. Many of their houses became run down early in this century, but are increasingly valued for their strong characters and consequently are now looking bright and cared for.

On the outskirts to the west there is a Jersey round tower, giving its name to First Tower. The parish extends to the stream, the mill brook, at Millbrook, at the entrance to Waterworks Valley. To the east, between the Howard Davis Park and St Luke's Church (3/3C), which is just in ST SAVIOUR'S PARISH, there is a beautifully kept war cemetery, where British and Allied airmen and sailors shot down or washed ashore during the Occupation are buried.

The town and parish teem with hotels and guesthouses; notable are the Hotel de France (3/3A) – first built as Hotel Imperial, it then became a Jesuit school for many years; the Ommaroo Hotel (3/3C) at HAVRE DES PAS has amazingly elaborate ironwork balconies, a wonderful piece of craftsmanship.

Again, do not overlook the rural northern part of this very surprising parish.

See also Fort Regent; Markets, The; Victoria College.

St Helier's Church (3/2B) As the church of the town and capital of Jersey (it is known as the Town Church), St Helier's has perhaps had more spent on it, and has been more altered, than is the case with the smaller country churches. The parish and church have taken the name of the saint who, according to tradition, was murdered in 555. Before man-made sea defences were built the church stood on the seashore. Before 1025, as with ST CLEMENT'S CHURCH, half its revenues were going to the abbey of Montvilliers, with the advowson passing to St Sauveur le Vicomte. North and south transepts were added to the first nucleus of a 12th-century church, with the crossing tower, but the nave was extended westwards only in 1804. It was probably in the 14th century that the roof was raised and the small Norman windows replaced by large ones with elaborate tracery.

A piscina that since 1866 has been in St Simon's Church in the town is convincingly suggested to have come from St Helier's Church, having been removed at the time of the Reformation. The font found its way to LA HOUGUE BIE and was later reinstated in GROUVILLE CHURCH.

There are some interesting monuments. Among them is the oldest, to Maximilian Norrys, 1591; there is one (though not contemporary) to the Parliamentary Bailiff, Michel Lemprière (in office 1643 and 1651-60); and one to General Anquetil who died in the retreat from Kabul in 1842. A recent plaque records the local artist, Jean Le Cappelain, Jersey's 'Turner'. In the floor under the crossing is a granite slab with the one word 'Peirson', and there is also a memorial tablet commemorating the courage of this young major (*see* Royal Square).

In the 19th, and the present, century many alterations have taken place, notably in 1864, a time when the whole church was heavily shrouded in ivy.

The cross and candlesticks on the altar were given by HM the Queen Mother as a thank offering for liberation after the Occupation. The church plate includes two wine cups of 1764 and two of 1777. A flagon is dated 1639 and another 1766. Seventeenth-century communion silver from ELIZABETH CASTLE has been deposited in St Helier's and is displayed, with other plate, in a special wall cabinet in the south transept.

ST SAVIOUR'S CHURCH and St Helier's are the two churches to have, or to have retained, a tower without a spire.

As the capital's church, and for some years now also the Dean's Rectorship, St Helier's is naturally the church where any special ceremonial services take place.

St Helier's Harbour (3/1C) It is quite astonishing – for a mercantile community – to learn how long it took Jersey to build a good harbour. In the 17th century even, HAVRE DES PAS was the main landing place, and that was a haven rather than a harbour. From about 1700 other small havens, such as Le Havre des Français and Le Havre des Anglais, were constructed at St Helier; both are now filled with pleasure craft. But such harbours

Cast ironwork, Havre des Pas, St Helier

were entirely tidal and no road led to them, so that all loading and unloading had to be done on the sands at low tide. About 1800 the facility was extended by the building of the old north and south piers; the merchants themselves constructed the road in front of their warehouses, many of which bear dates of around 1818, now called Commercial Buildings, or Le Quai des Marchands. In 1841 a new south pier was built largely to accommodate the enormous amount of shipping using it, as a result of the prosperous Newfoundland fishing industry. This enlargement was named the Victoria Pier and was where the young Queen landed, with Prince Albert, in 1846. The north pier, completed in 1853, was named the Albert Pier. This is the one that became most familiar to islanders, for it was where the mailboats run by the old Southern and Great Western Railways berthed. The steamers from England no longer carry the mail, as it has become airborne, and the boats are now referred to as ferries.

But still these piers were controlled by the tides, until dredging in this century made them accessible at all times. Now the pressure of bigger vessels, the busy holiday traffic, larger containers for freight, and the constant need for roll-on/roll-off facilities for visitors' cars, all contribute to the need for bigger and better harbours.

Gone are the days when the 9 am (weather permitting) arrival of the mailboat was an event awaited with excitement and watched by many islanders strolling on the sea walls. The quays would be thronged with people and with horse-drawn cabs to take passengers to their homes, and farm vans with produce. The scene during the potato season was one of great activity, and the highlight of the farming year.

St John's Church (2/3A) The earliest mention of this church, dedicated to St John the Baptist and also known as St Jean des Chênes, is in 1150 when it was given to St Sauveur le Vicomte. In early documents it is referred to as *ecclesia sancti Johannis Caisnibus*, or *Quercibus* indicating, as does its French name, that it was sited among oak trees.

The oldest part is the north chancel, and in its north wall is a blocked priests' door bearing the date, perhaps retrospective, 1622. The nave was added in the early 17th century, a date confirmed by the carved initials and arms of Thomas Lemprière of La Maison de St Jean.

In 1828 one of the supporting pillars between the north and south naves was removed, a dangerous architectural feat achieved also at ST MARY'S and TRINITY CHURCH, so that more of the congregation could see the preacher.

Maître Jacques Pitel cast a bell for St John in 1754 – the only one cast in Jersey still in use. In 1975 a ring of bells was installed, a difficult operation as there are two storeys in the steeple; these were used as school rooms before the building of a parish school, but the area is small and it must have been cruelly cold up there. The spire was rebuilt after lightning had struck it in 1733, during divine service. The rendering on the steeple was removed in 1772, an enormous improvement. The weathercock was placed on the spire in 1774 and has since been twice regilded. The fine carved pulpit dates from 1791, when it was a three-decker. The west end rose window was inserted in 1972.

The particularly handsome chandeliers, perhaps 17th century, should be noted, and also the copper alms box; it is the local pattern of collecting pot, dated 1677, bearing the initials of the donor. As in other Jersey parish churches much of the glass is by H. T. Bosdet. The church plate includes four 17th-century wine cups and an alms dish of 1677, as well as the earliest piece of dated Jersey pewter (1718).

In the north wall of the churchyard are many small square blocks of granite, with the initials and dates of those whose burials they marked. The water table here is so high that no further interments can take place in the cemetery, and these gravestones were removed in 1852 in order to make a pathway round the church. The elegant vestry to the north is quite modern, the work of St John's architects.

St John's Parish (2/3A) A small parish with some of the finest scenery in Jersey. The Route du Nord runs along its northern coastline; this road was made during the German Occupation in order to give work to those who direly needed it, but were determined not to work for the enemy. There is a dedication stone in the centre of a car parking area inscribed, 'This road is dedicated to the memory of the men and women of Jersey who suffered in the World War 1939-1945'.

The view varies considerably with the weather. If very clear Alderney can be seen, though this is usually a sign of rain to come. Frequently the coast of France is visible, and most often the islands of Guernsey and Sark with, nearer home, the rocky reefs of Les Dirouilles and Les Pierres de Lecq.

Roadside flower stand, St John's Parish

Inland this is an agricultural parish and the beautiful cows can be seen grazing in many fields. A curious feature on the cliffs is Le Lavoir des Dames, or Le Puit de la Chuette. Accessible only at low tide it is a hollow in the rock, 15 ft deep and about 24 ft square. It is not even certain whether it is man-made (though for what purpose?) or a natural phenomenon. With such a mystery it is natural that legends should have grown up around it. The headland of Ronez Point is a granite quarry.

Inland is the small tumulus of La Hougue Boëte, perhaps of about 3500 BC. It is attached to the manor of that name, though the existing manor house, slightly to the south, is of 18th-century date on earlier foundations. The fief of that name was extensive and spilled over into other parishes. The house St Blaize incorporates in its south wall a fragment of a medieval chapel dedicated to him, most appropriate for a parish that had so many sheep in medieval and post-medieval times.

Macpéla Cemetery, on the main road leading south, was started for the use of Independents who did not wish to be buried in Anglican graveyards. However, its heyday came in 1848 and succeeding years, when political exiles flooded into Jersey from countries that had seen revolutions. Victor Hugo was associated with Macpéla during his exile in Jersey in 1852-5, during which time he often made eloquent orations at funerals of *proscrits*.

See also Bonne Nuit Bay; Mont Mado

St Lawrence's Church (2/3B) Documentary evidence for this church is not as early as in some instances, but in 1198 John, later King of England, gave it to the abbey of Blanchelande. However, it is most likely that the nave, tower and transept, the oldest parts, date from before that. The south transept has an altar recess, unusual as many transepts have not survived alterations.

It is likely that parts of the church have been altered and rebuilt many times. It was roofed in stone some time after 1204, as so many of the island churches were. The saddle-backed tower was heightened in the 1880s.

What is certain is that the Hamptonne chapel was added on the north-east in the 1530s, so that its piscina is the latest to be made – only a few years before the Reformation was to hit Jersey so

St Lawrence's Church

ferociously. The chapel was the inspiration of the Rector, Sire Louis Hamptonne, and is an outstandingly fine piece of architecture with a vaulted ribbed ceiling. It is recorded that the north aisle was constructed in 1546, the last enlargement to be made. Some of the crocketed gables on the Hamptonne chapel were added by J. E. Trollope, the architect of the restoration.

In the east wall, on the outside, are some stones with incised designs, mostly some form of cross. Those with a cross with a circle round the intersection are Celtic and perhaps 9th century; those with a Calvary cross (steps leading up to the cross) 12th century.

The west doorway to the north aisle, now blocked, recalls the time when militia cannon were stored in the churches, from 1547, which is when this section was being constructed.

St Lawrence's and St Mary's are the only island churches to have retained their Calvinist communion tables, used on only four occasions in the year, and with the congregation standing round the table.

St Lawrence's bell is the oldest in the island and is inscribed: '*Cete cloche est pour la paroisse de St Lorans a Jarze 1592.I.W.*'

In the outside of the south-east buttress is a fine Hamptonne memorial stone, in Latin.

The most famous item in the church is a broken granite pillar of non-Jersey stone, found buried under the floor during the 1892 restorations. In the first instance it was a Roman Doric pillar, or part of one, in a 3rd-4th century Roman villa. Later the inscription was cut in the top, in insular majuscule script, probably in the 6th century.

US DI
LAU SER
RIGON D

The meaning of this message has been hotly debated over the years, but the most plausible theory is that it represents the name of a priest and where he came from, the most likely reading being:

Lau, from Rigond, Servant of God

This strongly suggests a Christian presence in this central part of Jersey in a period when we know St Helier and other Christian missionaries were active in the islands. Later, in the 8th or 9th century, the pillar was carved on the back with an elaborate three-cord plait design. What we do not know is when in its long and interesting history this artifact came to Jersey.

Excavations to the north of the church have revealed early medieval cist graves; one, of a youngish woman, has been carbon dated to about 1080, so that she could have known the Conqueror! Some of these graves lie under the 16th-century Hamptonne chapel.

The church plate includes four wine cups and a baptismal dish dated 1748. A piscina including an ancient lintel with a carving of St Lawrence's gridiron (on which he was martyred) was inserted during 1973 restorations.

A burial stone of some interest, set into the path south of the church, is dated 1586 and records the death of Nicolas de Treguz, from the bishopric of Nantes in Brittany, surely a Huguenot refugee.

As a postscript it is recorded that as late as 1860 some parts of the floor were 'in the original state of mother earth, grown green by age and damp'. A full restoration was begun in 1888 under the architect J. E. Trollope.

St Lawrence's Parish (2/3B) This parish whose only coastline is a strip on the south is perhaps the richest of all in mellow old houses, great and small. Most unfortunately the flightpath to Jersey Airport crosses it and is a real menace. It is also very well-watered, and Waterworks Valley or La Vallée de St Laurens, its eastern boundary, is beautiful at all seasons. So too is St Peter's Valley, part of its path being the western boundary.

Significant archaeological relics are few, but a considerable quantity of Bronze Age implements has been found near Bel Royal. At the junction of St Lawrence's, St Mary's and St Peter's parishes is La Pierre des Baissières, a large block of red granite with cupmarks on the top. The meaning of these marks is not known, but they must have had a particular significance to those who cut them there.

A small mill named Quétivel (not to be confused with Quétivel Mill in St Peter's) nestles in an idyllic situation. Documentary evidence, as well as place names, tells us that there were other mills along the many streams. Later, when water power was no longer used for grinding corn, these streams fed the waterworks reservoirs. The present company was founded in 1882, and gradually more and more of the island is being linked to mains water.

A beautiful and typical farm is La Ferme Morel, belonging to the National Trust of Jersey, as does the small early 17th-century cottage Le Rat just below it. Opposite is La Fontaine St Martin, one of the many natural springs believed to have magical properties.

Of larger houses there is Le Colombier, near the church, with its dovecot dated 1669; the main

house itself is dated 1776 but its predecessor to the west may well be 14th century. The house Les Saints Germains on the boundary with ST JOHN'S PARISH is late 17th century on the site of one far older. Avranches Manor, built in 1818, was again erected on the site of something far older. The name derives from a fief in TRINITY PARISH held by the owner, François Marett, in 1749; its full name is *Le Fief qui fut à l'évêque d'Avranches*.

In some ways the most interesting house in the parish is Hamptonne, or La Patente, taking the latter name from the Patente (Letters Patent) granted by Charles II when in Jersey to Laurens Hamptonne le Vicomte (Sheriff of the Court). Laurens had bought the property in 1637, a date to be seen above the big double arch on the roadside. There is a *colombier* bearing the date 1674, but it is known to have existed in 1445. There is a strong tradition that Charles II visited the house, and this may well be true. It is surely one of the most distinguished houses, historically and architecturally, in Jersey.

The *perquage* or sanctuary path for ST JOHN'S PARISH, and possibly for other parishes too, winds its way down St Peter's Valley and out to the sea at Beaumont.

Carrefour Selous, a broad crossroads, records the name of an English family Slow, which became assimilated locally. From it spring both a well-known dramatist and a painter, and 'Selous the Mighty Hunter'.

See also St Matthew's Church

St Martin de Grouville *see* Grouville Church

St Martin's Church (2/5B) The earliest known reference to St Martin's Church is in 1042, when William, Duke of Normandy, but not yet King of England, granted it to Cérisy Abbey, and it was known as *ecclesia Sancti Martini veteris* – St Martin le Vieux (the Old), as distinct from its neighbour St Martin de Grouville. The diocese of Coutances was in great chaos in the 9th and 10th centuries and it is quite possible that we are speaking here of a Dark Age foundation.

Often in the past the Dean of Jersey was the Rector of St Martin's (for some years now the Rector of St Helier's has been the Dean) and it was regarded as the leading and the richest church in the island.

The earliest part is the north chancel, with nave, transepts and crossing added, with a south

Opposite: La Ferme Morel. (Above) The 17th-century farmhouse; (below) the cider press and crusher

chancel and nave following. At one time Dean Richard Mabon (1514-45) was involved in, but did not complete, an additional north-east chapel, remnants of which are now incorporated in the vestry. Work was done on the spire in 1582, but it will have existed before that. It was struck by lightning in 1616, again in 1745, and yet again in 1837. It is said that one rector kept his pigeons in the spire. The 15th-century south chapel has a recess, in origin a holy water stoup, and a simple piscina. Three recesses of simple rectangular form mark the positions of fraternity altars. All parishes had fraternities before the Reformation, and St Martin's had three; they were a kind of mutual aid society. Another pre-Reformation relic is the head of a female saint, found under the floor during the 1877 restorations, and now in the museum at ST HELIER.

Along the north wall are sturdy buttresses, some dated 1745. One buttress in the south wall bears a deeply carved and much weathered decoration, probably late 15th century, of figures holding a heraldic shield. There is a sundial in the south wall and the bell was cast in 1768.

Opposite the lectern is a memorial to the Reverend Charles Le Touzel, the Rector, who lost his life in a most unusual accident in 1818. His horse collided with another, galloping in the opposite direction, when coming home on a dark and windy night; he fell and died of his injuries.

The church plate includes four wine cups, one inscribed Lorans Baudains (1545-1611) a philanthropic parishioner who endowed money to support young Jerseymen at Oxford or Cambridge, who would return 'to devote their services in and about the business of the Isle'.

The colours of the East Regiment, Royal Jersey Militia, are preserved here. They were presented in 1879, and laid up in 1925.

St Martin's Parish (2/6B) St Martin's parish forms the north-east corner of Jersey and extends from the middle of ROZEL BAY to GOREY village.

The parish is rich in prehistory. The gallery grave of Le Couperon (*see* Rozel Bay) stands above Le Saie, or Scez, a rocky bay, wonderful at low tide for children and marine biologists. The slopes above it are in spring dotted with the pale gold flowers of the Lent lily, *Narcissus pseudonarcissus*. Faldouet dolmen, a passage grave of about 2500 BC, is on high ground inland from Gorey, and like other dolmens it was covered with an earth mound, in this case removed only in 1839. Human remains were found within the grave.

At the bottom of a winding hill leading to Fliquet Bay is a Martello tower, the terminus of the submarine cable to France. Another Martello stands above Anne Port (taking its name from the fief of Anneville); this is the Victoria Tower, dated 1837, the last of these defences to be built. It now belongs to the National Trust. On the coast road is Geoffrey's Leap, a rock from which a legendary figure named Geoffroi is said to have jumped to his death.

A lovely valley leads from ROZEL MANOR to the sea in St Catherine's Bay; at the far end of the stream is a dam built by the Germans. It has created a valuable source of water as well as a beautiful serene area called La Mazeline.

Place names in St Martin are evidence of a great many medieval chapels, crosses and fountains. A more modern fountain is dated 1846 and is a roadside *abreuvoir* on Les Vaux, a small hill running from the church eastwards, where the initials of those who had the right to use it are inscribed. Many of St Martin's houses of the 19th-century are built of granite from LES ECRÉHOUS.

The Roman Catholic cemetery to the south of the church has the graves of some of the descen-

dants of the Young Pretender. The last was Charles Edward Stuart, Comte d'Albanie, who died in St Martin in 1882.

St Mary's Church (2/3A) This church was first mentioned in 1042, when William, Duke of Normandy, later King of England, gave its tithes to Cérisy Abbey near Coutances. It was then described as *Ecclesia Sancte Marie arsi monasterii*, St Mary of the Burnt Monastery, though the location of such a monastery is not known. It may have been on the site on which the church was later rebuilt. The earliest part of the church is the north-east chancel where traces of two round-headed Norman windows were uncovered during alterations in 1978. The east window now set between them was inserted in 1839, at a cost of £3 10s.

The roof, as with most of the parish churches, is stone vaulted, its supporting ribs corresponding with the medieval buttresses on the north wall. The tower, probably of the 12th century, with a 14th-century steeple, was followed by a north transept (now a modern north porch), and a north-west nave. The sturdy granite pillars were inserted where necessary when the south-east chapel was added. The date of this addition is a

Ploughing fields above Gorey

St Mary's Church with a Jersey bull in the foreground

matter of discussion, as scholars are divided about the incised stone in the apex of this wall: it was thought to be 1342 (MCCCXLII), but recent research suggests that it is 1542 (MVCCXLII); it is not impossible that an earlier stone was inserted into a later wall. The south-west extension was added in 1838, and a change of alignment inside the church shows the joins.

A simple oak table, one of only two surviving, is a relic of Calvinist times when communion was taken standing, a time when men and women sat separately in church.

The church plate includes two bowls and two cups, almost certainly locally made and probably early 18th century. The piscina, with rope moulding, survived the Reformation, but the aumbry to the left of the altar and the stoup in the south wall, next to where there used to be a door, were only recently uncovered.

Perhaps the most interesting relic is a priest's tombstone now lying sideways in the outside of the west wall. The crude and symbolic incising shows a man, flanked by a chalice and fish, emblems of Christianity (though some scholars see a design of stars in the firmament).

On Christmas Eve parishioners ring the church bell and may do so over a period of 24 hours; this custom also survives in the neighbouring parishes, but is less enthusiastically observed there. It is believed that it stems from the Norman occupation of 1461-8, when the north-west parishes were the last to be subjugated.

St Mary's Parish (2/2A) St Mary's coastline runs from GRÈVE DE LECQ in the west to the MOURIER VALLEY in the east, and the cliffs offer glorious views, as in ST JOHN'S PARISH, of the other islands and the French coast. A particularly fine viewpoint is the National Trust headland Le Col de la Rocque, a flower lovers' paradise for spectacular displays of heavily scented gorse and delicate wild daffodils, followed by bluebells, foxgloves, and finally blackberries, down to minute flowering plants that thrive even in the thin soil of the headland.

The parish is not rich in archaeology, though the name La Hougue Mauger records a dolmen where ritualistically broken querns were found.

A granite cross surmounted on a church pillar excites the curiosity. It is believed that both have

Overleaf: Daffodils, St Mary's Parish

Sea mist, St Mary's Parish

come from ST MARY'S CHURCH, though the actual cross may well be the remnant of a pre-Reformation cross near by.

St Peter's Valley begins in St Mary, and Gigoulande Mill at the head of the valley already existed in 1274; it was the only one in the island with a double overshot wheel, though sadly this has quite disappeared, only the site being known. Near by is The Elms, headquarters of the National Trust, a fine 18th-century house, though there are arches and other stone fragments of far earlier date. The south-facing arch has particularly fine chamfer stops and on the keystone is a cross rising out of a rose.

La Mare vineyard is interesting (*see pp. 38 and 41*) as it is the only commercial one in the island; years ago grapes used to be grown for home consumption, or under glass for sale and export. Jersey grapes were quite famous in the 19th century, as were pears of which a huge variety were cultivated. The most perfect were the Doyenne de Comice, exported up until the Second World War. La Haute Tombette nurseries display carnations growing in a glasshouse with many colourful exotic butterflies.

There is a rifle range at Crabbé on the north coast, originally for the troops and militia, but now enthusiastically used by clubs. Close by is a Youth Centre, the local contribution to the Queen's Jubilee Fund where young people can enjoy an active outdoor holiday.

St Matthew's Church (2/3B) This rather plain edifice, built in 1834 in ST LAWRENCE'S PARISH, is often called the Glass Church. It is a great attraction to tourists on account of its Lalique glass. It is orientated north to south, which is surprising as there appears to be plenty of space for it to have been sited with the customary alignment.

René Lalique became famous in the 1930s, and his work is now becoming most popular again. The work he did for St Matthew's, installed by the late Lady Trent in memory of her husband, Jesse Boot of Boots the Chemists, was among his earliest important commissions. Windows, screens, door panels and font are of his special opaque glass with a design of lilies, and over the altar is a giant glass angel. Illuminated against the white walls and off-white floor paving, with sapphire blue hangings, it is most impressive.

St Ouen's Church (2/2A) The dedication (Audoenus in Latin) commemorates St Ouen or Owen (609-683) who was Bishop of Rouen in 639. The advowson was given to the abbey of Mont St Michel by Philippe de Carteret of ST OUEN'S MANOR some time after 1135.

Nave, tower and chancel are the oldest parts, probably 12th to 13th century. Any transepts there may have been were absorbed by enlargements. The unique (to Jersey) round arches from chancel to south aisle are 13th century, and the north aisle is probably Tudor. There is a most unusual stone staircase, almost surely replacing a medieval one, giving access to the tower and, in former times, to a rood loft.

When pews were introduced after the Reformation (because of the interminably long Calvinist sermons) they caused much class jealousy, controversy and unseemly bickering, here as in all the parish churches. There is some late but admirable wood carving on some of the family pews, notably one for the Seigneur of St Ouen and one for Vinchelez de Bas Manor; all of these pews date from around 1680.

The 1865 restoration, here as elsewhere, removed the smokers' gallery and ejected the

Detail of altar in the Lady Chapel, St Matthew's Church

militia cannon, which could by then be housed in the parish arsenals. The font, lectern and pulpit, of Caen stone and marble, date from this period.

A new bell was installed in 1812 and replaced in 1814, and again in 1971. As in ST MARY'S and ST PETER'S parishes there is here the custom of ringing the church bell from noon on Christmas Eve and throughout Christmas day.

Of the church plate the oldest item is a cup dated 1604. Two cups dated 1638 are of special interest; they were given by Captain (later Sir) George Carteret, as a thank offering for his return from an expedition against the Turks of Barbary.

The gargoyles and window surrounds deserve attention, particularly those on the north. One window at least, on the south, with part of an incised cross, must be a very early tombstone re-used. Others show devices and animals, one has the IHS monogram, and several have hood moulds, probably of Tudor date. The two west doorways have very elaborate 15th century hood moulds with more modern additions clearly discernible.

St Ouen's Parish (2/1A) St Ouen's is the largest parish, covering the north-west corner of Jersey. Much of it is cliffland and rather windswept, but the sea views to the north and west are superb,

La Rocco Tower, St Ouen's Bay

as is the carpet of heather, gorse and creeping broom that covers this open moorland area.

The great western bay *(see pp. 18-9)*, skirted by La Grande Route des Mielles, erroneously called the Five Mile Road, actually embraces three parishes, St Ouen's to the north, ST PETER's in the centre and ST BRELADE's to the south. This is the surfers' paradise. During the summer beach guards are on duty watching for anyone in difficulties. The modern surfboards tend to present problems, not only to those riding them, but sometimes to other surfers and bathers.

The Val de la Mare Reservoir was created by the Jersey New Waterworks Company in 1962 and provides most enjoyable walks along its fringes. There is a possibility of its being enlarged to meet the ever-increasing demands for water.

The most noticeable archaeological site is the passage grave of Les Monts Grantez, *c*. 3000 BC, where skeletons were found. Near it is St Ouen's Windmill, Le Moulin de la Campagne, first mentioned in 1331, though the present structure is of early 19th-century date. La Hougue de Geonnais lies north of Vinchelez; the word *hougue*, usually indicating a burial mound, is widespread over the parish.

La Cotte à la Chèvre, which is hard to find, lies east of Grosnez. It is a Palaeolithic site, perhaps 120,000 years old. There are many caves round these coasts but the greatest care should be taken exploring them.

The two manors of Vinchelez de Bas and Vinchelez de Haut lie on either side of the road from Léoville to Grosnez. Originally in one ownership, the two fiefs were divided in 1606 after years of family wrangling. They shared a manorial chapel dedicated to St George, of which all that remains is a field name indicating its site and the base of a wayside cross. The present Vinchelez de Bas was rebuilt in 1818 and Vinchelez de Haut has been greatly altered over the years. A new church dedicated to St George was built in 1880.

There is a Battle of Flowers Museum in this parish where you can see exhibits made out of dried flowers and grasses which have been shown over the years at the annual floral fête. A working woodcraft showroom at L'ETACQ is a very popular venue for visitors.

St Ouen's Manor (2/2A) It is not known when the first manor was built here, but by 1135 the de Carteret family, from Carteret in Normandy, had land and probably a house in Jersey. When King John finally lost Normandy in 1204 the de

Carteret family relinquished their Continental possessions and became firmly rooted in Jersey. Their descendants have dominated island history ever since. The royal mace was given by Charles II in recognition of services rendered by members of this family.

In broad terms the central hall and adjacent towers are medieval. Licence to crenellate (i.e. fortify) the manor was given in 1483. The east-facing façade and most of the projecting wings are late 17th century.

On the death without heirs of Robert Carteret, son of John, Lord Carteret, the property reverted to the descendants of the main line, who happened to be four women. Naturally much litigation followed. Finally the manor and fief were inherited by Edward Charles Malet de Carteret (who had changed his name by sign manual from de Carteret Malet) in 1880. Now, a century later, the alterations he put in hand are becoming mellowed by time and weather, for he had inherited the manor in a sorry state of disrepair.

The chapel is dedicated to Ste Anne and is non-denominational. During the Parliamentary regime, and again during the German Occupation, it was used for secular purposes. Its windows, as well as some of those in the manor, were filled with glass by H. T. Bosdet at the time of the great restorations. In it may be seen a carved mica lamprophyre bowl of post-medieval date, with an outlet in the shape of a heart held by hands. It was brought here from another de Carteret property and its purpose is unsure.

The moat, now dry in part, *colombier* (dovecot), ramparts and field names recall jousting and treading the maze, reminders of its medieval history. The approach to the east terrace is through an arch which on heraldic grounds must be dated at about 1600. Near there is a tazza of limestone; in origin a fountain, it has elaborate heraldic decoration and dates from about 1550.

The Seigneur of St Ouen, senior of island seigneurs, is the first to greet the monarch on his or her arrival in the island; and if he is a Jurat he takes precedence over the other 11 Jurats on the bench.

St Ouen's Pond (2/1B) This pond, which is also called La Mare au Seigneur, constitutes the largest sheet of freshwater in the Channel Islands. Originally only a shingle bank separated it from the sea; the island in the pond is man-made. Two stretches of water flanking it to north and south are the remains of anti-tank ditches dug by the Germans during the Occupation.

The National Trust for Jersey bought the pond when the then Seigneur of St Ouen, in whose family it had been since 1309 at least, was forced to sell. The surrounding land is rich in wild orchids, particularly the Jersey, or loose-flowered, orchid and the southern marsh orchid. Much of this land now also belongs to the Trust.

There have been carp and eel here for centuries, and some other species are now established. The surrounding reeds used to be valuable for thatching, but the area's importance now is as a nature reserve and bird-ringing station. The reed bed provides cover for nesting birds. Then in spring and autumn it is an important feeding and roosting area for birds migrating along the west coasts of Europe. Flocks of wildfowl, including brent geese, teal, widgeon and shoveller, with smaller numbers of other duck like gadwall and goldeneye, join the resident mallard, tufted duck, coot and moorhen in winter.

St Peter's Church (2/2B) St Pierre dans le Désert (a reference to the open wasteland to the west) was first mentioned in 1053, and its advowson was given to St Sauveur le Vicomte in about 1090. There was a Priory of St Peter situated near by, where the monks were still in residence when the Maulevrier occupation began in 1461. This is surprising as other alien priories had been confiscated by the Crown in 1413, though a regranting within the Royal demesne is not impossible.

The chancel is the oldest part, followed by the nave and tower, probably in the 12th century, and transepts a century later. The spire was added and is 124 ft high, and was alone in escaping the cement cladding imposed on its counterparts elsewhere. With binoculars many incised initials can be seen, probably those of workmen who have laboured up there over the years. The spire was struck by lightning in 1612, 1643 and 1648. At its apex it now carries a red light as a warning to aircraft.

As so often the mullions and tracery of the windows are modern, but the surrounding stones of the aperture are probably 15th century. The west door with recessed arches is mainly 14th century. The whole north aisle was added in 1885 to accommodate troops from St Peter's Barracks: a rather tardy move as these had been built in 1815.

A curious stone, which might commemorate a farrier, or alternately might show instruments of the Passion, because of the incised designs flanking the cross, is built into a buttress in the west wall. In origin it must have been either a memorial stone or a coffin lid. There are shallow medieval buttresses on the north and east walls of the church; the heavy sturdy buttresses, mainly on the south, are far later. Indeed, one of the latter, at the south-east corner, proclaims a date of 1768.

There is a simple piscina beside the altar, and another more elaborate one is now in the Lady Chapel. The latter was found in 1951 in a nearby house that was being demolished to make way for airport extensions. Yet another, which may in fact be a holy water stoup, is in the south wall; it is moulded and square-topped and could be of the 15th century.

The bell was cast in Normandy in 1649 and is inscribed 'Mon nom est Elizabeth la belle' – perhaps a pun on 'belle' or perhaps a reference to Elizabeth, wife of Sir George Carteret, who was closely connected with the parish. The church plate includes two early wine cups and a baptismal dish dated 1671, and another dated 1775, a relic of Calvinist times when fonts had been removed and baptism took place from a shallow bowl.

The reredos behind the altar depicting The Last Supper is in Royal Doulton pottery, a gift during the 1886 restorations. In the north wall of the church there is a memorial tablet, made of alabaster, a very rare material in Jersey.

A war memorial tablet honours 8 parishioners killed in the Second World War, and 38 in 1914-18: an illustration of the appalling slaughter of the First World War.

St Peter's Parish (2/2B) This parish has sea coast on the south at Beaumont, and on the west. The western part is largely sand dunes, hence its name of St Pierre dans le Désert, but the inland part is valleys and pastures.

In the dunes near the pond are three large upright stones, Les Trois Rocques, likely to be the sole remainders of an unrecorded dolmen. Out to sea is La Rocco Tower, the last of the Jersey round towers to be built, completed in 1800. It was severely damaged during the Second World War, and pounding by the seas reduced it almost to a ruin. Then in the early 1970s a campaign was mounted and the tower was fully restored, half through voluntary contributions and half from a States subvention.

St Peter's Valley has always been regarded as very beautiful, and how lovely it must have been when the stream supported at least six watermills. Their names alone speak of the history of

Weather vane, near St Peter's Valley

Jersey: Gigoulande, Tostain, Gargate, l'Oumel, Quétivel and Tesson. During the war some were reactivated to grind flour, and then fell into disuse again. One, Quétivel, first recorded in 1309, has been restored by the National Trust and now stone-ground flour can be bought there.

On the edge of the Airport there is a pre-Reformation cross base, the only one surviving in its original position, named La Croix ès Bruns.

At the bottom of Beaumont Hill a Tudor cannon can be seen; it is dated 1551 and states that it was made for St Peter, the only one of the parish guns to survive.

The most important house was Le Manoir de la Hague. The old house, itself rebuilt in 1634, has long since disappeared; the present one dates from 1871, and it is now St George's Preparatory School. The *colombier* (dovecot), now the school library, was built, or rebuilt, in 1629.

Jersey Airport covers acres and acres of flat land; opened in 1937, it has frequently been enlarged since then and is now one of the busiest in the British Isles.

A German Occupation museum (the Bunker Museum) and the Jersey Motor Museum, situated near ST PETER'S CHURCH, give added attraction to this parish.

St Saviour's Church (2/4B) St Saviour's Church was in the possession of the Bishop of Coutances by 1145, and the advowson belonged to the Archdeacon of Val de Vire. It is often known as St Saviour of the Thorn (St Sauveur de l'Epine), but this name first appeared in 1646 and there is no medieval evidence for it. The church was heavily restored from 1895, often making interpretation difficult.

Here the oldest part, probably 12th century, is the nave and chancel, with the tower and transepts added later. Various additions were dedicated to St John, St Mary and St Martin, but never constituted free-standing chapels as is often suggested. The crossing carries a crenellated tower but no spire. As in most of Jersey's parish churches, the 15th century saw enlargement of windows and the insertion of Flamboyant tracery typical of that period.

A niche in the south-west buttress has a carved shell and the initials G. L., while the north-west buttress has the arms of Lemprière. This is generally thought to represent George Lemprière who was Constable of the parish in 1464 and died in 1515, and that it indicates that he had made the pilgrimage to St James of Compostela in Spain, thus giving an early 16th-century date for the west front.

Jehan Hue, who was Rector from 1461 to 1507, recorded a mass of detail about the church, its revenues, burials and gifts, including instances of the gift of an image or money to supply candles for specified statues. Jehan Hue is also remembered as the donor of a house and land where later, in 1496, a school was founded called St Magloire (or Mannelier) after the chapel that stood there. This school served the six eastern parishes, and a similar foundation, St Anastase, was created for the six western parishes. These schools ceased to exist after VICTORIA COLLEGE was founded in 1852.

There are four bells, the oldest dated 1656, and the three others 1968. The parish plate includes four wine cups of 1638 and a baptismal dish dated 1700.

Monsignor de Cheylus, Bishop of Bayeux, who was a refugee from the French Revolution, was buried in St Saviour's in 1797, but his tomb could not subsequently be found. Other Revolution refugees were buried at St Saviour's, but the tomb

and memorial that without doubt evoke the most interest and curiosity are those of Lillie Langtry (1853-1929) daughter of Dean Le Breton; she was the 'Jersey Lily', the most noted beauty of her time.

St Saviour's Parish (2/5B) This is a sprawling parish, reaching far to the east but having only a sliver of coastline at Le Dicq. On the shore there is Le Rocher des Proscrits, the place where Victor Hugo used to deliver many of his orations to his fellow exiles. A commemorative tablet is inserted in the side of the rock.

The valleys running north out of ST HELIER, Les Grands Vaux and La Vallée des Vaux, formerly contained watermills, but are now greatly built up. The Grands Vaux reservoir leads up to what was Le Moulin de Louis Paul, now recognizable by the house name upon it.

There used to be four manors in the parish: LONGUEVILLE MANOR; Maufant, an erroneous but early appellation; Grainville, now demolished and only known by the name of the school on the site; and Bagot, also largely demolished. The last-named had a chapel dedicated to St André, erected in 1495. A very ancient house is Le Ponterrin. Its roadside double arch, a fine example of this Jersey design, is dated 1643, but the house within the courtyard is far older, and probably the oldest surviving unaltered vernacular façade.

A distinguished house of more recent times is Steephill, built by the Robin family and designed by Ernest Newton in 1899. Government House, its neighbour, was built in about 1817 and became the official residence of the Lieutenant-Governor in 1822. It has since been enlarged and the grounds and ambience are delightful. Before it was purchased the Governors lived firstly at MONT ORGUEIL, then at ELIZABETH CASTLE, and then in various town houses. St Saviour's Hospital, the mental hospital, was built in 1865 and occupies a commanding position above QUEEN'S VALLEY.

Samarès Manor (2/5C) The third most senior in Jersey's hierarchy of manors, Samarès (Salse marais) takes its name from the saltpans that existed on the low-lying land to the south in medieval times. The manor has been in the hands of many owners, and has passed through the female line more than once.

The *colombier* (dovecot) dates from a very early period. An undercroft, said by tradition to be a chapel crypt, is the oldest surviving part of the manor. It is claimed that the chapel was dedicated to Ste Marthe, but there is no early evidence for this; that there was a seigneurial chapel is certain from a 1498 licence to celebrate Mass there.

It is not known who built the existing manor house. It may have been Jacques Jean Hammond who bought the property in 1754. Slight evidence of a house earlier than this can be seen in the thickness of some walls, and a granite fireplace in what would have been the east gable of the earlier building.

The grounds were already well known for their trees in about 1680, but the present beautiful garden is the creation of the late Sir James Knott who bought it in 1924; in early summer the many exotics, and especially the camellias, are a delight. The grounds are now open to the public and an exciting herb garden has recently been laid out, supporting the goods on view in the herb shop.

Seymour Tower (2/6C) There is here a strong tradition of association with St Samson. No one can say exactly what it was, but the saint is believed to have visited both Jersey and Guernsey, and a rock beside the islet on which the tower was later built is called *les settes Samson* (*settes* is a word for stones, usually paving stones).

Perhaps there was never a permanent garrison here, for when the Baron de Rullecourt (*see* Royal Square) landed in 1781, he planned to put some of his men ashore at this point. There had been a tower or redoubt here earlier, but after the disaster of that French landing, the States built the present square tower on the islet and named it after Field Marshal Henry Seymour Conway, the Governor. The construction, all in granite ashlar, is of the usual high standard of defence works of the time. It can be visited at low tide, if great care is taken. It makes a lovely expedition in summer weather.

Trinity Church (2/5A) More correctly known as the Holy Trinity Church, its advowson belonged to St Helier's Abbey, and was transferred to the Abbey of Cherbourg in 1186.

The oldest existing part of the church is the nave and tower; the latter has an arched quadripartite vault, all of 12th-century date. The nave, of similar date, was largely rebuilt in 1865. As at ST MARY'S and ST JOHN'S CHURCHES one central pillar, which is now in a nearby garden, was removed to improve the congregation's view of the preacher, and his of them no doubt. This was in 1830. The spire, the most vulnerable in the

Farmstead, St Peter's Parish

island from its height above sea level, was struck by lightning in 1629, 1646 and again in 1648. The mullions and tracery of many of the windows are comparatively modern.

Jersey's early bells were confiscated at the Reformation, leaving just one for each church, but a most interesting one by Paul Burdon was hung at Trinity in 1690. The arms of four princi-

pal parish families are engraved upon it: Duma-
resq of Augrès, Lemprière of Diélament, de
Carteret of Trinity Manor, and Guerdain of La
Guerdainerie.

There is a particularly fine mural tablet by
Henry Cheere to the memory of Sir Edward de
Carteret (1620-82), Gentleman Usher of the
Black Rod.

The altar is one of several pre-Reformation
altar tops, with the five consecration crosses of the
Passion, found at MONT ORGUEIL CASTLE in
service as a gun platform, and then returned to
ecclesiastical use.

In the granite-paved chancel are some fine
carved memorials let into the floor: one is to
Hugh Lemprière dated 1685, and one to Denis
Guerdain who died in 1742. Both were given by
the widows concerned; the latter is inscribed as
Sara Rs for Richardson! The pews in the south
chancel are perhaps the glory of this church.

They are very similar to two Jurat's chairs at the museum in ST HELIER. They are made of walnut and are misericords, that is the seat was hinged, and when raised a carved console allowed the priest some support during lengthy services, while appearing to be standing. They must date before 1500.

The plate includes the only piece of pre-Reformation silver to have survived in Jersey. It is a chalice with an eight-lobed base, though unfortunately the stem is a replacement: a modern careful replica, with no stem, was given in 1912. There are five 17th-century wine cups, and one dated 1762. A platter is dated 1619 and another 1654. An alms dish of 1834 bears the mark of the celebrated silversmith William Bateman. Two of the wine cups were stolen from Trinity Manor in 1680 and were replaced by new ones, which are likely to have been made by the Huguenot silversmith Jean Girard, whose daughter, Marie, married the Seigneur of Trinity.

A full restoration of the church took place in 1863 and now, more than a century later, urgent work is again needed. It may be hoped that the trellis between the two chancels, brightly coloured, will disappear and that new life will breathe into this ancient site.

Trinity Parish (2/5A) This is a large parish with a fine northern coastline which stretches from the ST JOHN'S PARISH boundary to the middle of ROZEL BAY.

Among the most ancient archaeological sites are the Belle Hougue caves where remains of a small deer were found, probably from about 300,000 BC. Several stones in the parish seem to have been Neolithic menhirs, and field name evidence is involved in some cases, as well as a probable Iron Age promontory fort at Belle Hougue Point. Here, too, there is a natural spring, known as La Fontaine des Mittes, believed to have miraculous healing powers, especially for eyes.

The area known as Le Castel Sedeman is a mystery, but it is not impossible that it was a Roman site. It does seem very probable that it was used as a camp of refuge when Pero Nino attacked the island in 1406, and advanced from the town area towards MONT ORGUEIL CASTLE, always an objective for raiders.

There is a small cist grave at Les Platons of about 1500 BC; this is the highest point in the island, 435 ft above sea level and there are radio transmitting masts here.

Diélament was an important fief, though the existing manor house is relatively modern, but the *colombier* (dovecot) was rebuilt in 1573 and is the largest in Jersey, capable of housing 1000 pairs of birds.

On the coast is a fort, L'Etacquerel, now disused but a fine example of an 18th-century coastal defence work, all in granite. The area called Le Jardin d'Olivet is famous as the site of a battle in 1549 when the French landed but were heavily defeated by the local militia.

The States Experimental Farm, situated near TRINITY CHURCH, is a splendid establishment, originally the gift of the Jersey-born benefactor T. B. Davis in memory of his son who was killed in the First World War. It runs a modern scientific advisory service and conducts controlled experiments into all aspects of agriculture.

A recent addition to the parish's amenities is the Orchid Nursery at Victoria Village where a world-famous collection of exotics can be seen, through the generosity of the late Mr E. Young, a dedicated collector of orchids.

Tunnel, The (3/2B) In any small town, modern traffic poses an insoluble problem. No sooner is a new multi-storey car park built than it is full to overflowing. However, the smooth movement of traffic is as important as parking, and for years it was felt that ST HELIER needed an additional west–east artery.

An imaginative scheme was to blast a tunnel through La Montagne de la Ville, under FORT REGENT. This was not a new idea: as long ago as 1843 a railway engineer had suggested just such a move. But Sir John Le Couteur, a prominent islander, recorded in his diary, 'I do not think the Ordnance would allow a tunnel anywhere near Fort Regent.' However, with Fort Regent now a leisure centre, and no longer a defensive position, the situation is changed, and a tunnel was made in 1973. It is a boon, and St Helier wonders how it ever managed without it.

Vallée des Moulins, La *see* Queen's Valley

Victoria Avenue (2/4B) The annual floral festival, misleadingly called The Battle of Flowers, takes place along this avenue hugging the south coast to the west of St Helier.

Originating in festivities celebrating the Coronation of Edward VII in 1902, this fête has continued ever since, apart from the war years, the exhibits growing ever more intricate and sophisticated. Over the years the venue for the fête has

The Battle of Flowers (States of Jersey Tourism Committee)

changed, but for a long time now the parade has been held on Victoria Avenue, between West Park and First Tower.

As you drive along Victoria Avenue and recall that a century ago there was no sea wall and no coast road, note the carved granite pillar, surmounted by a crown. This was erected in 1897, celebrating the Queen's Diamond Jubilee, when the road was named after her. Her statue, now in a small triangular park close by, was originally sited by the Weighbridge, in a small circular garden. When, however, this area became the bus terminal, a more suitable place for Victoria's statue had to be found – although the area had been more pleasing when it was a garden full of tulips, followed by summer annuals.

The paved promenade along the shore used to be the Western Railway line (*see* Railways in Jersey) until shortly before the Second World War. This makes a very popular walk for visitors, and on a warm summer evening it is delightful to see ELIZABETH CASTLE floodlit in the bay.

Victoria College (3/3B) As the ancient grammar schools of St Mannelier and St Anastase fell into decay, the need for a good boys' school became pressing. After Queen Victoria's visit in 1846 some of those most wishing to see a school established found an excellent opportunity in suggesting this as a permanent memorial to her visit. Plans went ahead, the final choice of architect being John Hayward.

Victoria College holds a commanding position above the town, and was built in the Gothic Revival style of local granite with Caen stone quoins (the latter have weathered badly and have had to be replaced).

The foundation stone was laid in 1850 and the school opened for pupils in 1852. Queen Victoria presented full-length portraits of herself and Prince Albert by Franz Winterhalter, which hang in the Assembly Hall. She and Prince Albert paid a second, short visit in 1859 to see and admire the school that bore her name.

In the grounds stands The Temple, a gazebo surviving from when this was the garden of a private house. It is Jersey's most distinguished example of this type of architecture, Georgian in feeling though of Regency date. It was most carefully restored some years ago.

Zoological Gardens *see* Jersey Wildlife Preservation Trust

WAYSIDE CROSSES

Before the Reformation wayside crosses abounded in Jersey; place names incorporating 'La Croix' testify to this. At least 17 are known, with cognomens such as La Croix Benard, La Croix ès Bruns, La Croix du Sacrement. These crosses were generally sited at crossroads: places where a decision of direction had to be taken, perhaps, and so a place where a prayer might be helpful.

It was in 1547 that an edict came from Edward VI with instructions to destroy every emblem of Roman Catholicism. The anonymous author of *Les Croniques*, writing in or about 1580, gives a vivid description of this event, and the reader is struck with the readiness, even eagerness, with which the islanders accepted the new type of worship. The form introduced in these islands was Calvinism

from Geneva. The prayers needed to be in French to be comprehended by the islanders, most of whom did not speak English.

This wholesale destruction removed statues, stained glass, and fonts (only three survived), stoups and piscinae (six have survived).

Jersey's wayside crosses were simple and not at all like the elaborate Calvaries of Brittany. They were of granite, octagonal in section and very tall with short cross arms. The head sections of less than half a dozen have survived, and some bases can be found, sturdy granite objects, sometimes octagonal, with a square mortice which supported the tall shaft. A few may have been wooden: the old name of the modern Five Oaks crossroads, for example, was La Croix de Bois.

THE BAILIWICK
OF GUERNSEY

Bust of Thomas de la Rue (Eric Peskett, 1963), founder of the famous printing firm, St Peter Port (see p. 109)

Previous page: Cobo Bay (see p. 120)

The Bailiwick of Guernsey Gazetteer

Airport (4/3C) The States of Guernsey Airport at La Villiaze was opened in 1939, a few months before the outbreak of the Second World War. Like its counterparts in Jersey and ALDERNEY, it takes advantage of the plateau at the upper end of the island. Since the war the original airport, which covered 126 acres, has been enlarged repeatedly to cope with the increasing proportion of travellers who come by air. In 1959 a concrete runway was laid and the airport extended westward, and since then there have been two major enlargements of the terminal buildings.

The road from the airport to ST PETER PORT has some of the worst ribbon development in Guernsey. The traveller with a little time to spare will gain a much better impression of the island by turning right on leaving the airport and following the main road to L'ERÉE.

Alderney (6) The northern isle of Alderney lies 8 miles west of Cap de la Hague, the rugged promontory forming the north-western corner of the Cherbourg peninsula. Between the two is the Race of Alderney. A mile to the north-west, across the notorious Swinge, lies the uninhabited island of BURHOU and Guernsey is some 22 miles to the south-west. Each of the Channel Islands has a strong character of its own and the northern isle is no exception. It is open and windswept, with an atmosphere of freedom and a slightly unkempt appearance which only adds to its charm.

Alderney is about 3½ miles long and 1¼ miles across at its widest point. The western two-thirds of the island consist of an elevated plateau, rising to 294 ft near the airport, surrounded by cliffs. The remainder of the island is low-lying, with sand dunes around the bays of Braye, Saye and Longis, and underlying Longis Common.

The delightful town of **St Anne** (6/2B) contains most of Alderney's population of 1700. With its narrow cobbled streets, whitewashed stone houses and superabundance of hostelries, it must be one of the most human towns in Europe. Its

Victoria Street, St Anne, Alderney

medieval heart is a group of farmsteads in the area of Marais Square, with narrow lanes or *venelles* running between the houses and radiating out on to the agricultural land of the Blaye. Many of these sleepy *venelles* survive, with only the occasional car to disturb the slumbers of the local cats.

St Anne was enlarged in the 18th century, when privateering brought wealth to the island, and again in the 19th century, when labour was imported to build the harbour and fortifications. The main shopping area, centred round Victoria Street and High Street, contains a mixture of 18th- and 19th-century houses, all in the local idiom and built of local stone, usually the hard Alderney sandstone. Sash windows are the rule, often with curved glazing bars giving Gothic points to the upper panes. Taken singly, the houses are of no particular architectural merit, and yet as a group they add up to a town of such character that, if it were in England, it would certainly be designated a conservation area.

From near the bottom of Victoria Street, La Rue des Butes leads to a level plateau, once the medieval archery ground and now a playing field. From Butes there is a magnificent view over Braye Harbour and the breakwater, with small boats butting through the turbulent Swinge, and the hazy isle of Burhou beyond.

Between Victoria Street and Le Pré – once a meadow and now market gardens – is the magnificent parish church of St Anne. This was built in 1850 when the population of Alderney was augmented by numerous military and civilian workers involved with the harbour and fortifications. It is one of the few Channel Islands buildings by an architect of international repute, having been designed by Sir George Gilbert Scott. Although usually associated with exuberant Gothic buildings such as St Pancras Station Hotel and the Albert Memorial in London, Scott designed for St Anne a dignified Romanesque church, cruciform in plan, with apse and square central tower. The pyramidal spire is a conspicuous landmark. *(See p. 21.)*

Continuing to the top of Victoria Street, close to its junction with High Street, is the old churchyard, the site of the medieval church that Scott's building replaced. All that remains of the old church is the clock tower. Although in the Channel Islands idiom, with squat cement-covered spire and spirelets, the tower was only added to the medieval church in 1767. Over the cemetery wall, in the former schoolroom of 1790, the Alderney Society has its headquarters, and a museum well worth visiting.

A few yards further to the west, at the end of High Street, is Royal Connaught Square and facing the cobbled square is the Island Hall, containing among other things an excellent public library. The building was once Government House and the home of the Le Mesurier family, hereditary governors of Alderney. The imposing three-storey Georgian façade of dressed stone dates from 1763, when the Le Mesuriers had become wealthy privateer owners. The side wings and rather heavy porch are later additions. The *venelle* to the west of the Island Hall is Les Mouriaux and facing it is Mouriaux House, built by the Le Mesuriers in 1779. It is a pleasingly proportioned house of two storeys and dormers, with almost contemporary side wings. During the 19th century the façade was rendered and the doorcase and window mouldings added, but the stucco has recently been removed to reveal once again the attractive random stonework.

Alderney has been inhabited since Neolithic times, and was formerly rich in megalithic remains. Most of these have been destroyed during the various spates of fortifications; the best surviving example is a small burial chamber in a clearing in the gorse beside an unfenced road above Fort Tourgis.

The Coastline and Fortifications The fortification of Alderney began in Roman times. The Nunnery (6/3A), a square fort with rounded corners standing on the shore at Longis Bay, is thought to be one of a chain of forts built along the Channel coast in the 4th century AD. At that time Longis would have been the island's main anchorage. Opinions differ as to whether the fort has ever been a nunnery: the name may have been coined by the soldiers stationed there when it was converted into barracks in the 18th century. Today it contains a number of flats.

On the clifftop to the south of the Nunnery is Essex Castle, begun in 1546 by Henry VIII in order to command Longis Bay. The outer walls on the north and west sides are original but much of the present building is Victorian, and again it has been converted into flats.

The coastline to the east and north of Longis Bay is low-lying but at Essex Castle spectacular sea cliffs begin, which continue westward along the south coast, and north again as far as Fort Clonque. At Cachalière (6/3B) a path descends to a concrete jetty from which the hard diorite rock from the nearby quarry was exported in the early

Clock tower of the old church, St Anne, Alderney

Mouriaux House, St Anne, Alderney (see p. 102)

years of this century. The cliffs around Telegraph Bay (6/2C) are particularly dramatic, with carpets of sea campion, thrift and prostrate broom on the clifftop, and a series of conical sea stacks far below. From the clifftop a steep path descends to the bay. Telegraph Bay has a good bathing beach at low water, but great care should be taken to avoid being cut off by the rising tide. The name refers to the tower that still stands on the skyline above the bay, and was used in the early 19th century for signalling to the other islands.

A little further along the cliffs, at the western extremity of Alderney, is a view of Les Etacs (6/1C), a rugged stack surrounded in the breeding season by a cloud of countless gannets. These large, magnificent sea birds took up residence during the German Occupation. When the people of Alderney returned from exile they found colonies on Ortac, an isolated stack between Alderney and LES CASQUETS, and on Les Etacs. The colonies flourished, although recently many young birds have perished as a result of becoming entangled in nylon netting which the adult birds collect as nesting material. During the summer the gannets can be watched as they wheel over the

colony, or dive headlong into the sea after fish. In winter they disperse over the Atlantic and North Sea, returning to breed the following spring.

To the north lies the Giffoine (6/1C), a broad expanse of heathland between the clifftop and the arable land of the Blaye. The Giffoine is mainly covered by gorse, both the common and the late-flowering western species, and is the habitat of the diminutive stonechat.

From the Giffoine a zigzag path descends the cliff towards a causeway leading to Fort Clonque (6/1C), a Victorian fort built off-shore in order to command the Swinge. Fort Clonque was built in 1854 to designs by Captain William Jervois, the military architect responsible for most of the Victorian forts on Alderney's headlands and islets. Jervois had a strongly developed aesthetic sense which sometimes overruled mere military considerations. Fort Clonque is particularly romantic, with rounded bastions full of loopholes, clinging to the offshore rock. The fort has been restored and converted into holiday flats by the Landmark Trust.

Brooding over the next headland is Fort Tourgis (6/1B), a large and rather derelict fortification containing barracks that once housed the Alderney Militia. From Fort Clonque to Fort

Tourgis the coastal path runs along the foot of a steep slope – once a sea cliff but now separated from the sea by a strip of low-lying ground. Below Fort Tourgis the path rounds a German bunker and continues past Platte Saline, a shingle beach where gravel is extracted, to Crabby. The sand of Crabby Bay is a depressing dark-grey colour, probably because spoil was dumped here from York Hill quarry (6/2B), which once yielded stone for the fortifications and now provides the cooling water for an electricity generating station. Nearby is Braye Harbour (6/2B).

The traveller who arrives in Alderney by sea (there is a hydrofoil service from the other islands) will probably leave the harbour area by Braye Street, between two rows of 18th-century buildings. On the left is a row of pubs and houses, whose backs face the sand dunes of Braye Bay. The first house, the Sea View Hotel, has been disfigured by an unsympathetic extension which obscures the rest of the row from the direction of the harbour. On the right are a series of warehouses. The buildings owe their existence to the smuggling and privateering activities of the Le Mesurier family, who built a jetty at Braye in 1736. This was the angled pier projecting across Braye beach from near the Sea View Hotel. The original jetty, roughly constructed of boulders, was enlarged in 1840 as the Douglas Quay.

In the 1840s the British Government, alarmed by the building of a naval harbour at Cherbourg, began work on 'harbours of refuge' (a euphemism for naval bases) at Braye in Alderney and St Catherine's Bay, Jersey. As third harbour, proposed at FERMAIN BAY in Guernsey, was never begun. The intention was to convert Braye Bay into a gigantic naval base by building two great breakwaters out to sea from opposite ends of the bay. Work began on the western breakwater, the only one built, in 1847. The attractive inner harbour, with the appearance of an old fishing harbour, was built to shelter and load the barges that built up the rubble mound on which the breakwater stands. On this mound were laid several courses of giant concrete blocks, with granite on the seaward side. The rest of the breakwater is of sandstone from Mannez Quarry (6/3A) at the eastern end of the island. A mineral railway was constructed to bring the stone from Mannez; it is still used in the unending task of maintaining the breakwater, though today it also carries tourists.

The anti-tank wall, Longis Bay, Alderney (see p. 107)

Above: Les Etacs at sunset, Alderney (see p. 104)
Opposite: Telegraph Bay, Alderney (see p. 104)

When the breakwater was begun nobody (except the Alderney fishermen, who had not been consulted) had anticipated the violence of the seas that would constantly attack it. Although it was eventually built to a length of 1600 yd, the outer 600 yd sustained such constant damage that it had to be abandoned, leaving only a dangerous submerged bank.

As in Jersey, the 'harbour of refuge' came to nothing, but the 1000 yd long breakwater that remains does provide the shelter without which the present harbour would be unusable. The jetty now used by the hydrofoils and cargo boats was begun in 1896, after a long dispute over who should pay for it; eventually it was the British Government.

Braye Bay has a fine sandy beach backed by dunes with marram, fennel, sea spurge, sea holly and sea bindweed. Overlooking it from the east is Fort Albert (6/2A), the largest and most impressive of William Jervois's creations, which was intended to protect the 'harbour of refuge'. Ramparts and gun positions are built into the hillside, with barrack blocks in an inner courtyard. Beyond Fort Albert is Saye Bay, a sandy

cove enclosed by a horseshoe of dunes, and on the next headland is Château à l'Etoc, a handsome fort now converted into flats. A further sandy bay, Corblets, a popular bathing beach, is defended by Fort Corblets (6/3A), now a private house.

The coastline of the eastern end of Alderney is rocky and inhospitable. A lighthouse, built in 1912, stands on the shore and there are two off-shore islets, Les Homeaux Florains and Houmet Herbé (6/3A), each with a ruined Victorian fort. Inland is the quarry that provided the sandstone for the breakwater, and the rough grassland of Mannez Garenne. From here there is a view across the Race of Alderney to Cap de la Hague in Normandy, where the nuclear reprocessing plant is only too evident.

The broad, shallow bay of Longis (6/3A), fortified since Roman times, was armed yet again by Jervois, who built an attractive fort on Île de Raz, an islet in the mouth of the bay. The fort, now a private house, is reached at low water by a causeway. The Germans regarded Longis Bay as a possible landing beach, for they built the concrete anti-tank wall that now separates the beach from the sand dunes behind.

In the Second World War, as in Victorian times, Alderney was the most heavily fortified of the Channel Islands. The population had been evacuated before the arrival of the Germans, and at the end of 1941 foreign workers of the Organisation Todt began to put into effect Hitler's extravagant plans to turn the island into an impregnable fortress. Concrete strongpoints were added to the Victorian forts and gun batteries were dug into the cliffs, and a great concrete control tower that still broods over Mannez Garenne. Thousands of foreign workers lost their lives in the construction of these fortifications, and the atmosphere of Alderney is still haunted by this unhappy period in its history.

Although Alderney is only slightly larger than SARK, the visitor will be struck by the great differences between the two islands. Perhaps the most obvious difference is the degree of fortification. Apart from three small French forts, Sark has had no significant fortification whereas Alderney, which lies close to the Channel shipping route, has been fortified since Roman times, so that today the fortifications are a dominant feature of the landscape.

A more fundamental difference is the pattern of settlement. Sark, which was settled from Jersey in the 16th century after a long period as an uninhabited island, has Jersey's pattern of scattered farmsteads with fields enclosed by hedges. Alderney, which has been inhabited continuously since prehistoric times, has inherited from the Middle Ages a central settlement, St Anne, surrounded by open fields. The farm buildings were clustered in St Anne, while the agricultural land was on La Blaye (6/2B, 2C), the plateau to the south and west of the town. The Blaye, which

Breaking up the earth, Val du Sud, Alderney

had no walls or hedges, was divided into blocks known as *riages*, each consisting of a group of parallel strips. Each farmer would own a number of strips, scattered among the various *riages*.

Today the population of Alderney has spread beyond St Anne and part of the Blaye is occupied by the airport. But the Blaye is still the main area of agricultural land, and except for the occasional electric fence it is still unenclosed. Alderney's is, in fact, one of the very few open field systems in the British Isles to have survived to the present day.

Bellieuse, La (4/5C) Villages are not a feature of the Channel Islands; typically, in Jersey, SARK and Guernsey the ancient farmsteads are scattered singly over the countryside, each one surrounded by its own fields. There are, however, a few nucleated settlements and one of the best preserved is La Bellieuse, the village centre of ST MARTIN'S PARISH. The first accurate survey of Guernsey, published in 1787, shows La Bellieuse as a group of farms clustered round the parish church, surrounded by orchards and fields. Most of the buildings are still there, and with the church they form a most attractive group. The houses are built of the local red-brown stone, with pantile roofs and in several cases the original small casement windows. Mercifully La Grande Rue, the main road through St Martin's shopping centre, misses La Bellieuse by a hundred yards and the cluster of old houses remains unspoiled.

In the Middle Ages the arable land of La Bellieuse was in the form of open fields at **Les Camps** and **Les Camps du Moulin**. The section of road between La Grande Rue and SAUSMAREZ

MANOR is still La Route des Camps (*camp* is the Norman form of *champ*, 'field'). The map of 1787 shows that by that date most of the fields of Guernsey had been enclosed, but there remained an open area at Les Camps du Moulin, crossed by five unfenced roads which intersected at the windmill belonging to the Seigneurs of Sausmarez. This was almost the last part of Guernsey to be enclosed; today it is heavily developed and the last vestige of the open fields is a tiny traffic island beside the Old Mill Housing Estate. The sails and machinery of the mill have long since disappeared but the granite structure remains, hemmed in by States houses.

Bourg, Le (4/4C) At the point where the Forest Road turns a sharp corner just before the airport is a group of old houses clustered round the FOREST CHURCH. It is an ancient site, where formerly there were several megalithic remains. Of these the only survivor is Le Perron du Roi, a menhir or standing stone which now forms the end of the wall, at the junction of the Forest Road and the road to PETIT BÔT BAY. It bears three cup marks or shallow depressions, which are characteristic of megalithic remains, and some lettering that is probably no older than the 18th century.

The German Occupation Museum, Les Houards, near Le Bourg (see also p. 27)

Le Perron du Roi was formerly the other side of the road, where it marked the boundary of the royal fief. It was one of the stopping places of the *Chevauchée de St Michel*, a colourful medieval ceremony whose main purpose was the inspection of the island roads. The *pions* or footmen danced around the stone, and it was used as a mounting block by the dignitaries.

The house opposite, to the right of the Forest Stores, was the ancestral home of Thomas de la Rue, founder of the famous printing firm. Beside the house is a roofed passage through which farm carts passed into the yard behind. The building beyond the passage is now a petrol station.

Behind the church, at Les Houards, is the Occupation Museum, containing a notable collection of relics of the German occupation.

Braye du Valle (4/5A) Until 1806 the greater part of the VALE PARISH was a separate island, divided from the rest of Guernsey by an expanse of tidal mudflats and salt marshes, the Braye du Valle. This extended from GRAND HAVRE to the inlet which is now ST SAMPSON'S HARBOUR. The northern shore ran from immediately below the VALE CHURCH to the north side of St Sampson's Harbour; the southern shore of the Braye extended from L'Islet, which was then nothing but a salt marsh, south as far as today's Brae-Side traffic lights and then eastward to ST SAMPSON'S CHURCH. There were two areas of saltpans, where sea water was evaporated for salt. One, near Capelles, was bounded by Salines Road, the Rue Sauvage and Basses Capelles Road. Le Grand Fort, which still exists as a raised footpath next to the Corbet playing field, was a dam separating the saltpans from the rest of the Braye. It would have contained sluices so that water could enter the saltpans at certain high tides and then be retained while it evaporated. The other saltpans were further to the east, where the district still bears that name.

At low tide it was possible to cross from the northern island, the CLOS DU VALLE, from below the Vale Church to L'Islet, but the only place where a crossing was possible at any state of the tide was St Sampson's Bridge (4/6A).

The draining of the Braye began in 1806, mainly for military reasons. The Lieutenant-Governor, Sir John Doyle, was concerned that the Guernsey roads were so bad that if the French landed on any of the western or northern beaches, his troops would be unable to reach the spot before the enemy had established themselves. In particular, he was afraid that the French might land at L'ANCRESSE BAY and occupy the isolated Clos du Valle.

The first step was the construction of a substantial barrier against the sea at each end of the Braye. The modern coast road running across the end of Grand Havre makes use of the western barrier. Behind it is the Vale Pond, the last vestige of the Braye to remain undrained. This brackish pond with its attendant salt marsh is run by La Société Guernesiaise as a nature reserve. A gap in the roadside wall gives access to a hide for watching the birds on the pond. The eastern barrier is now the site of the shopping centre at St Sampson's Bridge.

The draining of the Braye du Valle yielded 300 acres of fertile land, which was sold for £5000. This money paid for the building in 1810 of two more of Doyle's roads, leading to VAZON and ROCQUAINE bays.

See also The Military Roads of Guernsey.

Brecqhou (8/1B) The island of Brecqhou lies to the west of Great Sark, from which it is separated by the narrow Gouliot Passage. The island is half a mile long from west to east, and slightly less from north to south. Access is extremely difficult as it is entirely surrounded by cliffs, and the two landing places can only be used in calm weather. The centre of the island is fairly flat and windswept, sloping up from 100 ft in the north-west to 200 ft in the south-east, where the tallest cliffs face the Gouliot Headland of SARK. The tide runs strongly through the Gouliot Passage, precipitous cliffs towering on either side.

Brecqhou is one of the feudal holdings whose ownership carries a seat in Chief Pleas, the assembly of SARK. The island has a farm, a mansion and a helicopter pad.

Bréhon Tower A Victorian fortification on a rock of the same name in the Little Russel, the stretch of water between Guernsey and HERM. The oval tower was built in 1855 and replaced an obelisk which had previously served as a seamark. It was intended to command the northern approaches to ST PETER PORT HARBOUR and was garrisoned for some 50 years before it was abandoned. During the Occupation it saw service again as a German anti-aircraft battery and today, once more deserted by man, it supports a breeding colony of terns.

Burhou The low, uninhabited island of Burhou lies a mile off the north-west coast of ALDERNEY, across the turbulent passage known as the Swinge. The main island is about half a mile long and 300 yd broad; the smaller island of **Little Burhou** lies to the west and becomes separated at high water. Rabbits abound on both islands and the soil is honeycombed with their burrows, and those of puffins. Low maritime plants carpet the ground, particularly cliff sand spurrey on the main island and sea campion on Little Burhou.

In the past, when Burhou was hardly ever visited, it supported very large breeding populations of puffins, razorbills and storm petrels. Now that there are day trips from Braye Harbour when the sea is sufficiently calm during the summer, fewer sea birds are breeding there, though it is still possible to see puffins, razorbills, guillemots, shags and oystercatchers.

A stone cottage on the southern shore was destroyed by the Germans and within its ruined walls is a wooden hut which is let for short periods by the States of Alderney.

Burhou is surrounded by reefs of rock which have claimed a number of wrecks. Out to sea, between Burhou and LES CASQUETS, is the great square stack of Ortac, one of Alderney's two

gannetries. During the summer the 80 ft summit is a mass of birds at their nests, with other gannets wheeling round the rock or diving into the sea after fish.

Camps, Les, and **Les Camps du Moulin** *see* Bellieuse, La

Candie Gardens (5/2B) Between Candie Road and Les Vauxlaurens ('the valley of laurels' or possibly 'of the Laurens family') on a slope overlooking ST PETER PORT HARBOUR, is the former estate of Candie, which became the property of the States in 1886. Candie House, at the upper end of the estate, is now the Priaulx Library. It contains a valuable collection of books, including many of local interest, and is open free to the public.

In the Upper Gardens is an attractive early 20th-century bandstand, which has been incorporated into an award-winning modern museum, the Guernsey Museum and Art Gallery. Its architecture was inspired by the bandstand. In the garden are statues of Queen Victoria and Victor Hugo. That of Hugo is a romantic portrayal of the author striding out against a gale.

The Lower Gardens, originally the walled fruit and vegetable garden of Candie House, have been laid out as an extremely pleasant public garden

Statue of Victor Hugo (J. Boucher, 1914), Candie Gardens

and contain some interesting plants including palms and a fine maidenhair tree. Of particular interest are the tender plants against the south-facing wall, such as *Fremontia californica*, *Abutilon* and a lemon tree which produces fruit in good years.

The first greenhouse in Guernsey is said to have been erected in Candie Gardens by Peter Mourant in 1792. Two of Mourant's prototype greenhouses are still there, one at the top and one at the bottom of the Lower Gardens. They were built to last, perhaps by ship's carpenters, with heavy timbers and narrow panes. By modern standards the light within them must be poor, but they are still used for raising plants by the States Parks and Gardens Department.

Casquets, Les A reef of rocks composed of a hard, gritty sandstone, Les Casquets lie 7 miles west of ALDERNEY, close to the Channel shipping lane. The name means 'The Cascades', and certainly the worst seas that the Channel Islands ferries usually encounter are as they round the Casquets.

For centuries Les Casquets have been a notorious hazard to shipping, and some kind of light has

Medieval wall paintings, Castel Church

been maintained on the reef since early in the 18th century. In 1785 three lighthouses were built, lit first by coal and later by oil. When Trinity House accepted responsibility in 1877, one tower was improved while the other two were shortened and used for other purposes – painted white, they are visible from as far away as Guernsey. The modern light, 120 ft above the water, is powered by electricity generated on the reef.

Among the many ships claimed by the reef was the man-of-war *Victory*, lost with all hands in 1744. In 1899 the mail packet *Stella*, bound from Southampton to Guernsey, struck the reef while travelling at speed in thick fog, with the loss of 102 lives.

Castel Church (4/4B) The church of *Sancta Maria de Castro* was mentioned in a Papal Bull of 1155 as one of the possessions of the abbey of Mont St Michel. It was one of four Guernsey churches under the patronage of that monastery, to whom it had been given by Duke Robert, father of William the Conqueror. There is a tradition that the site of the church was formerly the stronghold of a pirate chieftain – the castle of the parish name. Certainly it is a magnificent site, commanding a panoramic view over the north of the island to ALDERNEY, HERM and the French coast beyond.

Like many Channel Islands churches, the Castel Church consists of a pair of parallel naves and chancels. Between the north nave and chancel are the four massive piers supporting the steeple. Piercing the south-east of the piers is a squint, directed at the place where the High Altar

would have been before the Reformation. There is some fine ribbed groining under the bell loft. The north transept is now a vestry; the south transept, if it existed, was swallowed up when the south chancel and nave were built.

The vaulting over the north chancel is decorated with a series of medieval wall paintings. In the centre is a figure with a chalice and flagon, and with an axe across his neck. He may be St Thomas à Becket. To the east is the Last Supper and to the west the 'fable of the three living and three dead'. The three courtiers in the latter scene can be dated by their costume to the first quarter of the 13th century.

The window over the west porch is of interest as it is the sole surviving example of a pointed sash window – a type common in Guernsey churches in the 19th century.

The female figure standing outside the west porch was found under the floor of the north chancel in 1878, when the church was undergoing the inevitable Victorian restoration, and was erected in her present splendid position beneath the trees. She is a Neolithic statue-menhir similar to mother-goddess figures that have been found in certain prehistoric tombs in France. Perhaps she was buried to prevent a veneration that persisted from an older religion.

The three flat stones at the statue's feet mark the position of the feudal court of Fief St Michel.

Castel Parish (4/3B) The largest of the ten Guernsey parishes, with an area of almost 4

square miles, and a coastline of 4 miles from Richmond to Port Soif. The population of the parish in 1981 was 7727, and with the amount of residential development that has taken place since then, the Castel may by now have overtaken the VALE PARISH as the most populous after ST PETER PORT.

CASTEL CHURCH is at the extreme eastern edge of the parish. In the Middle Ages there were, however, at least three chapels in the west of the parish: St Anne, near KING'S MILLS, St Germain (now quarried away) and St George, whose remains are still to be seen in the estate of that name. Since 1854 the COBO area has been served by St Matthew's Church, built in the Norman style from the red Cobo granite quarried near by.

The southern part of the parish contains some beautiful scenery. The TALBOT VALLEY and its tributary, the Fauxquets Valley, are unspoiled wooded valleys surrounded by fields. Candie Road runs down the spur between them, with delightful views in both directions. The Grantez, on the heights overlooking King's Mills, is an area of open fields exposed to the full force of the Atlantic westerlies. There are no trees but the

Left: Neolithic statue-menhir, Castel Church
Below: Feudal seat near Les Pellys, Castel Parish

Sunset, Albecq Bay, Castel Parish

fields are protected by broad, grassy hedgebanks rich in violets and primroses. Further north are the estates of SAUMAREZ PARK, La Haye du Puits and St George, and the farmland around Les Beaucamps, Les Effards and Le Préel. Here the hedgerows are rich in trees, particularly the straight-trunked Guernsey elm.

The Cobo Road runs along the foot of a scarp and divides the southern, upland part of the parish from the northern, low-lying part. It is this northern part that has borne the brunt of the postwar building; there are States housing estates at Rectory Hill, L'Amône and Les Genâts, and more recently, besides the ribbon development that characterizes this area, private housing estates have spread over the fields to form an extensive residential area between the Villocq and La Rue Cohu. La Mare de Carteret, once a marshy wilderness, is now the site of two schools. The public path from here to Saumarez Park is described in the Saumarez Park entry.

Fortunately Guernsey has never allowed building between the coast road and the sea, and the view from the road as it skirts the bays of VAZON, Albecq and Cobo is unforgettable, particularly when the warm red rocks glow in the evening sun *(see pp. 98-9)*.

Castle Cornet (5/3B) This magnificent monument, more than any other, encapsulates Guernsey's history; for built into it is the material evidence for every event of military significance from the separation from Normandy in 1204 to the German occupation of 1940. Until 1204 the Channel Islands lay at the centre of a great Norman empire, and had no military importance except as the haunt of a few pirates and outlaws. In that year, King John of England lost the Continental part of the Duchy of Normandy. Immediately the Channel Islands, as possessions of the English crown on the hostile, French side of the Channel, assumed immense strategic importance. Castle Cornet was built to defend the roadstead of ST PETER PORT, which was an important staging post on the route between England and her monarch's remaining possessions in southern France.

Before the Victorian harbour was built, the island of Castle Cornet lay more than a quarter of a mile offshore, and could be reached on foot only at low spring tides. The medieval fortifications

Firing the mid-day gun, Castle Cornet

are towards the summit of the island. Fragments of the 13th-century walls can be made out in places around the Citadel, and on the east side of the 'Prisoners' Walk'. They are of rubble masonry with narrow buttresses, similar to those of the medieval churches. In 1338, soon after the start of the Hundred Years War, the French stormed the castle and held it for seven years. The Barbican, an attractive entrance tower with pit, drawbridge and portcullis, probably dates from this occupation. It is built of small stones such as the builders would have found on the beach, for the quarries of Guernsey were not in French hands.

In the 15th century the castle was extended further; the Carey Tower facing the town, with its elaborately corbelled parapet, dates from 1435 and the machicolations surmounting the Barbican are of the same period. During the reign of Henry VIII gun emplacements were added for the cannon which were coming into use; the Mewtis Bulwark, near the Carey Tower, guarded the landward side while the Well Tower faced the sea.

By Elizabeth's reign artillery had progressed to the point where the castle and harbour would have been within range of each other. This necessitated much stronger walls, which were built outside the medieval castle. The present main gateway, the gun ports above it, and those covering it from the other side, are of this date. The gate faces away from the town, to protect it from gunfire from that direction.

During the Civil War Guernsey supported Parliament, but for eight years Castle Cornet held out for Charles I, receiving its supplies by sea from Royalist Jersey. During this time the town was under constant fire from the castle, while the castle received a severe battering from the town. The high wall between the inner and outer bailey probably dates from this period.

The 18th century is represented by the main guard, the married quarters and the fine Georgian hospital building, which now houses the Militia and RAF Museums. The brick guardroom is a typical piece of 19th-century British military architecture; the present century is represented by the concrete gun emplacements and pillboxes of Hitler's Atlantic Wall.

Castle Cornet is open every day in the summer. There is much to see, for beside the historic pile itself there is a splendid view from the summit, as well as several museums.

Overleaf: Castle Cornet at night

Catioroc, Le (4/2B) To the west of PERELLE, a spur of elevated land runs down to the coast at the point where the coast road rounds the western headland of Perelle Bay. Along the spine of this ridge runs Le Chemin Le Roi – once the King's Highway but now no more than a cart track. The land to the south of the track belongs to the National Trust of Guernsey, which maintains grassy picnic areas among the blackthorn scrub. Visitors are welcome free of charge at most National Trust properties, on condition that flowers are not picked or litter deposited. There is a small car park on the headland; the entrance to the footpath is marked by a stone.

Towards the foot of the spur, and in full view from the coast road as you approach from L'ERÉE, is the Trépied dolmen. This Neolithic burial chamber, roofed by three massive capstones, has a sinister reputation as the meeting place of a coven of witches. It is repeatedly mentioned in the records of a series of witch trials that took place early in the 17th century. According to some of the unfortunate victims the Devil, in the shape of a black goat, would sit on the centre capstone while the witches danced around him.

Three hundred yards offshore to the west of Le Catioroc is a minute islet, La Chapelle Dom Hue, which can be reached across the rocks at low tide. Here the monk Dom Hue is said to have established himself in opposition to the witches. The remains of his cell can still be seen.

Château des Marais (4/5B) A medieval place of refuge in the marshes inland from Belle Grève Bay, in ST SAMPSON'S PARISH. It is reached from Le Grand Bouet by following an unpromising-looking lane between housing estates. As the lane approaches the castle it becomes a causeway across the marsh, which in the Middle Ages would have been subject to flooding by the sea.

Le Château des Marais, or Ivy Castle as it is popularly known, is thought to date from the separation of the islands from Normandy in the 13th century. It was a place of refuge for the inhabitants against raiding parties from France. Excavations suggest that a *hougue* or hillock projecting from the marsh was partially levelled by removing many tons of material from the centre and dumping it round the edge. The central area, protected by a moat, formed an inner bailey while the dumped material provided a much larger outer bailey, protected by an earth bank.

During the Napoleonic wars the castle was hurriedly strengthened by throwing up two

Le Château des Marais, also known as Ivy Castle

concentric walls around the inner and outer baileys. Just inside the archway into the inner bailey is an 18th-century powder magazine and a 20th-century German concrete bunker.

Until recently the walls of the castle were ruinous and ivy-covered. They have now been repaired, the moat dug out and the whole area restored as an oasis in a rather depressing desert of States housing.

Clos du Valle (4/5A-6A) This is the portion of VALE PARISH that was formerly a separate island, cut off from the mainland of Guernsey by the tidal BRAYE DU VALLE. Although parts of it are now heavily developed, the Clos du Valle retains a strong northern character of its own. In the 19th century the main industry was quarrying and dressing stone, which was exported from ST SAMPSON'S HARBOUR. Numerous disused quarries remain, often filled with water, though some have become industrial sites, car parks or even, in one case, a yacht marina.

Forming a broad coastal strip along the west and north coasts, L'ANCRASSE COMMON provides an important amenity for the whole of Guernsey, besides being the common grazing land for the *habitants* of the Clos du Valle. The Common forms the eastern shore of GRAND HAVRE, with a car park, kiosk, loos and children's playground at Les Amarreurs, and more loos and a tea room at Chouet, which also has autocross car racing on the beach on certain days.

The Chouet peninsula is a relatively unspoiled headland with a Martello tower and a small quarry filled with oil that was collected from the beaches after the wreck of the *Torrey Canyon* in 1967. The vast quarry of Mont Cuet, with a concrete German watchtower balanced on its brink, is nearing the end of its life, though at the time of writing it is still providing stone for the North Beach reclamation scheme to the north of ST PETER PORT HARBOUR. From Mont Cuet a pleasant lane winds between small fields with drystone walls to La Jaonneuse Bay, where there is a leaning Martello tower.

Fort Doyle, on a little-visited headland in the extreme north-east corner of Guernsey, started life in 1803 as a battery of three guns, named after the popular Lieutenant-Governor of the time, who did so much to improve the island's roads. Most of the present building, complete with drawbridge, dates from 1855. Later, it became the shore base of the unmanned Platte Fougère lighthouse, a mile to the north-east. Near by is the flooded quarry of Beaucette, once a source of the grey stone called diorite, and now a yacht marina. From the lanes around, the masts of the yachts appear to be sprouting from the fields.

Off the east coast of the Clos du Valle are three islets, LES HOUMETS, and on the coast opposite is another flooded quarry, Noirmont, which is used as a fish farm.

Bordeaux Harbour is one of the most attractive corners of Guernsey. A small, sheltered cove with a slipway and a sandy beach, it provides moorings for a number of small boats. At low water the sea recedes, leaving the boats stranded. The road from L'Ancresse Common reaches the coast at this point, and from it there is a splendid view across the harbour, with the islands of HERM and JETHOU in the background. Immediately to the north of the harbour is the giant Bordeaux Quarry in which for the past few years most of Guernsey's rubbish has been dumped. The island has been fortunate in having a plentiful supply of holes in the ground for rubbish disposal.

A little way inland from Bordeaux is a hill, La Hougue du Moulin, surmounted by the conspicuous if not very beautiful Vale Mill. In 1771 the builder of the first mill on the site had to obtain special permission from George III, on the grounds that the *habitants* of the Clos du Valle had nowhere to take their corn for grinding without crossing the Braye. During the Occupation the mill was increased to almost double its former height by the Germans.

South of Bordeaux the coast road skirts the VALE CASTLE, passes a yard where formerly road metal was crushed for export, and then runs along the north quay of St Sampson's Harbour to the Bridge.

Cobo and **Le Guet** (4/3B) The west coast of Guernsey from VAZON BAY to Port Soif is composed of the warm red stone known as Cobo granite. It underlies the headlands of Fort Hommet and Grandes Rocques, and acres of it are exposed at low tide in the bays of Albecq and Cobo. *(See pp. 98–9)*. It also forms the Guet, a spur of high land overlooking Cobo, which ends abruptly in the sheer face of a quarry, from which came the stone for many of the houses and fortifications in the west of the island. On the very brink of the quarry is a Napoleonic watch house and battery; the Germans chose the same vantage point for a concrete observation post and gun emplacement. In 19th-century prints the Guet appears as a bare hillside surmounted by a watch house and signalling mast. Between the wars it was planted with pine trees and these have now matured to cover the hill.

Cobo is a popular bathing beach, and the headquarters of a windsurfing school.

Commercial Arcade (5/2B) A pedestrian shopping precinct in ST PETER PORT, linking High Street with Market Place. It was created in the 1820s by a Jerseyman, George Le Boutillier. The ambitious scheme involved the removal of a hillside, covered in terraced gardens, which stood between High Street and the cleared alleys where the markets now stand. The spoil – 125,000 cartloads of it – was dumped on the beach to form the South Esplanade, where the bus station is now. The arcade was originally intended to be covered by a roof – hence the even roofline of the buildings in each block – but the bankruptcy of Le Boutillier brought the scheme to a premature close. Today the paved streets and square Regency buildings form an extremely pleasant shopping area.

Crevichon *see* Jethou

Fermain Bay (4/5C) The east coast of Guernsey between FORT GEORGE and St Martin's Point has a character all of its own. Like the south coast it is a coastline of cliffs, but as it is sheltered from the prevailing westerly wind the vegetation is far lusher, with oak, sycamore, hawthorn and bracken covering the slopes and in many places descending right down to the highwater mark. From the cliff path there are sudden and spectacular views, framed by trees, with clear blue water below and CASTLE CORNET, HERM, JETHOU and SARK in the distance.

In the midst of this coastline is Fermain Bay, a pebble cove at the foot of a wooded valley. During the summer a boat service runs all day between ST PETER PORT HARBOUR and Fermain; alternatively, it can be reached by cliff path from the town or JERBOURG, or on foot (for there is no car park) by taking the lane that leaves Fort Road opposite the Fermain Tavern, and following the valley down to the bay. The stream, which carved out the valley at a time when rainfall was considerably greater than it is today, forms the boundary between ST PETER PORT and ST MARTIN'S parishes. After making its way between clumps of hydrangea, arum lily and pendulous sedge in the floor of the valley, the stream runs through a gap in the substantial sea wall and disappears among the pebbles of the beach.

Fermain has always been a potential landing beach in times of war; at low spring tides the remains of German anti-landing barriers can be made out, and there are several Napoleonic fortifications. Beside the gap in the sea wall is a 'Martello' tower, No. 15 of a series of 15 built in

THE CONSTITUTION OF GUERNSEY

As ancient fragments of the Duchy of Normandy that have remained for centuries loyal possessions of the English Crown, the Channel Islands enjoy a unique constitutional position; their relationships with the United Kingdom and the outside world are outlined in the Introduction (*see* page 121). Although there are many similarities, the constitution of the Bailiwick of Guernsey (which includes Alderney, Sark and the smaller islands) is quite separate from that of Jersey: it has its own legislature (the States of Deliberation) and judiciary (the Royal Court).

The Lieutenant-Governor is the Sovereign's personal representative in the Bailiwick, and normally holds office for five years. He acts as a channel of communication between the island authorities and the Queen and Privy Council, and is in addition Commander-in-Chief in the Bailiwick. The Bailiff, also a Crown appointment, is the island's chief citizen and is president both of the Royal Court and of the States. He also heads the administration of the island. He is assisted by a Deputy Bailiff.

Two further Crown appointments are the Procureur (Attorney-General) and the Comptroller (Solicitor-General). They act as legal advisers to the Crown and to the States, they institute criminal proceedings and are responsible for the drafting of legislation. The island legislates for itself on all internal matters, though draft laws have to be approved by the Privy Council.

The Royal Court consists of the Bailiff and 12 permanent jurors called Jurats. These are elected by the States of Election – an electoral college of about 100, consisting of the States of Deliberation, augmented by the Rectors of the 10 parishes, and extra parish representatives according to the population of the parish. The Royal Court has jurisdiction in criminal matters, and a variety of other duties which include the hearing of appeals against the decisions of various States Committees.

The 'grassroots' of Guernsey's democracy is the parish. There are 10 civil parishes, each with a 'parish council' or Douzaine elected by the people of the parish. Most parishes have 12 Douzeniers, though the Vale has 16 and St Peter Port 20. In addition each parish has a senior and a junior Constable. Now that they are no longer responsible for law and order, the Constables' present function is to preside at meetings, deal with correspondence, issue dog and gun licences and generally act as the unpaid executive officers of the Douzaine. Among the varied duties of the Douzaine are the inspection of roadside hedges after their statutory trimming, inspection of water courses, the regulation of buildings close to highways and reporting on applications for liquor licences.

Each Douzaine nominates one of its number to represent it in the States of Deliberation. Besides the 10 Douzaine representatives, the States consists of 33 People's Deputies, 12 Conseillers, the Procureur, the Comptroller and the Bailiff; People's Deputies are elected by universal suffrage on a parish basis, each parish electing from 1 to 10 Deputies, according to its population. There is a general election every three years. The Conseillers are elected by the States of Election, and hold office for six years.

The function of the States of Deliberation is to enact legislation, and to elect committees which are responsible to it for the day-to-day running of the island. There are about 50 of these standing committees, dealing with matters as varied as health, education, planning, fisheries, horticulture, police and the licensing of buses.

Guernsey's constitution has evolved over the centuries in response to a mixture of Norman and English influences, to meet the special needs of the island. It is not perfect, but with approximately one States member for every thousand souls in the population, the people of Guernsey are well represented, and with its strong tradition of unpaid public service and its freedom from party politics, it is something to be cherished.

the 1780s to a design peculiar to Guernsey. On the level ground above the wall is a Napoleonic gun battery, and picnics are now served from a watch house. On the spur to the north of the bay, commanding both Fermain and Soldier's Bay, is a gun platform, a powder magazine and the 'Pepper-pot', a quaintly but extremely solidly designed sentry box which today serves as a seamark.

The steep and crumbly section of cliff immediately to the north of the bay has in recent years become colonized by the fleshy-leaved mesembryanthemum or the Hottentot fig. This South African introduction is a useful plant for covering unsightly objects such as German bunkers, but it is not to be encouraged on the cliffs as it forms a heavy mat which smothers the native plants and in time falls off, taking part of the cliff with it.

At the foot of the cliffs on each side of Fermain is a shelf of rock which is just awash at high spring tides. This wave-cut platform was formed during the last of several mild intervals in the Ice Age, when the sea level was 25 ft above its present height. The platform is particularly well developed at Bec du Nez and at Divette, between Fermain and St Martin's Point. Standing on it

you can see at the base of the cliff the remains of sea caves and a pebble beach, now overgrown by vegetation.

In 1842 there was a plan to turn Fermain into a 'harbour of refuge' for the Royal Navy by building a breakwater similar to those planned for Alderney and St Catherine's, Jersey. In view of the problems subsequently encountered by these two projects it is fortunate that the Fermain plan was never put into effect, and the bay remains a popular bathing beach, despite the pebbles which occupy most of the bay except at low spring tides.

Forest Church (4/3C) The smallest of Guernsey's medieval parish churches, St Marguerite de la Forêt stands at LE BOURG, a cluster of old houses at the head of the Petit Bôt valley. The church was originally dedicated to the Holy Trinity, and by this name in 1048 it was placed under the patronage of Marmoutiers Abbey by Duke William of Normandy, later to become the Conqueror.

The two parallel naves and chancels are each vaulted in stone. The oldest part of the church appears to be the south chancel, much of which is now occupied by the organ. Traces can be seen,

Le Variouf, Forest Parish

of the intractable nature of granite this is an unusually elaborate example. The north doorway has a round arch of the characteristic Guernsey pattern, found in houses built before 1700.

In 1891 the church underwent the usual Victorian restoration. The old high pews were replaced by low pine ones and an organ was installed. The instruments that had hitherto provided the music are preserved in a case by the door: fife, piccolo, clarinet and two flutes. The windows were spared by the Victorians and most are still close to their original form, either square or round-headed, with chamfered stonework.

The Forest was the only church to be compulsorily closed by the Germans. Following an RAF raid on the airport in August 1940 it was thought to be too vulnerable to air attack, though it re-opened in 1941.

Forest Parish (4/3C) With an area of 1003 acres and a population of 1383, the Forest is second only to TORTEVAL as Guernsey's smallest and least populous parish. It is a parish with a strong sense of identity, having managed to retain its own primary school, despite the trend towards the amalgamation of parish schools.

Much of the northern part of the parish is covered by the AIRPORT, the terminal buildings and much of the runway being in the parish. The military road from town to L'ERÉE, built in 1810 by General Doyle, separates this northern part from the rest of the parish. The road enters the parish (as the Forest Road) at St Margaret's Lodge Hotel and leaves it (as Plaisance Road) at Passiflora Hotel. To the east of the airport a narrow, rural lane runs parallel to and north of the Forest Road. This is Le Chemin du Roi, which before Doyle's roadbuilding programme was one of the main highways of the island.

The church and main settlement of the parish are at LE BOURG at the point where the military road passes the head of the western of two valleys leading down to PETIT BÔT BAY. Another settlement, much more isolated and completely unspoiled, is at Le Variouf, where a row of tiny cottages and a few larger farmhouses cling to the side of a valley. Le Variouf is reached by taking the Petit Bôt road from Le Bourg, and following a lane to the right immediately below the Manor Hotel. Other groups of old houses, all built of the local red-brown stone, are at La Corbière, Le Bigard and Les Villets. More modern development, mainly of bungalows and glasshouses, is concentrated in a belt along the Forest Road, and between Plaisance Road and New Road.

both inside and out, of massive boulders, possibly the remains of a dolmen, on which this part of the church rests. Between the south nave and chancel are the piers supporting the tower; this is surmounted by an octagonal, cement-covered spire with four spirelets at the corners.

The northern part of the church, now used as the chancel and nave, appears to date from the 15th or 16th century. In the east wall of the chancel is a finely carved granite piscina; because

The coastline of the Forest extends from La Corbière to Petit Bôt. It is a coast of exposed cliffs interrupted by sheltered valleys, with a network of footpaths connecting with narrow lanes that wind between the fields. La Corbière is a small headland which may have been used as a place of refuge in antiquity, for a ditch and bank can still be made out across the neck of the promontory. In the Middle Ages there was a fort here: old documents refer to Le Château de Corbière, but all traces of it have disappeared.

Between La Corbière and Le Bigard much of the cliff land is owned by the National Trust of Guernsey. Le Bigard means 'the sheep pen': sheep were formerly common on the cliffs; many 19th-century prints show them devoid of trees and shrubs, grazed bare by the sheep. The walls that contained them are still to be seen, particularly when the vegetation has been destroyed by one of the summer fires which sweep across the cliffs every few years.

See also Le Gouffre.

Fort George (5/3C) An up-market housing estate on the site of a Georgian fort on the clifftop immediately to the south of ST PETER PORT. The fort, begun in about 1782, was intended to replace CASTLE CORNET as Guernsey's main strongpoint and the headquarters of the garrison. The main gateway, one of the few parts of the fort to have survived intact, bears over the dressed stone archway the date 1812 and the name of the Lieutenant-Governor of the day, Sir John Doyle, who did much to improve Guernsey's roads and defences. It is approached by a side road from the top of the Val des Terres.

At the heart of the fort was the Citadel, a star-shaped brick fortification surrounded by a dry moat. The Citadel has been demolished to make way for houses but the moat survives in places and accounts for the strange relief of the land. There were several outlying batteries on the clifftop, and the whole considerable area was enclosed by a substantial granite wall, part of which can be seen among the trees and bordering the field at the top of the Val des Terres.

After the Second World War the site was offered by the War Office to the States of Guernsey who sold it to a private developer for 'open market' housing. (In order to protect the island housing stock and ensure that prices remain within the reach of local people, incomers are only allowed to occupy certain dwellings. In practice, these are the more expensive houses – many of them in Fort George.)

Clarence Battery on Cow Point, the promontory between Havelet Bay and Soldier's Bay, has escaped development and is a pleasant vantage point within walking distance of the town. It is reached by the cliff path which begins near the Aquarium. Also associated with the fort is the Picquet House, near the foot of Cornet Street and now the bus company offices. It was built in 1819 as a guardroom.

In the military cemetery on the clifftop below the fort are the only remaining German war graves in the Channel Islands.

Gouffre, Le (4/3C) The whole length of Guernsey's south coast is of great beauty, and a cliff path extends from end to end. Access points, however, are limited. One is at Le Gouffre, where there is a bistro, an art gallery and room for a limited number of cars. It is approached from LE BOURG, by taking the lane to the right immediately in front of the FOREST CHURCH. The next crossroad is called La Croix, indicating that before the Reformation this was the site of a wayside cross. Evidence has been found for more than 50 of these crosses, often marking the route between an outlying settlement and the parish church. This one was on the route to Les Villets, a group of farmhouses at the head of the valley leading down to Le Gouffre.

Turning left at La Croix and following the lane through Les Villets, the road descends the valley to a platform overlooking a ravine which carries a stream over the cliff face. (Le Gouffre means 'the gulf' or 'ravine'.) The bistro stands on the site of a hotel which was destroyed by the Germans; at the turn of the century this was a favourite stopping place for carriage parties.

From the platform the cliff path can be followed in either direction along the shoulders of the ravine. The left-hand path is a broad track leading down to a tiny fisherman's harbour in the lee of La Moye Point, a peninsula of sheer granite cliffs jutting into the sea.

Grand Fauconnière *see* Jethou

Grande Mare, Castel (4/3B) An extensive area of marshland and meadow, formerly a lake, lying between KING'S MILLS and VAZON BAY. It originated as a valley cut by the King's Mills stream, which became silted up when its outlet to the sea was blocked by the shingle bank where the Vazon coast road now runs.

Guernsey has a number of place names with *mare*, indicating the former existence of a pond.

GUERNSEY CUSTOMS, CELEBRATIONS AND CEREMONIES

For an island with such a long history as Guernsey it is perhaps surprising that more local customs have not survived to the present day. In the Middle Ages there were numerous customs connected with Christmas, Easter and the Saints' days but at the Reformation in the mid-16th century the island came under the control of an extreme form of puritanism, and during the following hundred years most of the old customs were forgotten. Those that have survived are connected with secular festivals such as the New Year, and with the feudal system which is still alive in the island.

As in Scotland, New Year's Day has always been a public holiday, but now that England and Wales have followed suit the only public holiday that Guernsey enjoys besides the United Kingdom bank holidays is Liberation Day on 9 May, when they celebrate the end of the German Occupation.

A custom dating back to pagan times took place on New Year's Eve, when boys would prepare a grotesque figure called *Le Vieux Bout de l'An* – the end of the old year. The figure was paraded through the streets in a mock funeral procession, and was then either burned or buried on the beach. With the increasing anglicization of the 20th century the bonfire ceremony has moved to 5 November, a date that has no relevance in Guernsey. But the effigy is still called *Budloe*, a corruption of *Bout de l'An*.

Numerous tangible reminders of the feudal system survive in Guernsey. The island is still divided into manors or fiefs, each with its Seigneur. Feudal courts, where the officials of the Seigneur collected feudal dues and transacted the business of the fief, may take the form of a small building or simply a row of stone seats in a hedge. Several are mentioned in the Gazetteer. Although the duties and privileges of the Seigneurs are now purely nominal, a few feudal courts still meet regularly, and three times a year the Royal Court sits as the Court of Chief Pleas, at which the Seigneurs have to appear to pay homage to the Sovereign.

The most colourful and elaborate feudal ceremony in Guernsey, and perhaps in the British Isles, was *La Chevauchée de St Michel*, which is described in the Gazetteer under Pleinmont.

The law of Guernsey is based on the ancient customary law of Normandy, and although English law has had a good deal of influence in the last hundred years, the unwritten *Coutume de Normandie* still holds sway, particularly in the field of inheritance and real property. Until recently all written laws were drafted in French, and to this day meetings of the States are opened and closed by prayers in French, and members vote by saying *pour* or *contre*.

One Norman legal process that is still very much alive is the Clameur de Haro. Anyone who feels that his right to enjoy his property is being violated has only to collect two witnesses, kneel before the offending party and cry '*Haro! Haro! à l'aide mon Prince! On me fait tort*', followed by the Lord's Prayer, also in French. The other party must immediately stop whatever is causing the trouble, until the matter has been decided by the Court. Nobody knows what *Haro* means, but it is generally thought to refer to Rollo, the Viking chieftain who became the first Duke of Normandy in 911.

By raising the Clameur many a tree has been saved from felling, and many a boundary wall moved to its correct position. By this means an unlicensed priest was evicted from the pulpit in Sark in 1755, and the fortifications of Castle Cornet were saved from demolition in 1850. By this means in 1930 a householder in St Peter Port caused a workman to be fined a shilling for dropping plaster on his loganberries. As recently as 1975 a St Peter Port newsagent successfully prevented a crane jib on a nearby building site from violating his air space and frightening his customers; by invoking the mighty name of Rollo he caused the contractors to be fined £100, and the crane had to be removed. *See also:* Clameur de Haro *(p. 46)*.

Dr Peter Heylin, who visited the island in 1629, wrote that the Grande Mare was a lake about a mile in circumference and exceedingly well stocked with carp. In 1737 George II directed that the area should be let as a fee farm, in common with JETHOU, LIHOU and other marginal land belonging to the Crown. This provided sufficient security of tenure for the Grande Mare to be drained, for in a map of 1787 it appears as a chequerboard of hedges and ditches. These were swept away when the area became a racecourse early in the present century, the ditches being replaced by underground culverts. The racecourse was not a success, the culverts soon

became choked, and by the beginning of the Second World War the area was reverting to swamp. During the Occupation the peat underlying the central part was dug for fuel while in the north-west corner, opposite the Martello tower, the Germans extracted sand for their coastal defences. The large hole left by the Germans was subsequently used as a refuse dump; the area has now been landscaped and is occupied by a hotel putting green.

The present fee farm tenants have again drained the Grande Mare, both for a hotel and for agricultural use, though the *mare* still returns occasionally after heavy rain, for the area is below high-tide level. It is to be hoped that the drainage scheme will not be too successful, for wetland as a habitat for marsh plants and birds is becoming increasingly rare in the Channel Islands.

Grand Havre (4/5A) A tidal haven on the north-west coast of Guernsey, sheltered from the west by the Rousse headland and from the east by L'ANCRESSE and Chouet. Until 1806 Grand Havre formed the western entrance to the BRAYE DU VALLE. When this was drained a dike was built from below the VALE CHURCH to L'Islet. The modern coast road across the end of Grand Havre runs along this dike, which is still known as Le Pont St Michel, after the crossing place which formerly existed below the church.

The Rousse and Chouet headlands each have a round tower of the characteristic Guernsey design, built in the 1780s to repel an expected French landing. Fifteen were built, of which No. 10 at Chouet and No. 11 at Rousse were intended to guard Grand Havre.

Today Grand Havre provides an anchorage for a few small fishing craft but in former years it was a harbour of more importance, and even had a small shipyard. One of the attractive plants that grow in the dune grassland round the bay is hare's-tail grass, a small, annual grass whose white, oval heads look like a rabbit's tail. It is a native of south-west France and may have been accidentally introduced in the Middle Ages when Guernsey was an important staging post on the wine route between Bordeaux and England. Other flowers that will be seen near Grand Havre

are the tree lupin and fragrant evening primrose, both probably having escaped from gardens.

Guet, Le *see* Cobo and Le Guet

Hanois Lighthouse Les Hanois Reef, a mile to the west of Pleinmont Point (4/1C), is a notorious hazard to shipping, and claimed many lives before the lighthouse was built in 1860. Cornish granite and Cornish masons were employed by Trinity House. The stone was dressed on the newly completed Castle Breakwater, ST PETER PORT, and towed to Les Hanois by barge. The 117 ft structure is of the classical lighthouse shape, but with a modern helicopter platform on its head. The light, a double flash every five seconds, is visible for some 16 miles. *(See p. 139.)*

Hauteville House (5/2C) This massive house of about 1800 was the home in exile of the French author Victor Hugo. Between 1856 and his return to France in 1870 he stamped his extraordinary personality on the house, which is crammed with furniture, tapestries, medieval woodcarvings and macabre paintings. In the attic is the eyrie where Hugo worked, standing at a tall desk, or gazing out of the skylight at the low French coastline spread out on the horizon.

Herm (7) The islands of Herm and JETHOU lie 3 miles east of Guernsey, across the passage known

Opposite: Moonrise over the Common, Herm
Below: Herm village

as the Little Russel. Herm, the larger of the two, is about 1½ miles long from north to south and ½ mile wide at its broadest point. The northern third of the island, the Common (7/2A), is a low-lying plain of dunes from which rise two hillocks, Le Grand and Le Petit Monceau. The dunes are edged by sandy beaches rich in shells washed up from deeper water by the strong tidal currents that sweep past the island. This process has been going on for thousands of years, for the sand underlying the Common consists mainly of fragmented shells. For this reason the turf is rich in lime-loving plants such as salad burnet, rue-leaved saxifrage and the beautiful cream-flowered burnet rose. Some of these plants, as for instance the saxifrage, are so minute that they can only survive because the turf is kept closely grazed by the rabbits that abound all over Herm, particularly on the dunes.

The dune plain contains a number of Neolithic burial chambers – so many, indeed, that Herm must have been the burial ground for tribes dwelling in the other islands and even what is now France. The largest and best-preserved tomb is near the signpost at Robert's Cross (7/2A), where paths from the various parts of the Common converge. Others are hidden in the undergrowth near by. More fragmentary remains are on the shoulder of Le Petit Monceau to the north-west, on Le Grand Monceau to the east, and towards the north-east corner of the Common, where there is a small chamber surrounded by a partial circle of stones. These and many other monuments which formerly existed suffered at the hands of quarrymen in the 19th century. The stone obelisk La Pierre aux Rats, which overlooks the north beach, was built as a seamark to replace a large menhir or standing stone that suffered this fate. Others have doubtless been overwhelmed by the sea, for the sea level some 4000 years ago when the Neolithic monuments were built was very much lower than it is today. One such tomb may still be seen, at the top of the beach at Oyster Point (7/2A). Exposed since the Second World War by the erosion of the surrounding sand, it is only a matter of time before it too is destroyed by the sea.

The remaining two-thirds of Herm consists of fertile land rising to 200 ft. An ancient trackway runs north and south along the spine of the island, giving access to the fields used by the island farm. The walls of massive, lichen-encrusted blocks of granite which bound the track are said to have been built by medieval monks, who farmed the land until the Reformation.

The coastline of this southern part, from the Rosière landing steps (7/2B) to Belvoir Bay (7/3B), consists of cliffs rising in places to 150 ft. As in Guernsey, there is a continuous cliff path. From Rosière the path climbs towards the south-west corner of the island, passing the overgrown shaft of an abandoned silver and copper mine. As it rounds a spur of cliff at La Pointe de Sauze-bourge there is a panoramic view across the Little Russel to Guernsey, with Jethou and Crevichon (7/1C) in the foreground. The path continues up and down steps and round the indentations of the south coast until the view is across the Great Russel to SARK and BRECQHOU, with the coast of Normandy on the horizon.

Belvoir Bay is a sandy cove and a popular bathing beach, though it can be dangerous at low tide when strong currents sweep past. From Belvoir the path continues among the bracken and foxgloves to the Shell Beach (7/3A) and Common.

It is difficult to believe that 150 years ago this peaceful island was a thriving industrial centre. Yet the village clustered round the harbour, and the harbour itself, owe their existence to a quarrying industry which flourished in the first half of the 19th century.

Herm granite had a reputation for great hardness and many thousands of tons were exported to England. Besides demolishing many of the surface rocks, including several Neolithic tombs, the quarrymen cut three large quarries into the hillside facing Guernsey. One behind Fisherman's Cottage and another behind the hotel (7/2B) are now overgrown; the third, at Rosière, is used as the island rubbish tip.

The quarries were connected by a railway line to the arms of a large harbour, where stone barges were beached for loading. The broad, level path along most of the west coast of Herm is a legacy of this railway. The north arm of the harbour ran out to the small, green islet known as Hermetier or Rat Island (7/2B). All that remains of this arm is the low causeway which connects the islet to Herm at low tide. The south arm has been maintained and is still in use; this is where the visitor will land if there is enough water to enter the harbour. The small, beehive-shaped stone building beside the hotel tennis court was built as a lock-up. There were several hundred imported quarrymen, and it was essential to have somewhere where drunks could be safely deposited.

Opposite above: Shell Beach, Herm
Opposite below: Belvoir Bay, Herm

Like so many islands, Herm has had its share of eccentric occupants, and each has left his mark. The manor buildings (7/3B), at the top of the wooded hill from the harbour, were extended to their present form with battlements and machicolations by the German Prince Blücher von Wahlstatt, who leased the island at the turn of the present century. He also laid the metalled road up the hill and planted many of the trees, including the groves of pine and evergreen oak on the summit of the island. Behind the manor is a miniature fairy-tale tower, converted from a mill.

Standing near the manor house is the medieval chapel of St Tugual. This ancient, stone-vaulted building consists of a nave and north transept. Some excellent modern stained glass has been put in by the present tenant, and non-denominational services are held here every Sunday.

The present economy of the island is based on tourism and dairy farming. There is a fine herd of Guernsey cattle, with modern dairy buildings beside the camp site in Little Seagull (7/3B). Some ten families live permanently on the island; this population is increased greatly each summer by holidaymakers and the seasonal workers who look after them in the hotel, self-catering cottages and camp site.

Houmets, Les (4/6A) These three islets are off the east coast of the CLOS DU VALLE. All can be reached at low tide, but great care should be taken to avoid being stranded. The northern and most remote of the three is Homtolle, a diminutive, grassy islet a little way from the approach to Beaucette Marina. The middle and largest islet, Houmet Paradis, must once have been cultivated, for in the 17th century several Vale families owned strips of land there. In the 19th century stone was quarried, and the remains of the quarrymen's hut are still to be seen. Today the island, deserted and partially overgrown with brambles and honeysuckle, is run by the National Trust of Guernsey as a nature reserve. The third islet, Houmet Benest, is at the entrance to Bordeaux Harbour.

Ivy Castle *see* Château des Marais

Jerbourg (4/5C) In the south corner of Guernsey is a peninsula, some 1300 yd long and 880 yd wide, urrounded by steep cliffs and joined to the rest of ST MARTIN'S PARISH by a neck of land 500 yd wide. On the summit of the neck is the Doyle

Looking west from St Tugual's Chapel, Herm

Column, a granite monument commemorating Sir John Doyle, Lieutenant-Governor (1803 to 1816), who did much for the island, in particular by improving the roads. The present monument replaces a larger column, complete with staircase and look-out gallery, which was destroyed by the Germans. The view from the platform at the base of the column is magnificent, taking in all the other islands and part of the Normandy coast.

To the west of the isthmus a precipitous and daunting flight of steps descends to the bathing beach of Petit Port, where a large expanse of sand is exposed at low tide. From the other side of the Doyle Column a zigzag path leads down to the 'Pine Forest', a less precipitous section of cliff clothed in bracken, with a scattering of pine trees which descend almost to the water's edge. From the cliff path the views of the sea and the other islands, framed by pines, are particularly beautiful.

There is a car park near the Doyle Column and another, complete with loos, above Petit Port; from either of these it is possible to walk round the peninsula – a delightful and exhilarating exercise in any weather and at any time of year. Alternatively the road continues past the monument to another car park (also with loos) on the clifftop overlooking St Martin's Point. Here, on a low spur of rock reached by a narrow catwalk, is a navigation light and a fog signal emitting a high-pitched wail in groups of three that can be heard over much of the island.

The southern tip of the peninsula, only accessible on foot, ends in a series of great rocks, the Pea Stacks. The third stack from the end, which resembles a monk, is Le Petit Bonhomme Andriou.

During the Iron Age the Jerbourg peninsula was converted into a promontory fort by building a series of ramparts and ditches across the isthmus. Although these have been obscured by subsequent car parks, lavatories, bunkers and a beer garden, they can be clearly made out where they meet the coast at either end. From the cliff-top overlooking Petit Port they ran towards the Doyle Column, then down the other side to a tiny cove properly called Pied du Mur, but more commonly known as Marble Bay, because of a white quartzite rock that outcrops there.

The ramparts were enlarged in the 13th century to provide a refuge for the people living in the southern part of Guernsey against the raids that followed the separation of the islands from Normandy in 1204. In the 14th century a castle was built on the isthmus, but of this the only trace remaining today is the stone-faced bank on which the Doyle Column stands.

Jethou (7) At low water, when HERM harbour is dry, the boat carrying the visitor to Herm will pass close to the island of Jethou on its way to the Rosière landing. The channel dividing the two islands, the Percée Passage (7/2C), takes its name from La Pierre Percée, more usually called the Gate Rock, which the boat rounds as it approaches Herm. A circular hole bored through the rock was probably intended for mooring barges used in the 19th century for the export of stone.

Jethou, a steep-sided island some 600 yd in diameter, is much smaller than its sister island of Herm, though with a maximum of 248 ft above sea level it is slightly higher. The summit is a plateau where early flowers were formerly grown for export, and where the descendants of cultivated daffodils still bloom every spring. A series of terraces on the south-facing cliff, now overgrown by bracken, was probably also used for early bulbs. On the slope facing Herm is the Fairy Wood (7/2C), carpeted in spring with bluebells. A fine house faces north-west.

Robert, Duke of Normandy, gave Jethou to his shipmaster Restauld in 1031. Restauld subsequently became a monk and the island came into the hands of the abbey of Mont St Michel. When Henry VIII seized the alien priories and lands it became Crown property, and has remained so ever since. Among the tenants was Compton Mackenzie, whose novel, *Fairy Gold*, is set in Herm and Jethou.

Jethou has two attendant conical islets, each surmounted by a white seamark: **Grande Fauconnière** (7/2C) to the south-east and **Crevichon** (7/1C) to the north-west. Crevichon has the distinction of being the earliest recorded quarry in the Guernsey Bailiwick, for in 1564 it supplied stone to CASTLE CORNET. In the 19th century the States took the lease of Jethou for a time to secure the Crevichon quarry for their building projects; some of the dressed granite of ST PETER PORT HARBOUR came from the deep gash through the islet which is still a feature of the landscape.

Jethou is leased privately from the Crown, and is not open to the public.

King's Mills (4/3B) Although Guernsey does not have villages in the English sense, there are a number of groups of old houses that almost qualify for that description. One such is King's Mills or Les Grands Moulins, in the CASTEL PARISH at the point where the TALBOT VALLEY

opens out into the Grande Mare. The name derives from a series of three water mills that made use of the Talbot Valley stream. The Water Board pumping station at the road junction is on the site of the lowest of the three; the position of the waterwheel can be seen to the left of the building. Le Moulin du Milieu, the middle mill, is beside the Rue à l'Eau and the upper mill, Le Moulin de Haut, is in the Fauxquets Valley, beside the quiet wooded lane that begins at a green island near the bottom of the Talbot Valley.

Most of the houses in King's Mills were once farmsteads, their land extending up the hill behind, with meadows in the Grande Mare. Even at the close of the Second World War there were still a dozen working farms in the area. In the Middle Ages the open fields were at Les Beaucamps (*camp* is the Norman French form of *champ*, 'field'). The site is now a school.

L'Ancresse Bay (4/5A) L'Ancresse, a broad, sandy bay in the extreme north of Guernsey, is said to derive its name from *l'ancrage*, 'the anchorage'. The story is that Duke Robert of Normandy, father of William the Conqueror, was forced by contrary winds to take refuge here when, in 1030, he was attempting to reach England to do battle with King Canute. Robert's attempted invasion of England 36 years before his son's successful conquest was a historic event, but the chronicles differ as to whether his fleet took refuge in Jersey or Guernsey. Guernsey folklore says it was at GRAND HAVRE, and certainly this is a far more sheltered haven than L'Ancresse, which is wide open to the north.

That the sands of L'Ancresse have always been seen as a possible landing place for an invasion, however, is shown by the number of fortifications encompassing the bay. In particular, there is a greater concentration of 'Martello' towers here than in any other part of the island. These are not true Martello towers (*see* Vazon Bay) but are of a design peculiar to Guernsey. Fifteen were built, at a cost of £100 each, during the 1780s to repel an expected French invasion. Of these, Tower No. 4 stands on the Fort Le Marchant headland to the east of the bay; No. 5 is at Nid à l'Herbe, at the eastern end of the bay itself; and Nos 6 and 7 are behind the sea wall in the centre of the bay; No. 8, near the golf clubhouse, was demolished by the Germans; No. 9, looking distinctly drunk as it is founded on sand, is beside the track at La Jaonneuse to the west.

The approach to the bay is covered by a fort at the extremity of each headland. Fort L'Angle, later renamed Fort Le Marchant, is an attractive Napoleonic gun battery on the eastern headland. Until recently it was obscured by later barracks, now demolished. This headland is used as a full-bore rifle range and care should be taken when a red flag is flying on the Martello tower. Fort Pembroke, on the western headland, is little more than a powder magazine protected by a curtain wall, with musket apertures covering the bay. On the same headland is Star Fort, a star-shaped depression in the sandy turf. Its origin is obscure but it was probably dug by the Militia in about 1812.

The Germans' contribution to the defence of this possible invasion beach was a concrete anti-tank wall.

Today L'Ancresse is a popular bathing beach, and the landfall of the telephone cable linking Guernsey with England.

L'Ancresse Common (4/5A) In the extreme north of Guernsey is a broad coastal strip of rolling dune grassland punctuated by rocky *hougues* or hillocks. This is the common land of the CLOS DU VALLE. Although much of it is now occupied by an 18-hole golf course, the *habitants* of the Clos still have grazing rights over it. Until about 1920 the Common was fenced, the approach roads were barred by gates, and cattle and sheep were free to graze at large. There are still plenty of cattle, and the occasional donkey and goat, on the Common but today there are no fences or gates and the animals have to be tethered.

The sand underlying the turf is rich in shell fragments, especially towards the western end of the Common, and for this reason lime-loving plants such as salad burnet and rue-leaved saxifrage are plentiful. Snails also abound, having plenty of material with which to build their shells. Towards Fort Le Marchant the soil becomes peatier, and acid-loving plants such as heather and foxglove begin to appear. Where the turf is kept closely cropped, either by grazing animals or the golf club mowing machine, a close examination on hands and knees will reveal a great variety of wild flowers. One of the most attractive is the sand crocus, whose pale blue, star-shaped flowers are produced in April, but only open in sunny weather. In other parts of the Common there are dense thickets of gorse, whose yellow flowers may be found virtually all the year round.

One of the most attractive of the rocky *hougues* rising from the Common, La Rocque Balan, stands beside the road a little to the west of L'Ancresse Lodge Hotel. Before the Reformation it was the custom to assemble here on Midsummer's Eve with pots, pans, cowhorns and anything that would make a noise, presumably to frighten away evil spirits. For a hundred years, from the mid-16th century to the restoration of the monarchy after the Civil War, Guernsey was governed by a Calvinist regime during which all the old customs connected with the calendar were rigidly suppressed. Through these long years many customs were doubtless forgotten, but at some stage during the more permissive Anglican regime that followed, the custom of dancing at Midsummer on the summit of the Rocque Balan was re-established, and persisted until comparatively modern times.

L'Ancresse Common is rich in prehistoric remains, particularly Neolithic tombs. The largest of these is on La Varde, a sandy hill to the west of the road to Pembroke Bay. The summit of the hill, some 70ft above sea level, is shared by a Neolithic passage grave and a concrete German bunker. The entrance to the tomb leads into a passage which opens into a spacious chamber – the largest of any Channel Island dolmen – with a small side chamber. When the tomb was excavated in 1837 evidence was found that it had been repeatedly used for many burials. Finds from this and other tombs are in the Guernsey Museum and Art Gallery in CANDIE GARDENS. From the entrance to La Varde dolmen is a splendid view to the east towards HERM Common, another sandy area rich in megalithic remains.

Across the road to the east of La Varde, near a small pond, is a much smaller tomb, La Mare ès Mauves. Another small grave, in the rough between golf fairways 5 and 6 in the south-west part of the Common, is La Platte Mare. It is notable for a fine row of 'cup marks' or shallow depressions on the end of the northern propstone.

Near La Platte Mare is Les Fouaillages, a unique site discovered in 1978 and excavated between 1979 and 1981. Although the results of the excavation have yet to be published it appears to consist of a pair of small burial chambers in a triangular enclosure. Pottery from the site has been dated to 4500 BC, making it by far the oldest man-made structure in Guernsey, having been built by some of the first farmers in Western Europe. Les Fouaillages is best reached by following a track across the road from the car park at Lucksall on Les Amarreurs Road.

L'Erée (4/2B) A peninsula in ST PIERRE-DU-BOIS PARISH, forming the northern headland of

ROCQUAINE BAY. A pair of one-way lanes connects the main coast road with a car park on the headland overlooking the causeway to LIHOU ISLAND. Beside the car park is a memorial to the crew of the *Prosperity*, a cargo vessel lost with all hands off the west coast in 1974. Beyond the memorial, at the extreme tip of the headland, is a small Napoleonic battery.

Beside the lane leading from the coast road to Lihou Causeway is Le Creux-ès-Faies, a Neolithic passage grave which, as the name suggests, was thought by Guernseymen of old to be a fairies' cave. The tomb, which is 28 ft long, is built into a hillock which also contains a German bunker.

On the summit of L'Erée headland is the Martello tower of Fort Saumarez. Built in 1805, this is a 'true' Martello tower, being broader and of more solid construction than the earlier Guernsey round towers. Although the German concrete added in the Second World War has not improved its beauty, it does provide a focal point in the view from much of western Guernsey.

On the inland side of the coast road between L'Erée Hotel and LE CATIOROC is an open expanse of low-lying land, at present grazed by one of Guernsey's few flocks of sheep. The area is still known as L'Erée Aerodrome, for this was the first airfield in the Channel Islands, and from here for two brief months in 1935 Sir Alan Cobham ran a scheduled service to Bournemouth. In making the airfield all the hedges and walls were removed, but the *hougue* in the middle of the area proved too difficult to level and in 1939 the present AIRPORT was opened.

L'Erée Aerodrome is protected from the sea to the north by a lofty shingle bank on the seaward side of the coast road, La Rue de la Rocque. Characteristic shingle plants that can usually be found here include sea kale, sea rocket and yellow-horned poppy.

Lihou Island (4/1B) A small island of 38 acres, lying a quarter of a mile off Guernsey's west coast. It can be reached on foot at low tide, by a causeway from L'ERÉE headland. It is safest to cross at spring tides (the two or three days following new and full moon), when low water is in the middle of the day and allows a stay of two or three hours. When the causeway is awash the crossing should on no account be attempted. The island is windswept and treeless, consisting mainly of rough grazing. The house is on the site of a farmhouse which was destroyed by the Germans, who used it for target practice. From here a path encircles the island. The southern path passes the ruins of the priory of Notre Dame. This was certainly in existence in 1156, for the church of Notre Dame de Lihou is mentioned in a Papal Bull of that year. Peter Heylin, writing in about 1632, said that almost nothing was left of the priory of 'Lehu' except the steeple, but such was the veneration in which St Mary was held that sailors would still strike their topsails as they passed. The last piece of vaulting fell in a storm in December 1979, and today only a few fragments of wall remain.

At the western end of the island the craggy cliffs of gneiss overlook a large rock pool much beloved of bathers.

The tenancy of Lihou is a fee farm lease from the Crown; it last changed hands in 1983, when the 'mobile fixtures' included a flock of seaweed-eating sheep.

Little Burhou *see* **Burhou**

Little Chapel *see* Les Vauxbelets

Markets (5/2B) Until well into the 18th century in ST PETER PORT market stalls were set up in the alleys immediately around the TOWN CHURCH, while the butchers operated in Cow Lane, the *venelle* running down to the harbour beside Le Lievre's shop. At high tide the sea washed up Cow Lane and removed the worst of the blood and offal. The arcades now known as the French Halles and used as a vegetable market were built for the butchers in 1780. Above them were the Assembly Rooms, now forming part of the Guille-Allès Library. The present Meat Market (John Wilson, 1822) lies across Market Square. Wilson, who was active in Guernsey between 1815 and 1830, was in his classical mood, with Doric columns and round-headed arches. The States Arcades, adjoining the Meat Market, were added by Wilson in 1830. Over the arcading is a generous flag-paved balcony with stone balustrade and an ornamental canopy of wrought iron.

The Fish Market (John Newton, 1877) fills the triangular site between Market Street and Fountain Street and demonstrates Victorian municipal architecture at its best. It is a long, low building, red granite below and grey above, with an attractively rounded end and a patterned slate roof. The adjoining Lower Vegetable Market was added two years later to designs by another London architect, Francis Chambers. Externally the

Detail of the wall of the Little Chapel, Les Vauxbelets,
decorated with broken china (see p. 173)   (Y. Dedman)

THE MILITARY ROADS OF GUERNSEY

Sir John Doyle, who was Lieutenant-Governor of Guernsey from 1803 to 1816, and a man of considerable military experience, was greatly concerned at the state of the island's roads. He feared that if Napoleon's troops landed on beaches in the north or west, his own forces, delayed by the appalling roads, could not be brought to bear until after the French had established themselves. It would be particularly dangerous if the French landed at L'ANCRESSE BAY and occupied the CLOS DU VALLE, which was still an island. (Doyle remarked that he did not know whether he ought to be a general or an admiral, for whether the battle was a military or a naval one would entirely depend on the state of the tide.)

It was, therefore, primarily for military reasons that the draining of the BRAYE DU VALLE mudflats and salt marshes, which divided the Clos du Valle from the rest of Guernsey, was begun in 1806. Barriers against the sea were constructed at each end of the Braye; the modern coast road that now crosses the end of GRAND HAVRE uses the western one.

To reach the Clos du Valle, Doyle built a road, still called La Route Militaire, from the Halfway to the VALE CHURCH and on to L'Ancresse Bay. Another new road skirted Belle Grève Bay and continued as Grande Maison Road to St Sampson's Bridge, then via Vale Avenue and Braye Road to Camp du Roi and Landes du Marché. The sections of the Route Militaire and the Braye Road that cross the reclaimed land are most unusual in Guernsey in that they are perfectly straight. They cross at right angles in the middle of the Braye.

The draining of the Braye du Valle yielded 300 acres of fertile land, which was sold for £5000 and the proceeds used for building two more roads, to the bays of VAZON and ROCQUAINE, in 1810. The road to Vazon ran via the Rohais and the CASTEL CHURCH to Vazon Tower; the road to Rocquaine ran from FORT GEORGE, through ST MARTIN'S PARISH to LE BOURG, Les Paysans and L'ERÉE. In the next few years the St Andrew's Road was built from Mount Row to ST ANDREW'S CHURCH and LES VAUXBELETS, and the COBO road from the Rohais to SAUMAREZ PARK. Finally a road was cut from Saumarez Park, crossing the Vazon road at La Houguette, then via KING'S MILLS, Mont Saint and Le Felconte to Les Adams.

Doyle usually followed the course of existing roads, widening and straightening where necessary. In places, in order to straighten a tight corner, he cut diagonally across a field. These new cuts can be detected by the perfectly straight line of the new section of road, and the triangular pieces of field on each side. A footpath with granite kerbstones runs the length of one side of the military roads and milestones of grey granite, with the mileage in Roman numerals, give the distance from the TOWN CHURCH. Twenty-six of these stones are still to be seen – often, like the 2-mile stone at the Castel Church, built into walls. The furthest stone from the church, opposite Les Adams Chapel, is 7 miles from town.

Although built for military reasons, Doyle's roads proved to be of immense economic value to the island, making it possible for country people to bring their produce to town, and for those who worked in the town to live in the country. Apart from the Val des Terres no significant roadworks have been undertaken since Doyle's time. His roads are still the main roads of Guernsey.

design is far more overbearing and fussy, with stepped gables and leaded windows in abundance. The bronze tobacco plants sprouting from the roof commemorate the tax on tobacco which partly paid for the building. Inside, the ceiling is worth studying for the capitals are embellished with carved ormer shells and a variety of fruit and vegetables.

Today the markets are being strangled by the lack of nearby parking; the housewife can more easily buy her flowers and vegetables from the wayside stalls that are a modern feature of the Guernsey countryside. But the markets remain a big tourist attraction and it would be a tragedy if they ceased to exist.

New Town (5/2B) A grid of streets and Regency terraces built in ST PETER PORT between 1792 and

1843 by the de Havilland family, on the plateau above Clifton. Saumarez Street, St John Street and Havilland Street are crossed by Union Street, connecting by George Street and Allez Street with Vauvert. The houses of Saumarez Street are rather grand, with a variety of Doric and Ionic porches and doorcases. Most are now flats or guesthouses. Union Street is more modest but at the west end, facing down Havilland Street, is an extremely fine terrace of four tall houses of four storeys plus basements and dormers. The drawing rooms on the first floor have large 18-pane sash windows. Behind the railings on the opposite side of the road is one of the earliest known pillar boxes, installed in 1853 on the recommendation of the novelist Anthony Trollope, who as Post Office Surveyor had visited the island 15 months earlier to establish a daily postal service. With its granite pavements and largely unaltered houses the New Town must be one of the most complete pieces of Regency development to have survived anywhere in the British Isles.

Perelle and **St Apolline's Chapel** (4/2B) Perelle Bay, between LE CATIOROC and Fort Richmond, is one of the rocky bays of Guernsey's west coast. At low tide many acres of rock are exposed, from which *vraic* or seaweed used to be gathered for use on the land. The granite slipway opposite the Perelle Garage was built to allow horses and carts on to the beach to collect the *vraic* which was – and is – free for the taking, subject to certain rules. Many such slipways exist around the coast, constructed of stone setts with projecting edges which afforded a grip to horses' hoofs as they hauled the loaded boxcarts up from the beach. The *vraic* was either spread directly on the land, where it supplemented farmyard manure, or was dried and burned, and the ash used as fertilizer.

Opposite l'Atlantique Hotel is La Perelle Battery, a small brick-built Napoleonic fortification.

La Grande Rue, just inland from Perelle Bay, is the nearest thing to a village that the rural ST SAVIOUR'S PARISH can offer. Besides a cluster of old houses and farm buildings there is a hotel, a hairdressing salon, a disused school, a United Reformed Church, St Apolline Chapel and the Douzaine Room (the office of the parish council). La Grande Rue, one of the ancient highways of Guernsey, was straightened and widened for military purposes in 1814; the fifth milestone from the TOWN CHURCH is on the corner a little to the east of St Saviour's Hotel.

St Apolline's Chapel stands beside the road, at the corner of La Grande Rue and La Rue de Ste Apolline. It is a simple, attractive building of red granite with a small, arched doorway to north and south, and three narrow square-headed windows. The west gable, like that of many old farmhouses, is completely blank. The roof is of vaulted masonry, protected by a modern covering of tiles. Under the vaulting are the remains of some mural paintings. They are badly decayed, as for some years the building was used as a cowshed, but some details can still be made out which may possibly be part of a Nativity scene.

St Apolline is the only medieval chantry chapel still standing in Guernsey. We know approximately when it was built because in the Greffe (the record office in ST PETER PORT) is a charter of 1394 by which Richard II gave permission to

St Apolline's Chapel, Perelle

Nicolas Henry of La Perelle to endow a chapel which he had recently built on his estate, for the purpose of maintaining a chaplain who was to celebrate a daily Mass for his and his family's souls, and for those of Christian people generally.

After the Reformation the chapel fell into decay. For years it was used as a stable, until in 1873 it was bought by the States in order to preserve it. In recent years it has been restored for inter-denominational worship.

Opposite the chapel is la Ruette de la Bataille, an unmetalled footpath or 'green lane' which climbs the hillside overlooking Perelle.

Petit Bôt Bay (4/4C) A popular bathing beach on the south coast of Guernsey, Petit Bôt is a sandy cove beset on either side by steep cliffs, on the boundary between the FOREST and ST MARTIN'S PARISHES. The bay lies at the foot of two well-wooded valleys, one descending from LE BOURG and the other from the St Martin's side. In summer it is best to approach the bay from Le Bourg, as there is a one-way road up to St Martin's.

The road from Le Bourg follows a stream down the floor of the valley, garden shrubs mingling with the forest trees on either side. Near the bottom, beside the stream, is a naturalized patch of gunnera or 'giant rhubarb', a South American plant introduced by the Victorians. The road from the east passes meadows grazed by heifers and goats, before joining another stream where the woods close in. Growing among the liverworts in the bank of the stream are Cornish moneywort and opposite-leaved golden saxifrage.

The combined streams used to operate at least two watermills. The position of one is indicated by a waterfall that still cascades where the mill-wheel used to be; another was across the road, on the site of the tea room. For a time during the 19th century the lower mill was used for making paper from rags and old rope.

Pleinmont (4/1C) The 'Land's End' of Guernsey, Pleinmont is a cliff-girt peninsula at the south-west extremity of the island. From the Imperial Hotel at the western end of ROCQUAINE BAY you can either strike inland or follow a narrow road along the coast to Pezeries Point. The inland route, taking the right-hand turning immediately above the hotel, follows a valley to the clifftop at Pleinmont Point, where a landmark is provided by the aerials of a television relay station. There are several car parks on the clifftop, among acres of bramble, gorse and rabbit-grazed turf; it is ideal for a picnic, or for blackberrying in season.

The flowers of the cliffs are at their best in May and June. Gorse, which flowers nearly all the year round, is then at its most golden and in addition there are drifts of sea campion, thrift and ox-eye daisy. Of particular interest at Pleinmont is a prostrate form of broom, which survives on the windswept cliffs by growing flat against the rocks. Pleinmont Point is exposed to the full force of Atlantic gales, and in a storm spray reaches the tops of the cliffs. A little over a mile to the west is the HANOIS LIGHTHOUSE, guarding a reef on which innumerable ships have foundered.

By the cliff path a few paces from the junction of La Rue des Plains with La Rue de la Trigale are the ruins of Pleinmont Watch House, which figures in Victor Hugo's *Les Travailleurs de la Mer*. This Napoleonic structure, which had become known as 'Victor Hugo's haunted house', was destroyed by the Germans as it interfered with their lines of fire. The whole headland is sprinkled with German concrete fortifications.

The coast road from the Imperial Hotel to Pezeries Point passes first the sheltered fishing haven of Portelet. A slipway leads down to a sandy cove which is an excellent bathing beach. Overlooking Portelet, on the inland side of the road, are Trinity House Cottages, home of the keepers of Les Hanois lighthouse. But since the lighthouse is not visible from the cottages, in pre-telephone days the keepers' wives used to signal to their menfolk from the Varde Rock, on the spur of land immediately west of the cottages, where traces of a flagpole remain.

Beyond the Varde Rock a zigzag road descends to join the coast road; the land to the east of the zigzag, above the Varde Rock, is Le Vau de Monel, the first property to be acquired by the National Trust of Guernsey in 1960. It is a secluded, wooded valley with a terrace at the centre, affording a beautiful view of Rocquaine and Fort Grey, framed by trees. A house on this terrace was destroyed by the Germans. The property can be approached on foot through the pine trees from the coast road. Alternatively, there is a small car park at the upper entrance to the property, but this can only be reached from above as the zigzag is a one-way road.

The narrow coast road ends in a car park at Pezeries Point. The low promontory to the north-east of the car park is occupied by an attractive star-shaped fort, Le Château de Pezeries. This was already of some antiquity when a report of 1680 listed its armament as consisting of one 7 ft

The Hanois Lighthouse from Pleinmont Point

saker of 14 pounds. The fort was rebuilt and the tiny cottage-shaped powder magazine added in 1804.

Beyond the car park is a flat expanse of short turf overshadowed by an amphitheatre of cliff. Beside the path leading towards the foot of the cliff is a grassy mound surrounded by a circular ditch. This is La Table des Pions, associated with the colourful ceremony, La Chevauchée de St Michel. La Chevauchée, the most elaborate medieval ceremony in the Channel Islands, was organized by the feudal court of St Michel and took place every three years. It was ostensibly an inspection of the main roads of the island, to make sure that they had not become overgrown, but the opportunity was not missed for a good deal of jollification. The *pions* were footmen who attended the mounted dignitaries, and they had their breakfast at La Table des Pions, sitting in a circle with their feet in the trench. La Chevauchée de St Michel was last enacted in 1966 to mark the 900th anniversary of the Norman conquest of England.

Another path from the car park follows the brink of a rocky cove with a winding slipway, beautifully constructed of granite setts to enable horses and carts to gather *vraic* or seaweed from among the rocks. *Vraic* is no longer in general use as a fertilizer but it is still cast up, free for the taking, in great quantities in the rocky creeks of the west coast. The footpath continues through a gap in some rocks and across another stretch of turf to a small Napoleonic battery from which there is a splendid view to the west across the Hanois Reef.

In several places on the central plateau of the Pleinmont peninsula there are traces of the medieval open-field system. The most complete example of an open field remaining in the island is beside La Rue du Banquet, immediately above Le Vau de Monel. The field is divided into strips, with low baulks of earth dividing each man's strip from his neighbour's. La Rue du Banquet, still unfenced, runs along the common headland of the strips, where the ox teams turned when ploughing. Today the strips are ploughed by tractor; the baulks, though vulnerable, have so far survived.

Strip cultivation was the normal practice in the Middle Ages but the enclosure of open fields came early to the Channel Islands; in Elizabeth's reign it proceeded so rapidly that the antiquary William Camden, writing in 1586, said that there was very little open-field farming in Guernsey. The first accurate survey of the island, in 1787,

QUARRYING: A GUERNSEY INDUSTRY

Stone has been used as a building material from the earliest times in Guernsey, and small quarries existed all over the island to supply stone for the immediate neighbourhood. It is still striking how the old houses of the north tend to be built of the grey diorite of the VALE and ST SAMPSON's parishes, those of the CASTEL parish are of the red Cobo granite and those of ST MARTIN's and the FOREST parishes are of the brown, flaky Icart gneiss which outcrops along the southern cliffs. In the early 19th century Guernsey began to earn a reputation for hard-wearing granite which was exported in the form of paving setts and kerbstones. The peace that followed the Battle of Waterloo in 1815, combined with the invention of the macadamized road surface, greatly increased the demand. The diorite of the Vale and the intensely hard gabbro of St Sampson's were particularly valued for road metal and soon the north of the island became pock-marked with quarries. The industry reached a peak shortly before the First World War, when 400,000 tons of stone were exported annually, and St Sampson's was covered by perpetual dust from the stone-crushing plant between the North Side and VALE CASTLE. Today there is no export of stone, and at the time of writing all local needs are being supplied by two quarries.

The huge holes in the ground left by the quarrying industry have proved to be of immense value for water storage and for the disposal of refuse. The great Longue Hougue gabbro quarry near ST SAMPSON'S CHURCH is one of several that are used as reservoirs by the water authority. Many other quarries have been filled with refuse and returned to other uses, such as car parks or industrial sites; many smaller ones have been fenced off and are now overgrown with ivy, gorse and bramble. At present a vast quarry immediately to the north of Bordeaux Harbour is nearing the end of its life as a refuse tip and another suitable hole is being sought.

shows that hedges were universal except for Les Camps, in ST MARTIN'S PARISH and a coastal belt, particularly at L'ANCRESSE and Pleinmont. The pattern of the old strips is usually reflected in the hedges, which often survive when the land between has been swallowed by houses or greenhouses.

Rocquaine Bay (4/1B) Rocquaine is the most southerly of the west coast bays of Guernsey, extending in a broad, rocky sweep from PLEINMONT to L'ERÉE. (The headland to the west of the Imperial Hotel is described under Pleinmont.) From the Imperial Hotel to L'Erée Hotel the Rocquaine Road runs for 1½ miles round the bay, flanked on one side by a granite sea wall and on the other by fishermen's cottages, bungalows, intermittently flooded gardens and derelict greenhouses. Behind the coastal ribbon of development is a strip of low-lying meadows, and behind that again an escarpment that was once a sea cliff, at a time when the sea level was 100 ft higher than it is at present.

Towards the southern end of the bay, on a tidal islet reached by a short causeway, is Fort Grey Maritime Museum, open from May to October. Fort Grey was built in 1804 and is one of Guernsey's three 'true' Martello towers (the others are Fort Saumarez and Fort Hommet). Unlike the majority of Guernsey's coastal towers, which were built in the 1780s, these three have sloping sides and a much more solid construction. Because of its appearance with its outer curtain wall, Fort Grey is often affectionately known as the Cup and Saucer. Outside the outer

wall is a small powder magazine. The tower is whitewashed and serves mariners as a seamark. The museum is run by the States of Guernsey; its theme is the innumerable shipwrecks that have occurred on the rocks off Guernsey's west coast.

St Andrew's Church (4/4C) The parish church of St Andrew is pleasantly situated among trees and ancient tombstones on the side of a hill in the rural heart of Guernsey. There has been a church here since before 1048, when William, Duke of Normandy (later to become the Conqueror) placed it under the patronage of the abbey of Marmoutiers.

Like all the medieval churches of the Channel Islands, St Andrew's has been built in stages and in common with most of them it now consists of two parallel naves and chancels, with an arcade between them. At some stage, perhaps in the 18th century, one of the pillars of the arcade was

THE ROYAL GUERNSEY MILITIA

Until the island was demilitarized in 1940 Guernsey had a part-time military force of which it was justly proud. Nobody knows when the Militia was first raised, but it was certainly at least 600 years old. The need to have a force capable of defending Guernsey arose in 1204, when King John lost Continental Normandy to France, so that the Channel Islands found themselves between two opposing powers and close to the shore of the hostile one. At some time during the ensuing century a force of Guernseymen was set up to man the island's defences and this became the Militia.

At first the defence of the island would have been organized on a feudal basis, each Seigneur providing a number of men, but during the 16th century it was reorganized on a parish basis, with compulsory service for all male inhabitants. By the mid-18th century the Militia was 2000 strong, with companies of artillery to man the coastal batteries. Pride in the force was strong, though the troops were unpaid and not provided with uniforms. It was not until the Napoleonic wars that the British Government provided the Militia with uniforms and equipment.

By the beginning of the 19th century the force was over 3000 strong, and in 1831 the title Royal Guernsey Militia was conferred on it by William IV.

In the 1870s the Militia was reorganized as one regiment of artillery and three infantry regiments. The regular army provided staff for each regiment, and the States provided accommodation in the various arsenals which, beautifully built of dressed granite, are still a feature of the island scene. The grandest of these, the Town Arsenal, which housed

the Artillery and the 1st Infantry Regiment, is now the fire station.

In the early years of the present century the Militia was run on similar lines to a British territorial force, except that service was compulsory for every able-bodied man between 17 and 35. There were a limited number of vacancies each year, however, and in practice there were more volunteers than vacancies. For a fortnight each summer a training camp was held at Les Beaucamps, Castel, where today there is a secondary modern school. The barrack huts have been recycled and remain as a not very attractive feature of schools all over the island; the granite drill hall is now the school gymnasium.

During the First World War the Militia, for the first time in its long history, fought overseas and did so with the utmost distinction. In 1916 it was transformed into the Royal Guernsey Light Infantry, which included men from Alderney and Sark, and in June 1917 the 1st Battalion RGLI sailed for England and subsequently France. The battle honours of the RGLI read:

Ypres 1917
Passchendaele Cambrai 1917
Lys Estaires Hazebrouck France and Flanders
  1917-1918

The War Memorial carries a list of a thousand dead.

In 1928 the British Government withdrew its financial support for the Militia but the States continued to maintain a small voluntary force until 1940, when the Militia was disbanded to allow its members to join various units of the British Army.

removed in order to provide a clear view of the pulpit, with the result that one of the arches is very broad and awkwardly shaped. The church is unusual in having retained its original square-headed windows in the north and south walls, though in most cases they have obviously been enlarged. The tower, perhaps the last part of the church to have been built, is at the west end. It is square, of dressed granite with a castellated parapet and a squat tile-covered spire. The vaulting below the bell loft is groined, with a circular opening in the centre.

Across the road and down a short cul-de-sac, among winter heliotrope and 'mind-your-own-business', is La Fontaine de St Clair: one of the holy wells whose waters were traditionally used to cure certain ailments, particularly of the skin.

St Andrew's Parish (4/4B) The only one of Guernsey's ten parishes to be totally landlocked, St Andrew's is a predominantly rural parish of 1101 acres of fields, narrow lanes with elm-lined hedgebanks and a good deal of ribbon development. The western boundary of the parish extends in a fairly straight line from the middle of the airport runway in the south to Les Baissières in the north. The eastern boundary is more tortuous. From La Villiaze it runs to La Corbinerie, then follows a stream down the floor of a green valley past Havilland Hall and Le Foulon to the St Pierre Park Hotel. A stone in the wall at the bottom of the Rohais marks the spot where the parish boundary crosses the main road.

About the year 1020 Duke Richard II of Normandy divided Guernsey into two feudal holdings, granting the western fief to the Vicomte du Bessin and the eastern fief to the Vicomte du Cotentin. St Andrew's fell into the eastern fief, and its straight western border is therefore part of the oldest boundary in the island. The lane that runs behind LES VAUXBELETS, across Candie Road and down to Les Niaux Mill in the TALBOT VALLEY is part of this boundary and it is noticeable how the lane is sunk between massive earth banks on either side.

For centuries St Andrew's was a purely agricultural parish and the only contact its parishioners had with the outside world was a Saturday trip along narrow, muddy lanes to take their produce to market. This was changed in 1812, when La Route de St André was built from town into the heart of the island. The immediate purpose of the road was to facilitate the movement of troops and ordnance in the event of a French invasion. The invasion never came, but the road opened up St

The Hangman's Inn, Bailiff's Cross, St Andrew's Parish

Andrew's Parish, allowing the development we see today.

From the direction of Mount Row, La Route de St André enters St Andrew's parish at the bottom of the Vauxquiedor, passing the Princess Elizabeth Hospital on the left and Havilland Hall, a neoclassical stately home built by the de Havilland family, on the right. It next passes Bailiff's Cross, associated in folklore with Gaultier de la Salle, not a bailiff in the modern Guernsey sense but merely an official, who was hanged for murder in 1320 and made his last confession here. A stone with an incised cross is built into a pillar beside the Hangman's Inn.

The second milestone from town is beside the entrance to St Andrew's Brickfield, site of a large disused quarry and the source of many of the bricks used in the older houses and greenhouse chimneys. The road passes ST ANDREW'S CHURCH, standing at the heart of the parish near the head of the TALBOT VALLEY. After passing the church the next lane on the left leads past the German underground hospital, a series of damp tunnels in the hillside open in summer to the public. La Route de St André continues to Les Vauxbelets, passing round the south of the estate, with the third milestone a little way past the entrance to the Little Chapel.

The road continues to the Hougue Fouque, where a left turn brings you into La Villiaze Road, skirting the airport. On the right are the premises of an American firm making electronics equipment. A little further on and on the left is the

Guernsey Zoo: a small zoo in an attractive setting specializing in birds and small mammals.

St Apolline's Chapel *see* Perelle

St James-the-Less Church (5/2B) A Greek Revival church built in ST PETER PORT by John Wilson. Wilson was a little-known architect who was active in Guernsey in 1815-30. Although his work is practically unknown elsewhere, his Guernsey commissions show him to have been highly competent, both in the classical idiom and in a pseudo-Gothic style to which he was greatly attached. His classical work, in particular, has earned him the title of the Nash of Guernsey.

The western façade of St James, which faces up the main road as it curves round the grounds of Elizabeth College, has a massive Doric portico, its pediment surmounted by a graceful Ionic tower and cupola. The solidity of the Doric and the elegance of the Ionic demonstrate Wilson's mastery of the classical orders.

St James was built as a garrison church, and to serve the English settlers, the services in the TOWN CHURCH at that time being in French. It is an 'auditory church' with a spacious nave, a domed apse and a graceful horseshoe-shaped gallery supported on pitch-pine columns. In 1971, having become redundant, it was accepted as a gift by the States of Guernsey. There followed a long saga in which conservationists did battle (at one point it nearly became a police station) and in 1985 the building, now beautifully restored at States expense by the Friends of St James, was opened as a concert and assembly hall.

St Martin's Church (4/5C) The church of St Martin de la BELLIEUSE stands surrounded by a cluster of old houses a few yards from the busy shopping centre of St Martin's. The rounded, raised churchyard, supported by an ancient retaining wall, suggests considerable antiquity and this is borne out by the stone female figure serving as a gatepost at the entrance to the churchyard. *La Grandmère du Chimquière* (the Old Lady of the Cemetery) appears to have been carved in two stages. The shoulders, breasts and arms, which are only faintly represented, were probably carved in about 2500 BC. The face was touched up much later, perhaps in the Iron Age. La Grandmère formerly stood within the church-yard, but was broken in two and removed by a 19th-century churchwarden, in order to suppress the veneration in which she was still being held. The St Martinais were so incensed by this

vandalism that she was cemented together and erected in her present rather precarious position beside the road, where coins and flowers are still occasionally found on her head.

The church is dedicated to St Martin of Tours, a 4th-century Abbot of Marmoutiers. The oldest part – probably dating from the 11th century – of the present building appears to be the chancel, whose angles and buttresses rest upon great water-worn boulders. The nave was added later, together with the bell tower, supported on four piers standing between nave and chancel. At some stage a north aisle was added, giving the typical Guernsey double nave. The two spans of the roof are vaulted in stone, with groining under the bell tower. The octagonal stone spire, with its four attendant spirelets, may have been added to the tower at a later date.

Just inside the east jamb of the south door is a holy water stoup. It is the only stoup in Guernsey to have survived the Reformation but it is badly damaged, and now accommodates a poorbox marked *Pauvres*. It is said that the font is the original one, and that it was used for many years as a pig trough. If this is so, it is the only pre-Reformation font in a Guernsey church.

The south porch is one of the finest examples of Flamboyant work in the Channel Islands. This style, typified by the ogee moulding over the door, flourished in France in the late Middle Ages when in England the Perpendicular style was in favour. Allowing a time lag for the style to reach Guernsey, the porch was probably built in the early 16th century.

St Martin's Parish (4/4C) St Martin's, one of the 'higher parishes' on the elevated southern plateau of Guernsey, is largely residential with a scatter-ing of farms and glasshouses. The parish forms the south-eastern corner of the island, the boun-dary running from PETIT BÔT BAY to the Vaux-quiedor, taking in the Princess Elizabeth Hospital and returning to the coast at FERMAIN BAY.

The original parish centre was at LA BEL-LIEUSE. The modern shopping centre is a few yards away on La Grande Rue, which General Doyle widened in 1810 as part of his military road between FORT GEORGE and ROCQUAINE BAY. Besides La Bellieuse there are groups of old houses at La Ville Amphrey, Saints, La Fosse and La Villette. All are built of the reddish-brown Icart gneiss that underlies this part of the island. La Ville Amphrey is reached by following a lane which begins in an unpromising way beside the Old Mill housing estate. It ends in a peaceful

cluster of old houses and a wishing well, whose limpid water overflows into a stone trough to which cattle, until recently, were led to drink. From here, the water descends to the sea at Moulin Huet along a sunken way between high hedges, just wide enough for the stream and a narrow footpath. As it approaches the coast the lane becomes steeper and the water channel deeper, until it emerges near the car park above Moulin Huet Bay.

The St Martin's coastline is of cliffs interrupted by small bays, some of which are popular bathing beaches while others are less accessible. A footpath follows the entire coastline. From a short distance up the road to the east of Petit Bôt the path climbs to the top of the cliff at Mont Hubert, and continues past the coves of Jaonnet and La Bette to Icart Point. From here it descends to SAINT'S BAY, then up to the clifftop again until the well-wooded slopes of Moulin Huet are reached. The path continues high above the sandy beach of Petit Port, and out to the tip of the JERBOURG peninsula opposite the rugged chain of rocks known as the Pea Stacks.

From the Pea Stacks the path follows the clifftop above Telegraph Bay to St Martin's Point, where it turns north to follow a more sheltered and luxuriant coastline through the 'Pine Forest' to Marble Bay and the fishermen's mooring place of Bec du Nez. The path then rounds an eminence from which there is a view over Fermain Bay and CASTLE CORNET, and finally descends to Fermain. The cliff path continues to town, but when we have crossed the Fermain stream we are in the parish of ST PETER PORT.

See also Sausmarez Manor.

St Peter-in-the-Wood *see* St Pierre-du-Bois Church *and* Parish

St Peter Port (5) The main town of Guernsey, and a civil parish extending from the Bouet in the north to Fermain in the south, and inland as far as Ville au Roi, Le Foulon, Foote's Lane and the Ramée. The town is magnificently situated on the hillside overlooking ST PETER PORT HARBOUR. It is best approached from the sea, particularly in the early morning, when the red pantiles reflect the rising sun, or in the evening, when the spires of St Barnabas, St Joseph, Notre Dame, St James, Elizabeth College and Victoria Tower are silhouetted against the sky. It is a town of cobbled

Opposite: La Grandmère du Chimquière at the entrance to St Martin's Church (see p. 143)

Barrière de la Ville, Smith Street, St Peter Port

shopping streets, narrow *venelles* between blocks of old buildings, and precipitous flights of steps. It is also a modern banking centre with large office blocks, in the main sympathetically designed to blend with the older buildings.

The medieval town was clustered round the TOWN CHURCH (5/2B). Until the 19th century jettied houses and narrow lanes jostled right up to the walls of the church; many were cleared after an outbreak of cholera and more to make way for the markets. A few jettied houses remain in Church Square, High Street and Berthelot Street (5/2B), their overhanging upper storeys supported on granite corbels. The boundaries of the medieval town are still marked by *Barrières de la*

Overleaf: St Peter Port, viewed from Castle Cornet

The Constable's Office, St Peter Port

Ville. The present *Barrières* are carved stones dating from 1700, and bearing the names of the parish constables of the time, Nicolas and James Carey. One stands in Smith Street (5/2B) by the entrance to the main Post Office. Others are in Cornet Street, Fountain Street and the Pollet (5/2B), and there is one just outside the north-east corner of the Town Church, wedged between a pillar box, a telephone box and an advertisement stand. The *Barrières* mark the position of the gates in a wall which Edward III ordered to be built round the town in 1350. Very little of this survives but the *Barrières* retained their significance because the laws of inheritance differed between town and country. *Préciput*, whereby an eldest son could keep an estate intact, did not apply in the old town. *Préciput* was not abolished in the country parishes until 1954.

One of the delights of St Peter Port is its roofscape of steeply pitched roofs, mainly of red pantiles. The town owes the use of these to a law forbidding the use of thatch within the *Barrières de la Ville*, passed in 1683 after a disastrous fire.

Until well into the 18th century Guernsey houses, whether in town or country, were built in the vernacular style we now associate with the farmhouse. Solidly built in granite, they were simple rectangular structures with plain gables and small windows in the front and back walls. The more prosperous houses had a half-round *tourelle* containing the staircase, projecting from the back wall, the back door beside it. Houses of this type are still plentiful in Back Street, Contrée Mansell, Tower Hill, Cliff Street and the older parts of the town (5/2B), though in many cases the façades have been updated at some stage by enlarging the windows.

In the second half of the 18th century money flowed into the island from maritime trade, and particularly from privateering. This wealth is reflected in the Georgian town houses the leading families built themselves on the outskirts of the medieval town. Moore's Hotel in the Pollet, once the town house of the Saumarez family, is a substantial six-bay house of three storeys plus dormers, with a severely formal façade of grey granite, dating from about 1760. The Constables' Office (the parish administrative centre) in Lefebvre Street (5/2B) was the town house of the Le Marchant family, dating from 1787. It is a

The Town Church and High Street, St Peter Port

Post Office, Smith Street, St Peter Port

three-storey house of dressed grey granite with segmental headed windows and a Doric porch with Venetian windows above it. The archway between High Street and Lefebvre Street was the carriage arch at the entrance to the Le Marchant house. Near the archway, at the junction of High Street, Smith Street and the Pollet, is the Guernsey branch of Boots. Above its familiar fascia is the dressed grey granite façade of a pair of semi-detached Georgian houses, each of four storeys and a dormer, dating from about 1780. One was the childhood home of General Sir Isaac Brock, who died in 1812 in an engagement at Queenston Heights, near Niagara Falls, where there is a tall monument in his honour.

One of the glories of St Peter Port is its Regency architecture, notably in NEW TOWN (5/2B). The end of the Napoleonic Wars brought an influx of new residents and this, together with booming maritime trade, created such a demand for housing that development spread up the slopes around the town and on to the plateau above, fanning out into what was then the countryside. The Guernsey vernacular style was no longer considered accept-able and for inspiration the builders looked to England. Fortunately, this period of prosperity coincided with one of the most lastingly satisfying styles of English architecture. The focal point of the Regency town is ST JAMES-THE-LESS CHURCH, now a concert hall.

Up the hill and facing St James is Elizabeth College (5/2B), a boys' public school founded by the first Queen Elizabeth. The original Eliza-bethan school was in the Rue des Frères, somewhere near the science laboratories. In 1760 it was replaced by a schoolroom now known as the Ozanne Building in College Street. The remains of the entrance arch can be seen built into a wall opposite the top of Anne's Place. The present main building, by John Wilson, dates from 1826. Despite the battlements, Tudor hoods over windows and doors, and Gothic glazing, the building is Georgian in its symmetry and pro-portions. The porter's lodge by the road is in the same style. The central arch, now filled in, was the original entrance to the courtyard.

Castle Carey, a grandiose private house which overlooks the town from the north, and the

Grange Lodge Hotel were designed by Wilson in the same style. They, the College and St James are covered by an ochre-coloured stucco much beloved of Wilson. Known as Roman cement, much of it was made at Les Vardes windmill.

The Grange (5/1B), the main approach to the town from the west, was transformed from a country lane into a gracious residential street by a series of substantial villas standing well back from the road. A few are still private dwellings though most have been converted into flats; others have become merchant banks – a tendency the authorities try to discourage in residential areas.

Opposite Elizabeth College and facing up the Grange is Bonamy House, one of the finest Neoclassical buildings in the island. The bowed central bay, with Ionic pilasters, is flanked by three-light windows and the curved front door leads into a circular hall with niches for statuary. Like a number of other private houses of the period, Bonamy House was almost certainly designed by Wilson.

Bonamy House stands at the corner of the New Town. Most of the early 19th-century schemes, however, were not intensively planned like this Regency development but took the form of what we would now term ribbon development along the approach roads to the town. Besides the Grange, Regency villas are to be seen in Candie Road, Doyle Road and Queen's Road (5/1B), with terraces in many other roads. Victoria Road, which follows a valley from Trinity Square up to the top of the Grange, is of particular interest. The modest terraced houses that line the upper part of the road, though basically of the same design as their neighbours, are transformed by their detailing. Some have Classical doorcases and Georgian glazing; others have Gothic doorcases, pointed glazing and elaborate icicles hanging from the eaves.

Hauteville (5/2B), the steep street leading out of town to the south, contains some older houses but during the early 19th century the gaps were filled by substantial villas which command a splendid view over the harbour and across the sea to the smaller islands, with the French coast beyond. This was one reason why Victor Hugo chose HAUTEVILLE HOUSE as his home in exile.

Not all the Regency building was on the outskirts of the town; the COMMERCIAL ARCADE and the MARKETS were redevelopment schemes right at the centre (5/2B). Beyond the Markets is Fountain Street, designed by Wilson as part of the same development as the States Arcades. The terrace on the south side is extremely fine, the

shopfronts at ground level unified (except in one case, where the façade has been massacred) by a series of fluted Doric columns. Barclay's Bank at the eastern end of the terrace curves gracefully round the corner into Cornet Street.

By no means all Guernsey's Regency-style buildings went up during that period. Houses of the same style and proportions continued to be built until well into Victoria's reign. Gradually, however, Victorian exuberance gained the upper hand, particularly in public buildings such as the Markets, where stonework of contrasting colours and texture is embellished by scrolls and ornamental cornices, taking full advantage of the quarrying industry which was by then flourishing in the north of the island. Most exuberant of all is Victoria Tower (5/2B), which commemorates the Queen's first visit to Guernsey in 1846. This splendid folly stands between the Town Arsenal (now the fire station) and the car park where once stood the Odeon Cinema, and forms part of St Peter Port's unforgettable skyline. The pink granite tower tapers to a crenallated superstructure with smaller towers at the corners and an octagonal lantern.

In the second half of the 19th century houses continued to be built of stone, but with Victorian details such as gabled attic windows and ornamental bargeboards. Hundreds of such houses were built along new streets which were cut across the fields between the main roads radiating from the town.

The new residential suburbs required new churches. St John's (5/2A), dating from 1836 and serving the north of the town, is a simple building of grey granite, with a square tower with pinnacles. St Barnabas (Sir Arthur Blomfield, 1874) stands at the summit of Tower Hill, overlooking the Bordage. Though now unused and deteriorating, the steep, red-tiled roofs and pyramidal granite spire still form an important part of the skyline. Holy Trinity Church, Trinity Square (originally a Nonconformist chapel of 1789), was reconstructed as an Anglican church. It is a handsome building with Dutch gables.

St Stephen's, Les Gravées (5/1B), was built in 1862 to serve the western part of the town. It is of red Cobo granite, with courses of grey stone. The architect, G. F. Bodley, was an important figure in the English Gothic revival, and the church is designed on Tractarian lines. It is in the Early English style, with narrow lancet windows below and round clerestory lights above. The stained

Castle Cornet and the Victoria Marina (see p. 152)

glass at the east and west ends is by William Morris; the figures in the main east window must surely be by Edward Burne-Jones.

St Joseph's Roman Catholic church (5/1B) of 1846 was designed by A. W. N. Pugin, one of the best-known architects of the Gothic revival. It is a fine Gothic building of grey granite, with much softer sandstone quoins. The copper-clad spire, 150 ft from the ground, was added in 1885.

Examples of buildings of this century are the States Office (1911), a rather austere but modestly proportioned building in grey granite on the Esplanade which once housed all the States departments (today they are scattered in large office blocks all over the town), and the neo-Georgian police station (1955) in St James Street (5/2B). Perhaps the most outstanding modern building is the church of Notre Dame du Rosaire (rebuilt 1968, A. Seguin), which serves the French Roman Catholic community. The roof of the original church, damaged during the Second World War, was in the form of an upturned boat, and the rebuilt church takes up the nautical theme. There is a superb timber-lined ogee-shaped roof, and soaring behind the altar is a mast with halyards and flags. The triptych behind the altar, the statuary and windows are in the modern idiom and of extremely high quality. The elegant bell tower was added in 1980. Notre Dame is in Burnt Lane, and can be reached by flights of steps from Vauvert and Mill Street. Burnt Lane (5/2B) is one of the delightful alleys which climb the slopes above Vauvert, Fountain Street, St Julian's Avenue and many other parts of the town.

St Peter Port Church *see* Town Church

St Peter Port Harbour (5/3B) This extensive harbour, which we owe mainly to the foresight of the Victorians, handles all Guernsey's maritime traffic with the exception of bulk cargoes. These are unloaded at ST SAMPSON'S HARBOUR.

On Christmas Day 1982 a diver noticed the timbers of a ship protruding from the mud between the pierheads. The ship turned out to be of Roman age, suggesting that even in the 2nd century mariners sought refuge here, protected from the west and north-west by Guernsey and from the south by the islet where CASTLE CORNET now stands. The wreck has now been excavated, and the timbers are being conserved before being put on display.

The medieval harbour was simply a beach, with a single jetty where the Albert Pier now stands. In 1750 a second jetty was built on the site of the Victoria (Crown) Pier, enclosing the basin which is now the Victoria Marina. The tall, gabled houses and cellars that still face the harbour stood on the beach, and at high water the sea washed up the alleys between them. By the beginning of the 19th century a quay had been built along the front, with an arch over Cow Lane through which horses and carts could pass between the harbour bed and the town. Cow Lane is the alley between Albion House and Le Lièvre's shop. The name recalls that in the days before refrigeration, meat was imported on the hoof, unloaded on to the harbour bed and driven up Cow Lane to the town.

By the mid-19th century the harbour had become wholly inadequate and in 1853, after prolonged deliberation by the States, work began on the great outer harbour. A new south pier was built out towards Castle Cornet; the broad emplacement where boats are laid up in winter and cars parked in summer was intended for ship-building yards which had been displaced at the landward end of the pier. The model yacht pond was built in 1887 to commemorate Victoria's jubilee; in the First World War it was used by the French for parking seaplanes and in the Second by the Germans for parking their vehicles. Today there are those who would like to use it for parking cars. The attractive battlemented lighthouse at the end of the Castle Breakwater was designed by the local artist Peter Le Lièvre.

Much of the dressed granite for the harbour came from Crevichon, an islet off JETHOU. The infilling material was excavated from the cliffs to the south of the town, where a promenade was constructed past La Valette to Cow Point. Two tunnels were dug. The first, by the bathing places, has since collapsed so that today the road passes through a cutting. The second is now occupied by the Aquarium; from the end there was a view over Soldier's Bay.

The new north, or St Julian's, pier was eventually extended as far as the White Rock to provide a berth for the steam packets, which could at last unload their passengers at all states of the tide without transferring them to boats. The 'New Jetty', where today the car ferries berth, was constructed of concrete piling in 1926.

The Victorian harbour, enclosing some 80 acres of water, was adequate for Guernsey's needs for over a century. It is only within the last decade that it has been outgrown, largely because of an enormous increase in the number of local and visiting yachts. Already there are two marinas within the harbour and a private one in the north of the island. Now work is well advanced on a fourth, immediately to the north of St Julian's Pier.

St Pierre-du-Bois Church (4/2C) St Peter's Church stands near the head of La Vallée, one of the valleys leading down from the southern plateau to ROCQUAINE BAY.

In plan the church is unlike any other in Guernsey, having a central nave and chancel, with two side aisles flanking the nave. To the west of the nave is a square, battlemented tower, with a porch on its northern side. The slope of the site is such that in spite of past attempts to level the floor, the east end is still 4 ft 8 in higher than the west. Because of this the octagonal granite pillars between the aisles increase in height from east to west.

The church was in existence in 1030, when Duke Robert of Normandy (father of William the Conqueror) placed it under the patronage of the abbey of Mont St Michel. ST SAVIOUR'S CHURCH was under the same patronage, and it is not surprising that the two have several features in common. Each has a tower at the west end, well built of dressed stone with moulded windows and one or more diagonal corner buttresses. The tower, the rather flat arcading and the Flamboyant tracery in some of the windows suggest that much of the present church dates from the late Middle Ages. An unusual feature for the Channel Islands is that the roof is not vaulted, but is of timber. This points to a date later than the 13th century, the period when the devastating French raids that followed the separation from Normandy in 1204 rendered a fireproof roof essential.

Several pre-Reformation features have survived. In the south wall of the chancel is a piscina, and built into the tracery of one of the windows of the north aisle is the plinth for a statue. Secured to the wall in the chamber beneath the tower is a great stone slab which was the altar; traces of the five consecration crosses can still be made out. At the Reformation it was used as a tombstone; the depression cut for a monumental brass can easily be seen.

St Pierre-du-Bois Parish (4/2C) The parish of St Peter in the Wood extends across the south-west corner of Guernsey, from the south coast cliffs to ROCQUAINE BAY and L'ERÉE. It is bound up with the TORTEVAL PARISH, for a detached portion of St Peter's divides the former into two halves. It is

La Longue Rocque des Paysans (see p. 154)

a rural parish of windswept upland fields, steep-sided valleys and low-lying coastal meadows.

The detached part of St Peter's includes a rugged section of cliffs around Mont Hérault, which is reached by a twisting lane from Pleinmont Road. The lane leads to Mont Hérault Watch House, built on the brink of the cliff in Napoleonic times, in the form of a traditional Guernsey house. The main part of the parish meets the south coast between Havre de Bon Repos, a rocky cove encompassed by precipitous cliffs, and the Prévôte Watch Tower. The lane to the Prévôte runs along the shoulder of an attractive hanging valley, part of which is National Trust property. The lane ends in a car park at the foot of a vast concrete tower erected by the Germans on the site of another Napoleonic watch house: in both wars Havre de Bon Repos was evidently regarded as a possible landing place, despite the surrounding cliffs.

The parish reaches its highest point near Pleinmont Road and then slopes away to the north, dissected by several small and very beautiful valleys carrying streams to Rocquaine Bay. At the head of one of these valleys is ST PIERRE-DU-BOIS CHURCH. The settlement clustered round the church is one of the rare examples in Guernsey of a village in the English sense. On level ground above the sloping churchyard is a village green with a war memorial. Across the road is the douzaine room (the office of the parish officials) and not far away is the old parish school, now converted into flats. The area is known as Les Buttes, for here were the medieval archery butts.

Running the length of the parish, from the AIRPORT to L'ERÉE, is the military road built in 1810 by General Doyle, in order to move his troops rapidly to the west coast in the event of a French landing. The main carriageway was to be 14 ft in width and a footpath 4 ft wide was constructed along the whole length of the road, which was partially financed by selling the reclaimed land of the Braye du Valle. The section known as Les Paysans Road, from Les Islets Arsenal to Les Adams, is particularly attractive, with views over open fields to the west coast. Standing in the middle of a field to the west of the road, just past a milestone which bears no number but is in fact the sixth from town, is La Longue Rocque des Paysans. This rugged column of grey granite stands 11½ ft above the ground, and is the largest prehistoric menhir still standing in the Channel Islands. At the bottom of the hill, opposite Les Adams Chapel, is the seventh milestone from the TOWN CHURCH, and the senior milestone of Guernsey.

The high land of St Peter's parish ends rather abruptly in an escarpment running parallel to Rocquaine Bay, but some distance inland. This is a stranded sea cliff, formed at the end of the Tertiary era, before the Ice Age, when the sea level was 100 ft higher than it is today. Although much obscured by erosion in the million years that have elapsed since its formation, the stranded cliff can be traced from PLEINMONT to Mont Saint and then by KING'S MILLS and the Castel Hill to town. The low-lying land between the cliff and the sea tends to be marshy, as names like Les Marais and La Claire Mare indicate, and much of it is below sea level at high tide. This has not prevented a proliferation of bungalows and greenhouses along the coastal strip; nevertheless there remain in St Peter's a number of unspoiled low-lying meadows, still managed in the traditional way. In the early summer they are too wet for grazing and the grass is allowed to grow for hay. When the hay has been taken there remains enough moisture in the soil for the meadows to be used for grazing, at a time when the grass in the drier upland fields is no longer growing.

In May and June the low-lying meadows are extremely rich in wild flowers: ragged robin, cuckoo flower, bugle, yellow flag and wild orchids. Particularly striking is the Jersey orchid, whose spike of loosely arranged claret-coloured flowers may stand 2 ft or more high. It is abundant in certain meadows in Jersey and Guernsey, but is found nowhere else in the British isles. Growing with the Jersey orchid are heath, spotted and southern marsh orchids. Since drainage and building are reducing the area of marshland every year, the local natural history and historical society, La Société Guernesiaise, has acquired a number of meadows in St Peter's in order to preserve a rapidly diminishing habitat. They are not open to the public as they are let to a farmer, on condition that they are not ploughed and the hay is allowed to stand until the orchids have flowered.

The west coast of St Peter's Parish is described under ROCQUAINE BAY, L'ERÉE and LIHOU ISLAND.

St Sampson's Church (4/6A) Christianity, according to tradition, was brought to Guernsey by St Sampson, who built a chapel on the beach at the spot where he first set foot on the island. The chapel became St Sampson's Church, which is thus traditionally the oldest church in the island. St Sampson, a Welsh missionary, was one of the founders of the Breton church in the first half of the 6th century. He became Bishop of Dol in about 552, and may well have included the Channel Islands in his diocese. Although there is no concrete evidence for his presence in Guernsey, the fact remains that St Sampson's Church has been dedicated to him since the earliest records in the 11th century. This probably indicates that the dedication is at least pre-Norman: they would have been unlikely to pick a Celtic saint. Certainly the church was hard by the shore and until well into the 19th century the sea at high tide came up to the churchyard wall. The land now lying between the church and ST SAMPSON'S HARBOUR was reclaimed from the sea when the south quay of the harbour was built.

St Sampson's differs in several respects from any other Channel Island church, and it certainly appears to be extremely ancient. There is no worked stone in the main structure of the church, and every arch, column and buttress differs from its neighbour. The squat, saddleback tower is undoubtedly the oldest church steeple in Guernsey, and may indicate what the other steeples looked like before the present spires were added. Its nearest parallel is St Brelade, Jersey, which was also built on the beach. The church still has nearly all its original small windows.

There is a central nave and chancel, the chancel being flanked by two side aisles. The west gable of the nave is stepped in the Scottish manner, again unlike other island churches. The oldest part appears to be the chancel, whose external buttresses indicate that it was once free-standing.

Then the north aisle was added, followed by the tower. Like most of the medieval churches of the Channel Islands, the older parts of the church are vaulted in stone, the vaulting coming to a point at the top in the manner of a Gothic arch. Similar vaulted roofs are found in Ireland, and it has been suggested that the idea may have been brought to the islands by Celtic missionaries such as St Sampson. On the other hand it has also been suggested that the vaulting dates from the 13th century and was built to replace the original roofs of timber and thatch, which were found to be too vulnerable in the raids that followed the separation from Normandy in 1204.

The south aisle was built later in the Middle Ages, possibly in the 14th century, and has a wooden roof. The projecting vestry was built after the Reformation, as a meeting room for the Consistory, the Calvinist parish council which regulated with the utmost severity the lives of the parishioners.

Over the priest's stall in the sanctuary is a tablet recording the death of Thomas Falla, who fell at Seringapatam in South India in 1799 when a cannon ball weighing 26 lb lodged in his thigh. So great was the inflammation that it was not until after his death that the surgeon discovered it.

St Sampson's Harbour (4/6A) St Sampson's Harbour, which today handles all Guernsey's imports of oil and other bulk cargoes, owes its existence to a great export industry in stone which sprang up in the 19th century. Until the beginning of that century it was a tidal creek forming the entrance to the BRAYE DU VALLE, with sandy beaches to the north and south. ST SAMPSON'S CHURCH stood on the verge of the southern beach. The creek had a muddy bottom on which ships were beached to be loaded and unloaded at low water.

When work began on the draining of the Braye du Valle in 1806 a barrier was built across the eastern end of the Braye, at the former crossing place still known as St Sampson's Bridge. Today this is a thriving shopping centre, as well as forming the western end of St Sampson's Harbour. Before 1806 the Braye must have provided a continuous supply of mud to the harbour, for as soon as the Bridge was filled in the mud was scoured away by the sea and boulders began to appear in the harbour bed. These proved such a hazard that shipowners refused to allow their vessels to enter the harbour until a pier had been

St Sampson's Harbour

built. This first pier is the one that projects into the harbour from the north side. It was built in 1820, largely for the export of oysters, but with the expansion of quarrying it was soon inadequate and in 1841 the South Quay was built straight across the sandy bay on which the church stood, the area between the church and the quay being filled with ships' ballast and quarry rubble. Later in the century the North Quay was built across the northern bay and again ships' ballast was used to reclaim the land behind it. Disposal of the ballast – mostly chalk and clay – which the stone ships had to carry on their return journey was a problem, and when the areas behind the quays had been filled further land was reclaimed. Much of the flat land now used for industrial purposes to the north and south of St Sampson's Harbour was reclaimed from the sea in this way.

St Sampson's Harbour, after a period of decline, is again in full use for since 1964 it has handled practically all Guernsey's bulk cargoes such as oil, liquid gas, timber and coal. There is also a shipyard with a slipway which can handle vessels up to 230 ft in length.

St Sampson's Parish (4/5A) St Sampson's is often regarded as the 'industrial north' of Guernsey, and certainly parts of the parish are something of an industrial wasteland, especially the areas to the south and west of ST SAMPSON'S HARBOUR. Besides modern industry the evidence of the once flourishing quarrying industry is everywhere. Some abandoned quarries have been filled with refuse and put to other uses. Some are used for water storage, and many smaller quarries have simply been fenced off and left. The parish also has more than its share of glasshouses, particularly on the reclaimed land of the BRAYE DU VALLE, much of which lies within its area.

Amid all the development there are still oases of green agricultural land, which give a rural character to much of the parish. The St Sampson's countryside has a strong northern character of its own, with bracken-covered hillocks or *hougues*, and field boundaries composed of great grey boulders. If a parish can be said to have a colour St Sampson's is grey, for the buildings, roadside walls, kerbs and field hedges are all composed of the local grey stone.

A busy main road sweeps around the Belle Grève Bay and once carried a tramline between St Sampson's bridge and ST PETER PORT. The town terminus was opposite the Picquet House. Tram sheds at Hougue à la Perre are still in use for buses; the tramlines remain embedded in the concrete floor.

At Richmond Corner the road to St Sampson's Bridge, Grandes Maisons Road, strikes inland while Bulwer Avenue continues along the coast, passing the depot where tomatoes are graded, packed and palleted for export. Bulwer Avenue continues to the south side of St Sampson's Harbour, passing builders' yards, scrapyards and storage tanks for oil and liquid gas. Behind the oil tanks lies an area of land which has recently been reclaimed from the sea and is at present settling before being allocated for various industrial uses. Much of the site is earmarked for boatbuilding, and a slipway is planned. Between Bulwer Avenue and the parish church is the huge Longue Hougue Quarry. This supplied gabbro, the hardest of all Guernsey's rocks, in the days when the export of stone was an important industry; today it stores water. Overlooking Richmond Corner is the green hillside of Delancey Park, run by the parish as a public recreation area, and beside it is a school.

Midway around the sweep of Belle Grève Bay is the Halfway. From here the Vale Road strikes inland to the St Clair Hill traffic lights, where you can either turn left to Oatlands and L'Islet, or follow La Route Militaire across the Braye de Valle into the VALE PARISH. All the military roads have straight stretches, but where it crosses the reclaimed land of the Braye, La Route Militaire is dead straight for three-quarters of a mile.

Oatlands is an old property now converted into a craft centre where visitors can buy a range of locally made products, many of which can be seen in the course of creation. Standing in a field behind the buildings are the kilns where clay plant pots were fired in the days when tomatoes were commercially grown in these. L'Islet, a little further to the north, was once a remote salt marsh on the shore of the Braye du Valle. Today it is a well-populated settlement with shops, garage and even a supermarket.

A small, detached portion of St Sampson's parish lies on the west coast and extends from Baie des Pequeries to Port Grat. Between these two bays the coast road passes beside Pulias Pond, a small brackish *mare* separated from the sea by a bank covered in blanketing mesembryanthemum. Although the pond is of no great scenic value, for it often contains an assortment of oil cans and bicycle frames, it is extremely attractive to wading birds and is often visited by ringed plover, turnstone, sandpiper, redshank and dunlin. This detached part of the parish also contains Les Vardes quarry, which now supplies virtually all the aggregate for the island's roads and buildings.

St Saviour's Church (4/3C) The church of St Saviour stands on the brink of a steep slope that falls away to the valley known as Sous l'Eglise, which itself falls away to Le Beauvallet, one of the three tributary valleys of ST SAVIOUR'S RESERVOIR. On the plateau on the other side of the church is the district known as Les Buttes, where archery practice took place in the Middle Ages. Every parish had its butts, usually on level ground near the church, and in most cases the place names La Butte or Les Buttes have survived to the present day. At the entrance to the churchyard from Les Buttes is a standing stone with a large, deeply incised cross on the front and a smaller cross on the back. It is thought that this may be a prehistoric menhir, 'Christianized' when the site became a place of Christian worship.

There was certainly a church on the site before the Conquest, for it figures in a document of about 1030, when Duke Robert of Normandy placed it under the patronage of the abbey of Mont St Michel. The present building, however, dates mainly from the 14th and 15th centuries, though much of it was rebuilt in the 17th century after being struck by lightning.

St Saviour's is the largest of Guernsey's country churches, and the one that most resembles the TOWN CHURCH in the quality of its masonry, much of which is in the French Flamboyant style. It consists of a pair of parallel naves and chancels, each with a vaulted roof. In the north-west corner of the church is a square, battlemented tower, surmounted by an octagonal lead-covered spire. A chapel projects from the south of the church in the manner of a transept. To the north-east of the church is an extension, built in the early 18th century to house the parish artillery, and now used as a vestry.

Between the two naves and chancels is an arcade of seven arches which gives a clue to the stages in which the church was built, for the pillars are of three patterns. The two at the western end are low, octagonal columns with capitals, in much the same style as the tower. The remaining four pillars have no capitals, the arches springing directly from the shafts of the pillars; of these, the two in the centre of the church have octagonal shafts, while the pair at the east end are round. It has been suggested that the original, central part of the church was extended eastward

when the two round pillars were inserted, and then at a later date the west end and tower were built; these are of an imported stone, presumably from France.

The tower, of dressed stone, displays the most sophisticated masonry in the church. The vaulting under the bell loft is groined, with a circular hole in the centre. The buttresses are more elaborate than those of the rest of the building, having string courses and carved finials. The corner buttress is set diagonally, a sign in the Channel Islands of the late Middle Ages.

During Evensong on Sunday, 30 January 1658 the tower was struck by lightning and much of the western part of the church destroyed. The spire and upper part of the tower had to be rebuilt, together with the western gable and part of the side walls of the nave. During the rebuilding the north-west doorway was inserted; it is a typical Guernsey domestic arch of the 17th century.

During the Occupation the Germans used the tower as an observation post, cutting peepholes through the lead covering of the spire.

From the bend in the road at the bottom of Sous l'Eglise, an attractive stone-paved footpath climbs the hillside towards the church. It ends in a flight of steps up to the churchyard. Beside the steps is a stone seat. This is the feudal court of Fief Jean Gaillard; the de Gaillards were a Gascon family who were influential in the Channel Islands in the 14th century. Here feudal dues would be collected and minor offences dealt with by the Seigneur's officials.

From Sous l'Eglise the Germans dug a labyrinth of tunnels under the churchyard. The unsightly spoil from the tunnels still lies in the floor of the valley and only in the last few years has it become partially hidden by trees.

St Saviour's Parish (4/3C) The parish of St Saviour forms a long rectangle extending from the AIRPORT to the west coast. The inland portion of the parish, between the airport and the church, is fertile plateau land with scattered farms. In the neighbourhood of Le Gron are several tourist attractions: the Strawberry Farm, Guernsey Woodcarvers, a goldsmith and silversmith, and the West Riding and Trekking Centre. From the plateau three valleys converge to form the three arms of ST SAVIOUR'S RESERVOIR. The parish church stands on an escarpment overlooking the middle one of these valleys. Below the reservoir is the 'village' of PERELLE. The low-lying land between here and the coast has been largely developed for glasshouses and housing.

The coastline of St Saviour's is a rocky one extending from LE CATIOROC and Perelle Bay to the headland of Fort Le Crocq at the western end of VAZON BAY. At low tide many acres of rock are exposed, and from Le Catioroc Point it is possible to walk to the tiny islet of Chapelle Dom Hue, where the foundations of a chapel, or possibly a hermit's cell, may still be seen.

St Saviour's Reservoir (4/3B) Two of Guernsey's main industries, tourism and horticulture, consume a great deal of water in the summer, when rainfall is at its lowest. As much water as possible is therefore collected and stored in the winter: two-thirds of it in disused quarries in the north of the island, and the remaining third in St Saviour's Reservoir.

The concrete dam just above Mont Saint holds back a lake with three tongues, extending up three valleys and collecting water from a large catchment area to the west and north of the AIRPORT. Below the dam is the original pumping station which abstracted water from the Rue à l'Or stream before the dam was built. Beside it and disappearing under the dam are the remains of the old road from PERELLE to ST SAVIOUR'S CHURCH. When the water level is low the road can be seen climbing out of the reservoir in the direction of the church. The present modern road skirts the eastern tongue of the reservoir and then rejoins the old road. From here (as Le Neuf Chemin, the 'new road', although it appears on a map of 1787) it runs straight up the hill towards

St Saviour's Reservoir

the church, passing the old parish school, now Le Mont Variouf School. Just above the school is a minor crossroad; 100 yd up the lane to the left is the feudal court of Fief des Gohiers. The rude stones that served as seats for the court officials are in the broad grass verge, among some hydrangeas. The lane leading west from the school is La Rue du Moulin. At the point where it passes the tip of the middle arm of the reservoir are the remains of a watermill, Le Moulin de Beauvallet. From here an unmetalled footpath or 'green lane' climbs through an unspoiled valley towards the church. The entrance to the path is marked 'No horse riding'.

Trees have been planted round the reservoir and the view across the water from the dam is most attractive. There is a car park at each end of the dam and from the western end is a public walk along the shore of the reservoir and back through the pine trees.

Saints Bay (4/5C) and **Icart Point** (4/4C) The road to Saints Bay leaves La Grande Rue in ST MARTIN'S PARISH, opposite the lane that allows traffic up from LA BELLIEUSE. It is a narrow road with much ribbon development, and negotiating it usually involves a good deal of stopping and squeezing into driveways. After half a mile the road passes a group of old houses, orientated in the typical Guernsey manner with their gables facing the road. A little further again and the road forks; one can either continue down a steep hill to Saints Bay, or turn right to Icart Point.

The lane to Saints follows a stream down the floor of a steep-sided valley, and ends in a slipway

on the beach. There is no parking or turning space for cars, and it is wise to leave them at the top of the lane. The bay is one of the few inlets on the south coast sufficiently sheltered for boats to be left at moorings. A tiny fishermen's harbour on the west side of Saints Bay is reached by a track which leaves the lane a little way above the bay and meanders along the cliffside to the harbour and a Napoleonic gun battery. On the way it passes a 'Martello' tower, No. 14 of a series of 15 built in the 1780s to a design peculiar to Guernsey.

The Icart road makes its way along a wind-swept plateau on the summit of the Icart peninsula. Before long a superb view opens to the left, across Moulin Huet Bay to the Pea Stacks. After passing Saints Bay Hotel the road turns to the right, crosses the tip of the peninsula and ends in a car park on the clifftop. The headland in the distance is La Moye Point and slightly to its right is PETIT BÔT BAY.

The Icart car park, a large one with loos and a tea room, is one of the few points from which the public have easy access to the cliffs, and the path for 50 yd in either direction tends to be rather congested. Beyond this distance humanity thins out and the cliffs assume their usual remote beauty. The path to the north-west follows the top of a steep section of cliff which plunges 300 ft to the sea. Far below are two small bays, La Bette and Le Jaonnet. The second bay, Le Jaonnet, can be reached by scrambling down a steep track that leaves the cliff path a little over a quarter of a mile from the car park. It has a good sandy beach at low tide, and because of the difficult access it tends to be deserted.

The cliffs support a variety of vegetation. Le Jaonnet means 'the furze brake', and indeed the slopes above the bay are covered in furze or gorse, which used to be used as fuel in the great bread oven every farmhouse possessed. Other parts are clothed with bell heather, with bracken and bluebells where enough soil has accumulated, and with blackthorn scrub in the more sheltered places. On exposed rocks beside the path grow English stonecrop, Portland spurge and autumn squill. On the inland side of the path a drystone wall, encrusted with orange and grey lichens, forms the boundary of the farmland beyond.

Turning in the other direction from the car park and walking to the south-east, it is a short distance to Icart Point. As you round the headland another spectacular view opens up, across Moulin Huet Bay to the JERBOURG peninsula.

The Icart headland has given its name to the rock, Icart gneiss, which forms the main part of the southern plateau of Guernsey and outcrops in the cliffs along much of the south coast. Of Precambrian age, it is one of the oldest rocks known in western Europe, being at least 2500 million years old. It is a rather flaky, reddish-brown rock which can be seen in old walls and houses throughout the parishes of St Martin and the FOREST.

Sark (8) The delightful island of Sark is unlike any other. The only motor vehicles are farm tractors, conveyance being by horse-drawn carriage, by bicycle, or on foot. The island is surrounded by cliffs of outstanding beauty and the interior, apart from a few substandard 20th-century buildings and a tangle of overhead wires, is unspoiled.

Sark lies at the heart of the Channel Islands, being 7½ miles east of Guernsey, 19 miles south of Alderney and 12 miles north-west of Jersey. The 9-mile boat journey from ST PETER PORT takes the visitor across the Little Russel to HERM and JETHOU, which are usually passed on the port side, then across the Great Russel, past Brecqhou and round Sark, usually by the north, to La Maseline Harbour (8/3B) on Sark's east coast. The island is 3 miles in length from north to south and 1½ miles across at its widest point. A narrow waist, La Coupée (8/2B), separates the main island, Great Sark, from the much smaller Little Sark.

Unlike the other Channel Islands, Sark has not been continuously occupied since ancient times and little is known of its history before it was permanently settled in Elizabeth I's reign. A monastery certainly existed in the wooded valley below La Seigneurie (8/2A), on the site of the property known as La Moinerie. It is said to have been founded in the year 565 by St Magloire, nephew of St Sampson, whose community of 62 monks undertook the education of children from the neighbouring French mainland. The monastery was sacked during the Viking raids of the 9th century. The island must have had a settled population in the early Middle Ages, for it figures in the archives of the diocese of Coutances, but by the early 16th century it was inhabited only by bands of pirates. In 1549 it was occupied by the French, who built three small forts, traces of which are still to be seen: Le Grand Fort covered the landing place at L'Eperquerie in the north (8/2A); another on the Hog's Back covered the bays of Dixcart and Derrible (8/3B) and the third, at Vermandaie (8/2B) in Little Sark, covered La Coupée. The French were evicted after four years

A farm cottage, Little Sark

Sark prison, built 1856 (see p. 165)

but the vacuum left by an uninhabited island so close to France was a cause of concern both to the English government and to the other islands. The solution was proposed by Helier de Carteret, Seigneur of St Ouen in Jersey, who offered to settle the island and guarantee its defence in return for the fief of Sark. In 1565 he received Letters Patent from Queen Elizabeth, granting him the fief on condition that Sark was permanently settled by at least 40 men capable of bearing arms. Accordingly he divided the island into 40 *tenements* or holdings, each with a proportion of fertile plateau and marginal cliff land. The largest holding, in the middle of Great Sark, he reserved for himself – the property is still known as Le Manoir. Other *tenements* were grouped to take advantage of the streams, and to command the landing places: La Moinerie, for instance, was one of a group commanding Le Port du Moulin (8/2A) and Le Petit Dixcart commanded Dixcart Bay (8/3B). Little Sark was divided into five *tenements* and the island of BRECQHOU formed a sixth.

The settlement patterns of Sark and Alderney make an interesting comparison. In ALDERNEY, which has been occupied continuously since ancient times, the farms are clustered together in St Anne and the cultivated land is not enclosed by hedges. In Sark the Elizabethan settlers, coming to an uninhabited island, brought with them the pattern of scattered farmsteads and enclosed fields they had been familiar with in Jersey.

When de Carteret died in 1581 he left a self-contained community of 40 tenants, each armed with a musket and each with a strong incentive to defend his island. The 40 *tenements* still exist, each tenant having a seat in the island assembly, Chief Pleas. Wherever you look in Sark the farmsteads, fields and hedgebanks built by the Elizabethan settlers are still to be seen.

Great Sark consists of a fertile plateau almost entirely surrounded by 300 ft cliffs except at the northern extremity, where the windswept Eperquerie Common (8/2A) descends nearly to sea level and breaks into a string of sea stacks.

Although Sark's coastal scenery is unsurpassed, access to the cliffs is often difficult as they become very overgrown in summer and there is no continuous path along them. If the visitor wishes to savour the coast as soon as he arrives, instead of climbing the full length of Harbour Hill he can follow the road for 100 yd and then take a path to the left. The path climbs the cliff above Creux Harbour (8/3B) and makes for the landing place at Les Lâches near by. Turning inland again he can take another path that runs out on to the spine of the Hog's Back, a bare-topped headland between Derrible and Dixcart Bays. At the tip of the headland is an old cannon, partially embedded in the ground. A level area near the cannon is the site of one of the forts built by the French during their occupation of 1549.

From Dixcart Bay there is the choice of climbing inland through the wooded Dixcart Valley (8/2B), or following a clifftop path to La Coupée past some of Sark's most spectacular coastal scenery. La Coupée (8/3B) is a narrow isthmus between two bays that have all but met in the middle. Across the summit, just wide enough for a horse and carriage, is the road to Little Sark (*see below*). To the east the cliff falls sheer to a forbidding, stony bay far below. To the west is the more inviting Grande Grève, a sandy bay that can be reached by a zigzag path from La Coupée.

The west coast is more difficult to see, as the only points of access are a few paths leading to the main vantage points. From Le Grand Beauregard a path leads through fields to the Pilcher

The Moulin and a tractor, Mill Lane, Sark

monument, a clifftop obelisk commemorating Jeremiah Pilcher who, with four companions, attempted to cross to Guernsey in a small boat one stormy night in 1868. His body was found near the Isle of Wight. Far below is Havre Gosselin (8/2B), a deep-water anchorage surrounded by towering cliffs. A track from the monument leads down to a landing place. Another path, this time from Le Petit Beauregard, leads to the Gouliot Headland overlooking the island of Brecqhou across the narrow Gouliot Passage (8/1B).

From the road just north of the Seigneurie (8/2A) a lane to the west follows a wooded valley to a pleasant bay, Port du Moulin, where once stood a watermill (perhaps the first mill in the Channel Islands) belonging to St Magloire's monastery. The dam of the millpond, L'Ecluse, gave its name to the old property, now holiday flats, beside the path a little way up from the coast. A path below L'Ecluse leads to a square window cut through the cliff face by an eccentric 19th-century Seigneur. The 'Window in the Rock' frames a magnificent view north along the coast with Les Autelets (the Altar Rocks) in the foreground.

L'Eperquerie Common, on the wild northern tip of Sark, has a network of footpaths among the heather and gorse. One on the eastern side leads down to what is perhaps Sark's original landing place. The name is derived from the poles (*perques*) which were used for drying fish. Another landing place, Banquette, is reached by a path from Le Grand Fort. Access to the next bay, La Grève de la Ville (8/3A), is by a path from La Ville Roussel, which zigzags down the cliff beside an overgrown stream.

Perched a little way down the cliff on the next headland, Pointe Robert, is a lighthouse which the boat from Guernsey passes just before it reaches La Maseline Harbour (8/3B). The concrete jetty at La Maseline, where the modern visitor makes his landfall, was begun in 1938 but, because of the German occupation, was not completed until 1947. Before this the delightful Creux Harbour, immediately to the south of La Maseline, was used. Le Creux ('The Hole') refers to the tunnel driven through the rock in 1588 to give access to the pier from Harbour Hill. The beautiful miniature harbour, its granite pier overshadowed by towering cliffs, dries at low spring tides. It was not until 1947 that Sark had a deep-water berth.

The half-mile haul from the harbour to the 'village' on the plateau is up Harbour Hill, a

La Coupée, looking towards Little Sark (see p. 160)

winding road following a wooded valley. If the traveller gets past the Bel Air Tavern he soon reaches a crossroad at La Hèche ('The Gate'). The road continues as the Avenue – once the dignified approach to Le Manoir but now the shopping centre. Apart from the *tenements* Sark is not noted for its architecture, and the Avenue has the air of a dusty shanty town. It is, however, entirely delightful. Cycles with capacious shopping baskets lean against the trees outside the shops and the atmosphere is friendly and unhurried.

A pair of parallel roads, one from each end of the Avenue, serves the north of Great Sark. The first, from La Hèche, leads eventually to a group of *tenements* established by de Carteret to guard the landing places at L'Eperquerie and Banquette. Two of the *tenements*, Le Fort (8/3A) and Le Grand Fort, take their name from one of the French fortifications, which Elizabethan settlers doubtless used as a source of building stone.

The second road, from near Le Manoir, passes first St Peter's Church (8/3B), a plain granite building with a square western tower. The church was built in 1820 to replace an outbuilding at Le Manoir which had been used for worship since the Elizabethan settlement. The chancel was added in 1880. The road continues northwards, passing the main gates of La Seigneurie on its way to L'Eperquerie Common.

The Seigneurie (8/2A) grounds and beautifully maintained walled garden are open to the public on certain days, and are well worth a visit. The property became the residence of the Seigneurs of Sark in 1730, when Susanne Le Pelley, widow of a Guernsey privateer owner, bought the fief. Almost the first act of the new Dame de Sercq must have been the erection of the romantic Gothic dovecot that is still to be seen behind the house: the possession of a *colombier* was the prerogative of the lord of the manor. The Georgian façade of the original part of the house dates from 1732, when the windows were enlarged using Jersey granite. A Victorian wing with Dutch gable and an ornate tower (for signalling to Guernsey) were added in 1854.

The land between the two parallel roads opposite the Seigneurie gates is known as Les Camps. The name suggests that here were the open fields of the medieval settlement, and indeed some of the Elizabethan hedges do seem to follow the layout of an earlier strip system.

Returning to the Avenue and following it to its western end we arrive at Le Manoir (8/3B), where the road curves round the end of a row of single-storey cottages. Here, in 1566, Helier de Carteret

Above: La Seigneurie (see p. 159)

established himself with his wife. Their first dwelling is said to have been the cottage nearest to the road. The building next to it served as the island church until St Peter's Church was built. Across the road from the cottages are the Greffe (island office), the school and the prison. Behind the cottages and facing south towards his old home in Jersey is the fine two-storey house which Helier and his wife subsequently built. In common with most of Sark's old houses it follows the Jersey pattern. The windows were enlarged and fitted with Georgian glazing in 1810. Opposite Le Manoir a footpath leads across fields to Stocks Hotel and the Dixcart Valley while the road, now Mill Lane, continues westward with a slight kink to avoid the mill at the highest point of the island. The sails are gone from the seigneurial windmill and today it is used as a tourist shop, but over the door are the arms of Helier de Carteret and the weathervane bears the date 1571.

The next road junction, La Vaurocque, offers the choice of continuing westward past the

Opposite: Great Sark. (Above) Tidal pool at the landing place at L'Eperquerie (see p. 159); (below) the Window in the Rock (see p. 163)

Beauregard duckpond to Havre Gosselin and the cliffs overlooking Brecqhou, turning right to follow a lane that eventually connects with the road leading north past the Seigneurie, or turning left towards La Coupée and Little Sark.

Little Sark, barely 1 mile in length and a ½ mile wide, is even more remote and peaceful than the main island. La Coupée is crossed by a concrete road built in 1945 by German prisoners-of-war, which then continues along the spine of the island, passing the ruined French fort of La Vermandaie (8/2B) on the right. The five *tenements* of Little Sark – La Sablonnerie, La Pipeterie, La Duvallerie, La Moserie, and La Donellerie – are grouped around a spring near the centre of the peninsula. In the middle of a field opposite La Sablonnerie (8/2C) are the remains of a windmill. After passing La Sablonnerie, now a hotel, the road turns left on its way to some barracks, built during the Napoleonic wars and now converted into a private house. From here a path descends to a landing place at Rouge Terrier.

The rough coastal land at the southern end of Little Sark contains evocative reminders of a 19th-century mining venture. Mineral veins containing silver, lead and copper run from Port Gorey (8/1C), an inlet in the south coast, to the

Pot, a cauldron-shaped cavity in the eastern cliffs. The richest silver lode, known as Sark's Hope, was extensively mined but never yielded economic quantities and after a series of disasters the mines were abandoned. Most of the shafts have been filled in but their position is still indicated by whitish spoil heaps. One shaft, near the road to the barracks, has been used as a rubbish tip. The desolate ruins of an engine house and several chimneys are reminders of the ill-fated venture.

Saumarez Park, Castel (4/4B) Although the fief or manor of Saumarez was granted in the 14th century to the de Saumarez family, it belonged for at least 300 years to the Le Marchants. It then reverted to the de Saumarez family by marriage.

The original part of the present house was built in 1721 by William Le Marchant: his arms, together with those of Elizabeth Knapton, his wife, appear on the main gates in the north-east corner of the park. In 1783 the property passed to James Saumarez, later Lord de Saumarez, the famous admiral of the Napoleonic wars, whose descendants extended the house and laid out the park. The façade, of beautifully wrought red granite with grey granite dressings, dates from 1850.

In 1938 the property was bought by the States of Guernsey. The house, now the Hostel of St John, is a home for elderly people; the park is open to the public. The trees planted by the de Saumarez family are now mature, and in more recent years the planting has been continued by the States. Full use is made of the idyllic setting for fêtes, agricultural shows and the Battle of Flowers. The stable block has been converted into a folk museum, run by the National Trust of Guernsey. It contains an extensive collection of agricultural implements, horse-drawn vehicles, furniture, costume and tableaux of cottage interiors, and is open from April to October.

The Saumarez property once extended to the Mare de Carteret and Grandes Rocques. The fourth Lord de Saumarez, a man of enormous energy who started to learn Spanish at the age of 80, created a scenic path from his house to the coast, including a footbridge over La Route de Carteret so that his children and guests could cross the road in safety. He also added the baronial touches to the house which is now the Grandes Rocques Hotel. The States have recently re-opened the path as the 'Heritage Walk'. To walk this from Saumarez Park, it is advisable to

Saumarez Park, Castel

leave cars in the car park at the northern end of the park. The original path began by crossing Home Farm. This is now run by the States as an artificial insemination centre, and is not open to the public. The path now begins a quarter of a mile down the Ruette de la Tour; the entrance is on the right, near a reservoir. The path winds between clumps of trees, with views over the west coast, and descends through a disused quarry to the Route de Carteret, which is crossed by the footbridge. The path now follows a canal – presumably also something to do with the fourth Lord de Saumarez – and skirts the Mare de Carteret School playing field to emerge on the Cobo Coast Road, beside a water pumping station.

Sausmarez Manor (4/5C) Sausmarez Manor, whose imposing manorial gates with heraldic beasts border Sausmarez Road, is the seat of the Seigneurs of the Fief de Sausmarez, a feudal holding covering much of ST MARTIN'S PARISH. Apart from a gap between 1557 and 1748, it has been in the possession of the de Sausmarez family since 1254. As would be expected, the manor contains features dating from several periods, but the beautiful Queen Anne façade, which faces the road across a croquet lawn, dates from 1714. Very few early 18th-century houses survive in Guernsey and this must be the finest example. The façade is of dressed grey granite with red granite quoins, of three storeys plus dormers, and the hipped roof is surmounted by a balcony and gazebo. The sash windows are of a very early type, with 24 panes and only one section opening.

The manor is open to the public on certain days in the summer, and is well worth a visit. The pictures are particularly interesting, and include a series of family portraits with the strong de Sausmarez features running firmly throughout.

The square building beside the gates is the manorial court of Fief de Sausmarez. Here the officials of the fief collected feudal dues and tried manor offences. The projecting upper storey was probably added in the 18th century.

Talbot Valley (4/4B) A picturesque valley running for a mile and a half from St Andrew's Brickfield to King's Mills. For most of its length the floor consists of meadows grazed by cattle. The steep sides have been terraced at some time in the past, but today many of the slopes are wooded. A road runs the length of the valley, a little way up from the bottom to avoid flooding.

Sausmarez Manor (see p. 167)

(see p. 167)

The Talbot Valley contains the remains of no fewer than six water mills. Near the head of the valley were two mills, Les Moulins de l'Echelle, one of which retains much of its machinery. These mills were supplied by a millpond by the lane running from ST ANDREW'S CHURCH to the head of the Talbot Valley. The lane is still called L'Ecluse ('The Dam'). A little further down the valley is another mill, Les Niaux, which has been restored and given a new wheel by its owner, who uses it to generate electricity.

Below Les Niaux the millstream has been diverted from the valley bottom; its course can be seen across the valley from the road, following a contour around a side valley. It then passes under Candie Road, where there is a roadside drinking place for horses and cattle, and thus to the mill-pond above Le Moulin de Haut (*see* King's Mills). At this point the road, now La Rue à l'Eau, crosses to the south side of the valley and runs beside the millstream to Le Moulin du Milieu, now a house, while the Talbot Valley proper continues through the property known as Le Groignet to the water pumping station, on the site

Torteval Church (4/2C) Torteval is the only one of Guernsey's ten parishes not to have retained its medieval church. The old parish church was allowed to fall into such a state of disrepair during the 18th century that it was demolished and replaced by the present building in 1816. The architect was the versatile John Wilson, designer of the ST JAMES-THE-LESS CHURCH. Torteval must have been one of his first commissions in Guernsey and is not his most distinguished building, although the round battlemented tower surmounted by a lofty, circular spire has a certain grandeur and is an important landmark in the south-west of the island. The view from the battlements is magnificent.

Like St James-the-Less, Torteval is a hall church: a rectangular box, with an apse at the east end. Unlike St James, there is no classical façade or stucco, the entire building being of severe grey granite. The side walls are supported by rounded external buttresses, made necessary by the lack of main tie beams in the construction of the fine timber roof.

The medieval church of Torteval was originally dedicated to Our Lady. The present dedication to St Philip seems to rest on the story of a shipwreck of Philip de Carteret mentioned in *La Dédicace des Eglises*, a 17th-century document now thought to be fictitious.

Torteval Parish (4/2C) The smallest of Guernsey's parishes, Torteval covers an area of only 760 acres and has a population of 881 souls. It is also the most thinly populated parish, with 1.7 persons per acre. Torteval is divided into two almost equal parts by wedges of the two parts of ST PIERRE-DU-BOIS PARISH which meet in the centre. The western half is the headland of PLEINMONT. The eastern part includes the parish church with an associated settlement at the head of one of the miniature valleys that descend to ROCQUAINE BAY. At the head of another valley, to the north-east of the church, is *Le Colombier*, Guernsey's only surviving manorial dovecot. It is a round tower, open to the sky, the inner wall honeycombed with hundreds of pigeon holes. It was in existence by 1330, and was restored in the 1950s. *Le Colombier* is on private property behind a farmhouse of that name, and is not open to the public, but it can be clearly seen from the surrounding lanes.

The eastern part of the parish has some rugged and beautiful coastal scenery centred around Les Tielles, where there is a car park poised above a particularly precipitous section of cliff. It is

of the last mill, Le Moulin de Bas, near King's Mills. Here the valley opens out into the GRANDE MARE.

The slopes to the north of the road in one section of the valley are owned by the National Trust of Guernsey and are open to the public. Cars may be left in a disused quarry beside the road. The Ron Short Walk, commemorating a member of the Trust who negotiated the purchase of many of its properties, begins a few yards to the east of this and climbs to the shoulder of the valley to take advantage of the views over this entirely unspoiled part of Guernsey.

reached by following a lane that leaves the Pleinmont Road a little to the east of TORTEVAL CHURCH. Further east again is Le Creux Mahié, a creek with the largest cave in the island, said to be some 200 ft long and extremely difficult to reach. Also at Le Creux Mahié is a sewage treatment plant. There are no main drains in the rural parts of Guernsey; houses have cesspits which have to be emptied by the yellow-painted tankers that are to be seen busily negotiating the lanes on their way to the nearest discharge point – Creux Mahié serves the south-west of the island.

Town Church (5/2B) The parish church of ST PETER PORT stands at the heart of the town, overlooking the quay. It is a handsome building, generally acknowledged to be the finest of the medieval churches of the Channel Islands. There has been a church on the site at least since 1048, when Duke William II of Normandy (soon to become William the Conqueror) gave the patronage of the church of *Sancti Petri de Portu* to the abbey of Marmoutier. The age of the present building can only be guessed at, though much of it appears to date from the 14th and 15th centuries. The nave may well be older than this, possibly even 12th century; the arches would have been pierced when the aisles were added at a later date. The chancel and the hugely massive piers that support the tower are of the 14th century. The ribbed vaulting under the tower is exceptionally fine. During the 15th century transepts were added, but the cruciform plan has since been obscured by the addition of side aisles to the nave and chapels to the north and south of the chancel. The north transept has been swallowed by these additions, and by the north porch with priest's room above it which were added in the early 16th century. The south transept is so long – longer even than the nave – that it still projects to the south of the building.

The position of pre-Reformation altars is indicated by no fewer than six piscinae; to see the total number the visitor will have to burrow behind the organ.

The handsome central tower, a simply proportioned square structure with battlements, probably dates from the 15th century. The present octagonal spire, of lead on a timber frame, was added in 1721. From the ground can just be made out an inscription with St Peter's keys, the date and the names of the dean, churchwardens, carpenter and plumbers. A substantial hood housing the clock bell projects from the north-west face of the spire.

During the Civil War, when the town, which was for Parliament, was under constant fire from Royalist artillery in CASTLE CORNET, the church was in the firing line and any medieval tracery and glass that may have existed in the windows was destroyed. In 1839 some of the windows were enlarged and the present stone tracery dates from that time. It follows the Flamboyant style which flourished on the Continent in the late Middle Ages when in England the Perpendicular style was in favour. But it must be said that the tracery of the Town Church is crude and heavy when compared with, for instance, the east window of the Hamptonne Chapel in St Lawrence's Church, Jersey.

In June 1944 most of the glass was again destroyed when a bomb exploded in the Old Harbour. Of the larger windows only that at the end of the south transept escaped. The windows are the weak point of an otherwise magnificent church.

During the 18th century the church, being the only large building in the town, was used for meetings, storage and all sorts of secular purposes. The Militia kept their guns in the north aisle of the nave and the parish fire engines were garaged in what is now the Lady Chapel; the remains of the doorway that was made to gain access can still be seen on the outside of the east gable, below the window. The remainder of the church was filled with a clutter of box pews, galleries, memorials projecting from pillars and a three-decker pulpit. All this was swept away in an extensive restoration begun in 1822. Box pews and galleries were removed; the corbels that supported the galleries can still be seen projecting from the walls. Wooden ceilings were replaced by plaster; the moulded ribs of the vaulting bear the stamp of the presiding architect, John Wilson. Many of the memorials also went, although ample survive to provide us with a lively commentary on island history over the centuries.

In 1886 the church underwent its second restoration of the century. A new floor was laid to provide a more efficient barrier between the quick and the dead. The present altar and rails, choir stalls, chancel screen, pulpit, font and pews all date from this Victorian restoration.

Vale Castle (4/6A) The coast road from ST SAMPSON'S HARBOUR to Bordeaux skirts round the foot of a fortified hill, the Vale Castle. There is a car park on the seaward side of the road and a footpath leads up to the castle gate. The climb is well worth it for, besides the interest of the fortifications, there is a panoramic view from the ramparts over Bordeaux Harbour and the islets to the north, the Little Russel with HERM and JETHOU beyond, and the entrance to St Sampson's Harbour.

Very little is known of the early history of the castle, though its main function was probably as a place of refuge from pirate raids for the inhabitants of the CLOS DU VALLE. It is mentioned in an old ballad which describes an invasion in 1372 by a French force under Evan of Wales, who is said to have landed at VAZON BAY, fought his way across the island to CASTLE CORNET, re-embarked his troops, and then laid siege to the Vale Castle. He was finally paid to go away.

The present fortifications date from the 16th to the 18th centuries and consist of an arched gateway and gate tower, a curtain wall round the hill with a ditch and bank below, and five half-round towers. The level area inside the walls formerly contained barracks, and is now an occasional venue for pop festivals.

The castle was excavated in 1980. It was found that any earlier remains on the summit had been removed when the top of the hill was levelled in the 18th century. However, outside the walls some evidence was found that the castle had been a place of refuge in the 15th century, and in the last days of the excavation evidence was found that the site had been an early Iron Age hill fort.

Vale Church (4/5A) The church of St Michel du Valle stands on the north shore of the BRAYE DU VALLE overlooking GRAND HAVRE, the Vale Pond and L'ANCRESSE COMMON. Although the hillock it is built on is only some 30 ft above sea level, the surrounding land is so flat that the church stands out as a landmark from many directions, particularly as you approach the Vale along the Route Militaire. Before the draining of the Braye, the church stood on the shore of the northern island, the CLOS DU VALLE, and people who lived in the part of the parish on the Guernsey mainland, the VINGTAINE DE L'EPINE, either had to wade to church at low tide or use a boat.

The antiquity of the site is demonstrated by a tombstone, found in the churchyard in 1933 and now in the church, which bears a cross, an alpha and omega and an inscription that suggests Celtic work of the 7th or 8th century. This stone, together with the dedication of St Sampson's Church to a Celtic saint, provide evidence, however slender, that there was a Celtic presence in the north of Guernsey in the Dark Ages.

Like most of the medieval churches of the Channel Islands the Vale consists of two parallel naves and chancels, each vaulted in stone. The most notable feature of the church is the Romanesque decoration of the south chancel. This is unlike anything to be seen in the other Guernsey churches, and is taken to be monastic work, for the church was a dependency of the great abbey of Mont St Michel, and a Benedictine priory once existed at the Vale. A single gable of the priory buildings survives beside the road to the south of the church.

The south wall of the south chancel is decorated with blind arcading, with a row of sedilia below. The roof of this part of the church is groined. The chancel arch has at some stage almost collapsed, and in order to support it the south wall has had to be strengthened by two massive external buttresses. Near the chancel arch, above the pulpit, is carved the head of a long-eared dog and one of the pillars between the nave and the aisle bears a lion's head. There are three piscinae; the one in the north chancel, in carved granite, is particularly fine. The east window of the north chancel is unusual in retaining its original stone tracery; it is in the Flamboyant style, which flourished on the Continent in the late Middle Ages and was contemporary with English Perpendicular.

The steeple is at the western end, and was added after the main part of the church had been built. The tower is surmounted by an octagonal, cement-covered spire with four spirelets.

Vale Parish (4/5A) ST SAMPSON'S and the Vale, Guernsey's two northern parishes, are confusingly intertwined, each having a detached part within the other. The two parts of the Vale parish are described separately in the Gazetteer under CLOS DU VALLE and VINGTAINE DE L'EPINE. Before the draining of the BRAYE DU VALLE in 1806 the two parts of the parish were separated at high tide by the sea. Today, though connected by road, the two portions of the parish are still separated by part of St Sampson's.

With an area of 2185 acres the Vale Parish is second in Guernsey only to the CASTEL, and with 8316 inhabitants it was in 1981 second only to ST PETER PORT in population.

Vauxbelets, Les (4/4C) On the side of a quiet valley in ST ANDREW'S PARISH are the massive buildings of Les Vauxbelets College, built early in the present century by a French religious order, the de la Salle Brothers. Besides farming

the land, the Brothers at one time ran an agricultural college, a French secondary school, a local boys' school and a teachers' training college. Today there is a language school and the remaining buildings are used for a variety of purposes.

Les Vauxbelets has become a tourist attraction because of its well-known **Little Chapel**. This minute church, decorated from top to bottom with shells and pieces of broken china (see p. 135), was begun in 1914 and added to over the years by one of the monks, Frère Déodat, whose numerous friends kept him supplied with china. Access to it is by the track to the farm buildings from Bouillon Road. The farm buildings house, among other enterprises, Guernsey Clockmakers.

Vazon Bay (4/3B) The broad sweep of Vazon Bay, a mile as the crow flies from end to end, is one of Guernsey's most popular bathing beaches. The northern, rock-free end is also the venue, at certain weekends, of motorcycle and car racing. When not in use for these purposes the bay is occupied by sea birds and waders. A visitor in the early morning will usually see dunlin, sandpiper, turnstone, oystercatcher, curlew and black-headed gull, as well as the ubiquitous herring gull and a few scavenging crows.

It was here, in May 1372, that a French fleet anchored and a party of mercenaries under Evan of Wales landed on the dunes. Evan fought his way across the island and besieged VALE CASTLE.

The Vazon coast road runs along a shingle bank which separates the bay from its low-lying hinterland, the GRANDE MARE. The small round tower beside the road is one of 15 built round Guernsey in the 1780s to repel another French invasion, which fortunately never came. These small Guernsey towers, often wrongly referred to as Martello towers, are of a design peculiar to the island: vertical-sided, with a diameter of about 20 ft, two storeys of loopholes and a well in the roof which was intended for a gun.

On the headland to the north-east of the bay is Fort Hommet. Built in the early 19th century to guard the entrance to the bay, this is a 'true' Martello tower – broader and more solidly constructed, with steeply battered sides. Both towers are built of the warm red granite of this part of the west coast.

Occasionally, when a storm has scoured away the overlying sand, a bed of peat is exposed at low tide. This contains the stumps of oak trees as well as acorns, hazelnuts and the pollen of oak, hazel

and alder. The peat bed continues under the shingle bank into the Grande Mare, and is the remains of a great forest that extended beyond the present shoreline of the islands, at a time when the sea level was lower and the climate even damper than it is today.

Vingtaine de l'Epine (4/4A) This part of the VALE PARISH lies to the south-west of the BRAYE DU VALLE, and has always been part of the main island of Guernsey. The coastline of the Vingtaine extends – interrupted by St Sampson's – from Port Soif to GRAND HAVRE. It is a rather desolate but attractive coastline of small, rocky bays alternating with grassy headlands. Port Soif is a sandy, horseshoe-shaped cove to the east of Grandes Rocques. The coast road skirts the bay, bordered by sand dunes with marram grass and yellow sea radish. Between Port Soif and the next cove, Portinfer, is an expanse of dune grassland rich in flowers such as Portland spurge, autumn squill and the cream-flowered burnet rose. Although a large car park has been made out of an old quarry, this part of the coast is seldom crowded. Portinfer is a rocky bay with sand exposed at low tide. The next headland has been suburbanized for various sporting purposes. At the rocky Baie des Pequeries the coast road enters a detached portion of ST SAMPSON'S PARISH as it passes Pulias Pond and Les Vardes quarry, before arriving at Grand Havre.

The hinterland of the Vingtaine has suffered more than its fair share of development, with residential and glasshouse areas interspersed with pockets of agricultural land. Before and after the Second World War there was much ribbon development, but this is no longer allowed and more recent housing has been in the form of estates. La Rue des Marais is a narrow, winding lane between La Hougue du Pommier and Les Rouvets. For more than half a mile it is bordered on both sides by ribbon development. Behind the northern ribbon of bungalows and greenhouses is a large area of agricultural land extending as far as the Scout headquarters at Les Mainguys. Les Meilles, once a broad, sandy common inland from Port Soif, has more recently been allocated for housing. It is already partly developed, and more estates are planned.

At the centre of the Vingtaine is the green hillock of Noirmont, surmounted by the remains of a mill. Another green oasis of elevated land is at the northern end of the Rue Sauvage, where La Grande Maison and La Maison de Haut stand among small fields and overgrown quarries.

Torteval church (see p. 169)

Glossary of Channel Islands Terms

Abreuvoir A watering place, mainly for farm animals.

Alien priories Priories belonging to French, usually Norman, religious houses, confiscated by Henry V in 1413.

Bailiff Chief Magistrate in each Bailiwick, and President of the Royal Court and States.

Bailiwick District under the jurisdiction of a Bailiff.

Buttes Butts, archery ground.

Clos An enclosed field; the word is widespread in Jersey, less so in Guernsey.

Colombier A dovecot.

Constable The elected civic head in each parish. In Jersey he has a seat in the States. In Guernsey each parish has two Constables, elected by parishioners. They hold office for two years, first as junior then as senior constable, and run the parish but do not have a seat in the States, where each parish is represented by one member of its Douzaine (parish council).

Côtil A sloping field, usually cultivated.

Courtel/courtil An enclosed field; the word more commonly used in Guernsey.

Creux Cave, hole.

Fief An estate held directly or indirectly from the Crown, on condition of certain services, which varied considerably.

Governor From 1648 each Bailiwick had a separate Governor, who was usually non-resident, and who appointed a resident Lieutenant-Governor. Since 1835 (Guernsey) and 1854 (Jersey) there has been a Lieutenant-Governor only.

Hougue Rocky outcrop, hillock; of Norse origin.

Jurat One of 12 honorary Justices who sit in the Royal Court with the Bailiff.

Landes Land originally left uncultivated.

Lavoir/douet à laver Communal place for washing clothes.

Mare A pond, often coastal, and often now filled in.

Mielle Sand dune.

Perquage In Jersey only; sanctuary path that leads from a parish church to the sea.

Pilotis/pilotins Stone 'mushrooms' upon which a corn or hay rick was supported.

Proscrit Banished exile, many of whom came to the islands in the mid-19th century.

Royal Court The Court of Justice in each Bailiwick.

Seigneur Lord of the Manor (fief). He held rights on the land of his fief but did not necessarily own the freehold. The Manor House was his residence.

States Island Parliament in each Bailiwick. The Channel Islands are not represented in the Westminster Parliament.

Tourelle Stone-built projection from a house containing a stairway.

Vergée Local land measurement; in Jersey 2 and in Guernsey 2½ vergées to an acre.

Vinery A glasshouse holding in Guernsey.

Vingtaine A subdivision of a parish, varying from two to six in each parish.

Vraic Local term for seaweed; it was extensively used in the past as a fertilizer.

Weights Large beach stones used as farm weights with the number of pounds incised on them.

Bibliography

Balleine, G. R. *The Tragedy of Philippe d'Auvergne.* Phillimore 1973

—*All for the King.* Société Jersiaise 1976 (*See also* Syvret, M., below)

Barber, A. *Walks with a Car in Guernsey.* Bailiwick Publications 1984

—*Walks with a Meal in Guernsey.* Bailiwick Publications 1986

Binney, M. *Victorian Jersey.* Save Britain's Heritage 1985

Bois, F. de L. *Walks for Motorists: Jersey.* Frederick Warne 1979

—*The Parish Church of St Saviour.* Phillimore 1976

Brett, C. E. B. *The Buildings of the Town and Parish of St Peter Port.* Ulster Architectural Heritage Society (for National Trust for Guernsey) 1975

—*Buildings in the Island of Alderney.* Ulster Architectural Heritage Society (for the Alderney Society) 1976

—*The Buildings of the Town and Parish of St Helier.* Ulster Architectural Heritage Society (for National Trust for Jersey) 1977

Chartier, H., and J. J. Vaupres *Recollections of Jersey en Cartes Postales.* Publications du Pélican 1982

Cottrill, D. *Victoria College, Jersey, 1957-1972.* Phillimore 1977

Coysh, V. *Alderney.* David and Charles 1974

—*The Channel Islands: A New Study.* David and Charles 1977

Cruickshank, C. *The German Occupation of the Channel Islands.* Imperial War Museum 1975

Davies, W. *Fort Regent.* Published privately 1977

Garis, M. de *Dictiounnaire Angllais-Guernesiais.* Phillimore 1982

Hawkes, K. *Sark.* David and Charles 1977

Jean, J. *Jersey Sailing Ships.* Phillimore 1982

Jee, N. *Guernsey's Natural History.* Guernsey Press 1972

—*Guernsey Cow.* Elek 1977

—*Landscape of the Channel Islands.* Phillimore 1982

Johnston, D. E. *The Channel Islands: An Archaeological Guide.* Phillimore 1980

L'Amy, J. H. *Jersey Folklore.* La Haule Books 1986

Le Feuvre, G. *George d'la Forge, Jèrri Jadis.* Don Balleine Trust 1973

—*Histouaithes et Gens d'Jèrri.* Don Balleine Trust 1976

Le Maistre, F. *Le Dictionnaire Jersiais-Français.* Don Balleine Trust 1976

Lemprière, R. *Portrait of the Channel Islands.* Robert Hale 1970

—*History of the Channel Islands.* Robert Hale 1974

—*Customs, Ceremonies and Traditions of the Channel Islands.* Robert Hale 1976

—*Buildings and Memorials of the Chanmnel Islands.* Robert Hale 1980

Le Scelleur, K. *Channel Islands' Railway Steamers.* Patrick Stephens 1985

Le Sueur, F. *A Natural History of Jersey.* Phillimore 1976

—*Flora of Jersey.* Société Jersiaise 1985

McCammon, A. *The Coinage of the Channel Islands.* Spink & Son 1984

McCormack, J. The Guernsey House. Phillimore 1980

Marett, Sir R. *The Maretts of La Haule.* Published privately 1982

Marr, L. J. *A History of the Bailiwick of Guernsey.* Phillimore 1982

—*Guernsey People.* Phillimore 1984

—*Bailiwick Bastions: The Fortifications of the Bailiwick of Guernsey.* Guernsey Press 1985

Mayne, R. *Mailships of the Channel Islands.* Picton 1971

—*The Battle of Jersey.* Phillimore 1981

—*Channel Islands Silver.* Phillimore 1985

Mayne, R., and J. Stevens *Jersey Through the Lens.* Phillimore 1975

Pocock, R. H. S. *The Memoirs of Lord Coutanche.* Phillimore 1975

Robinson, G. W. S. *Guernsey.* David and Charles 1977

Sinel, L. *Jersey Through the Centuries: A Chronology.* La Haule Books 1984

—*The German Occupation of Jersey.* La Haule Books 1984

Skelley, B., and J. Clark *Jersey Remembered.* La Haule Books 1985

Stevens, C., J. Arthur and J. Stevens *Jersey Place Names: A Corpus of Jersey Toponomy.* Société Jersiaise (in preparation)

Stevens, J. *Old Jersey Houses:* Vol. I 1965, Phillimore 1980; Vol. II Phillimore 1977

—*Victorian Voices.* Société Jersiaise 1969

—*A Short History of Jersey.* Société Jersiaise 1972

—*Le Moulin de Quétivel.* National Trust for Jersey (n.d.)

—*Jersey in Granite.* Royal Trust Company of Canada 1977

Stevens, J., and J. Arthur *St Mary's Church, Jersey* (n.d.)

—*Longueville Manor.* Published privately 1981

Stevens, P. *Victor Hugo in Jersey.* Phillimore 1985

Syvret, M., and J. Stevens *Balleine's History of Jersey,* revised and enlarged edition. Phillimore 1985

Note: La Société Guernesiaise: *Annual Report and Transactions* (from 1888); back numbers and offprints from the Candie Museum. La Société Jersiaise: Annual Bulletin (from 1875); back numbers and offprints from The Jersey Museum.

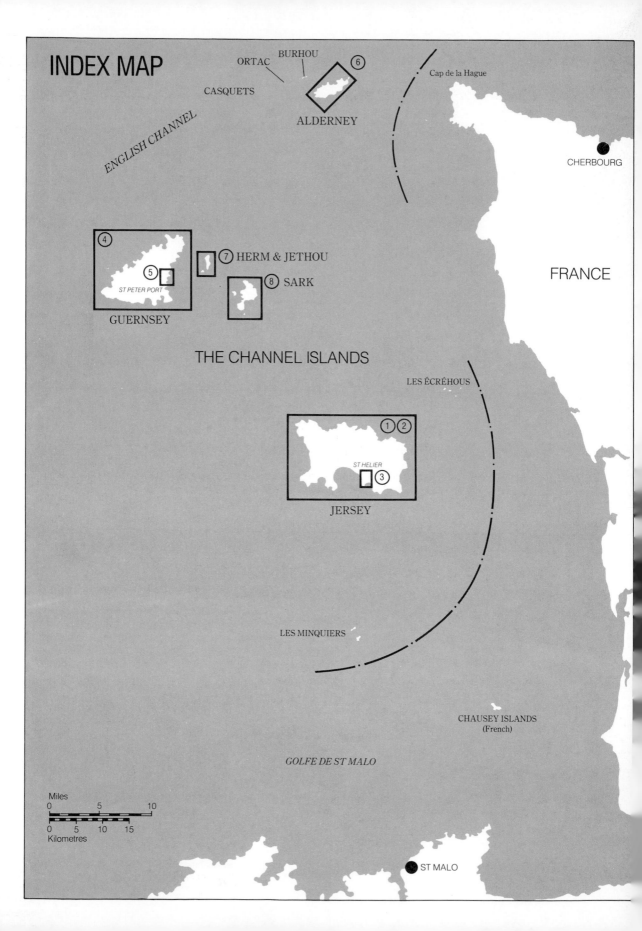

INDEX MAP

ORTAC
BURHOU
CASQUETS
⑥
CHERBOURG
Cap de la Hague
ALDERNEY
ENGLISH CHANNEL
FRANCE

④
⑦ HERM & JETHOU
⑤
ST PETER PORT
⑧ SARK
GUERNSEY

THE CHANNEL ISLANDS

LES ÉCRÉHOUS

① ②
ST HELIER
③
JERSEY

LES MINQUIERS

CHAUSEY ISLANDS
(French)

GOLFE DE ST MALO

Miles
0   5   10

0   5   10   15
Kilometres

ST MALO

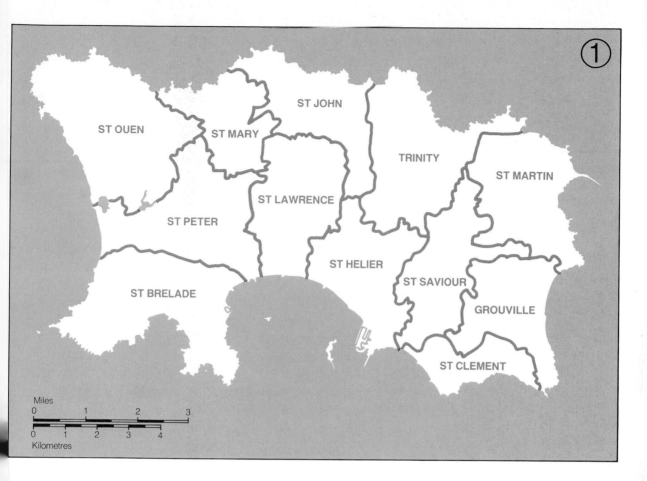

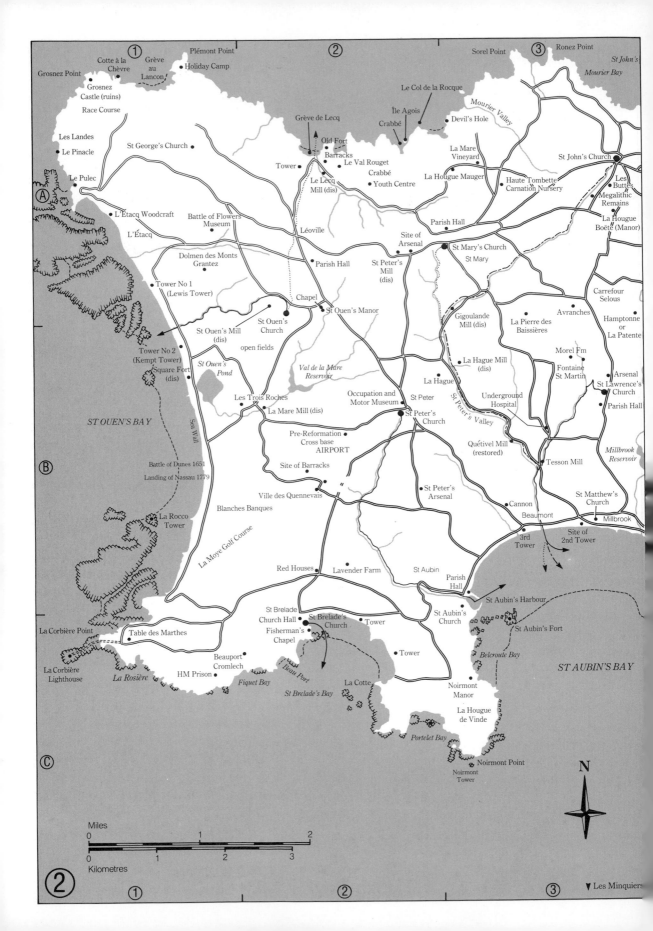

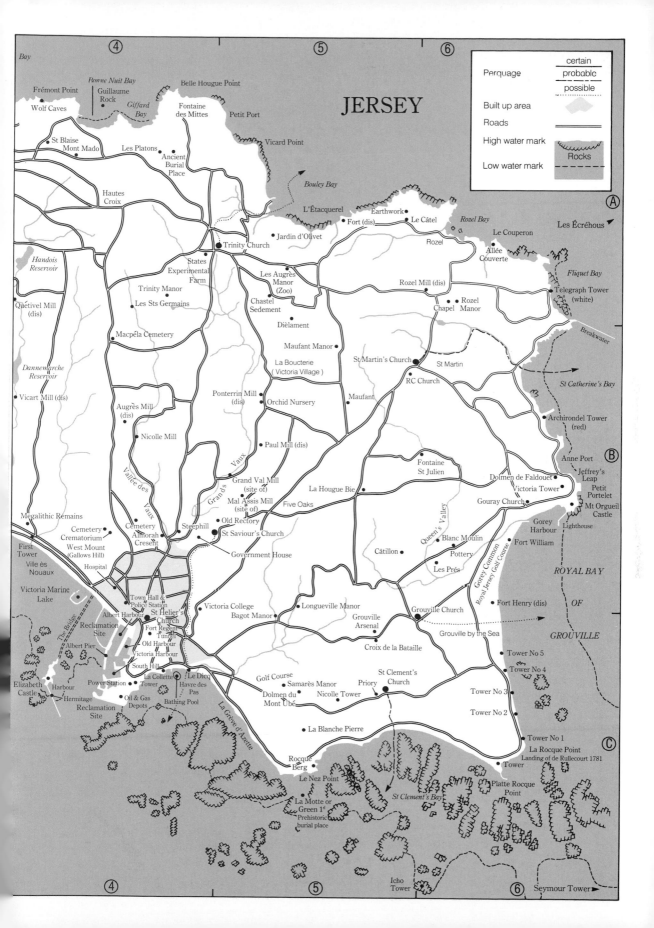

The States Offices, St Helier, Jersey

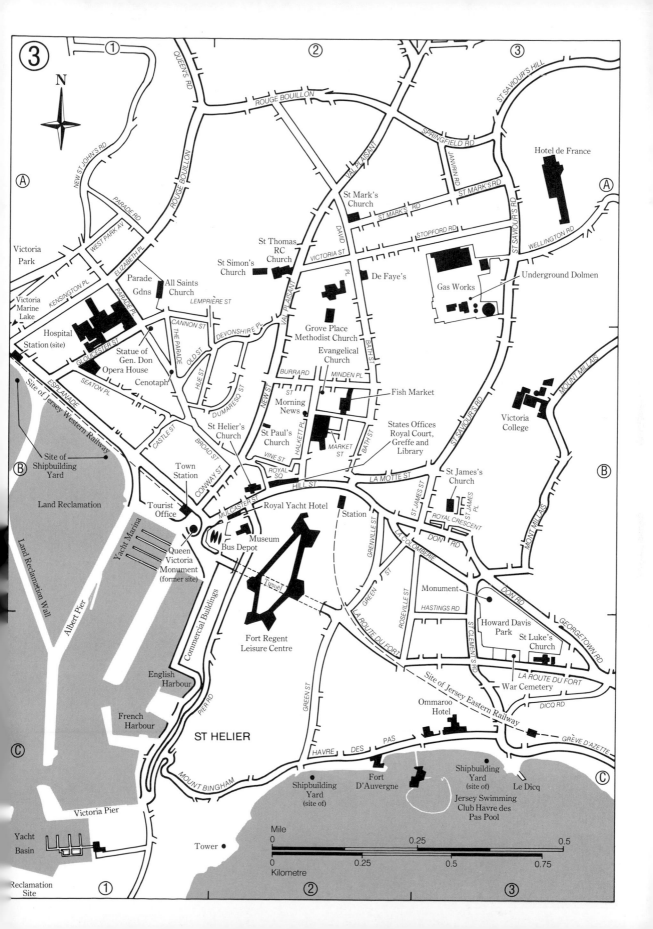

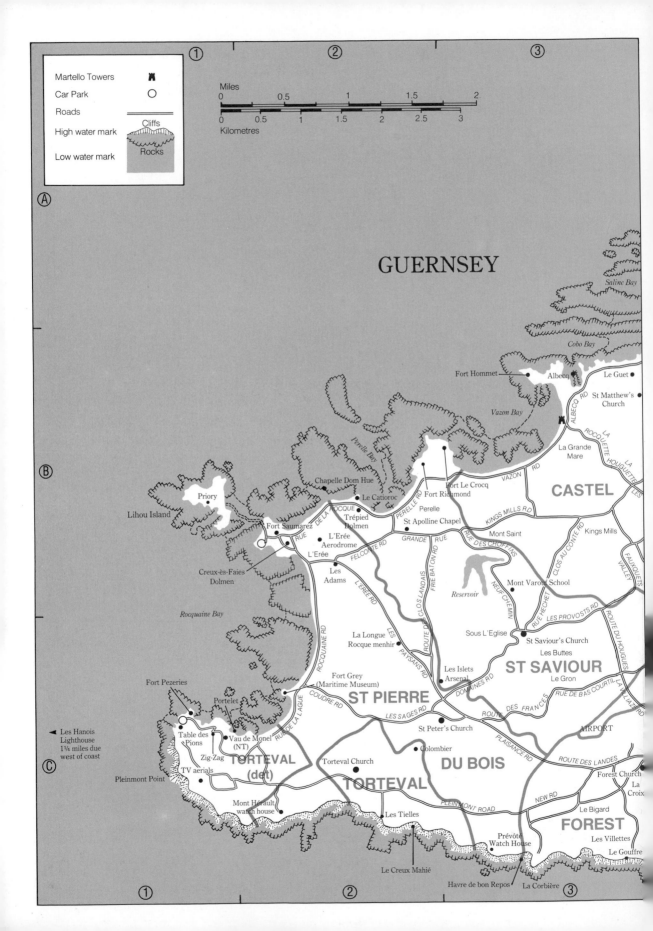

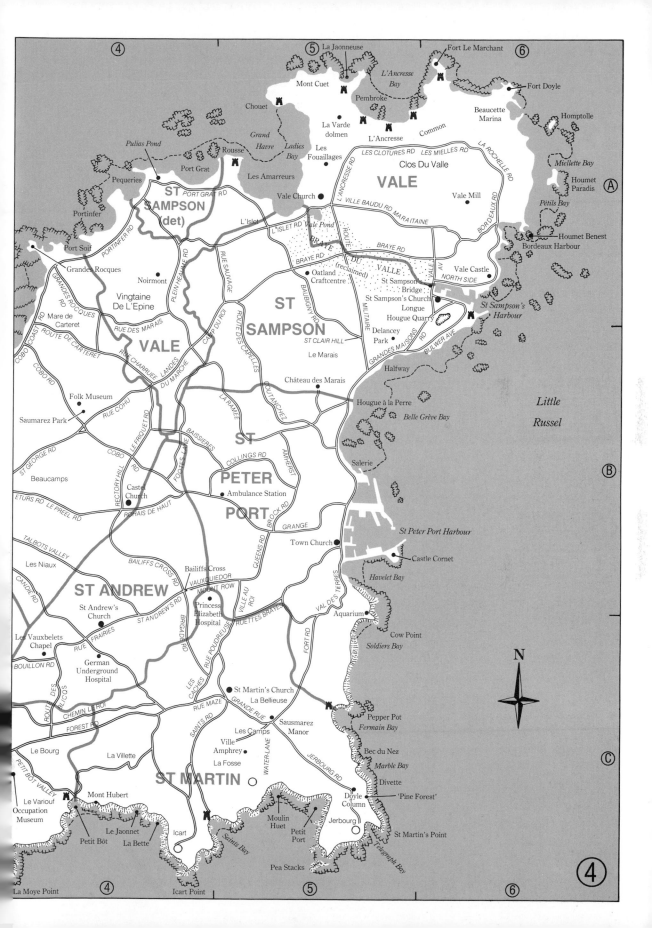

Ironwork and flowers, Ann's Place, St Peter Port, Guernsey

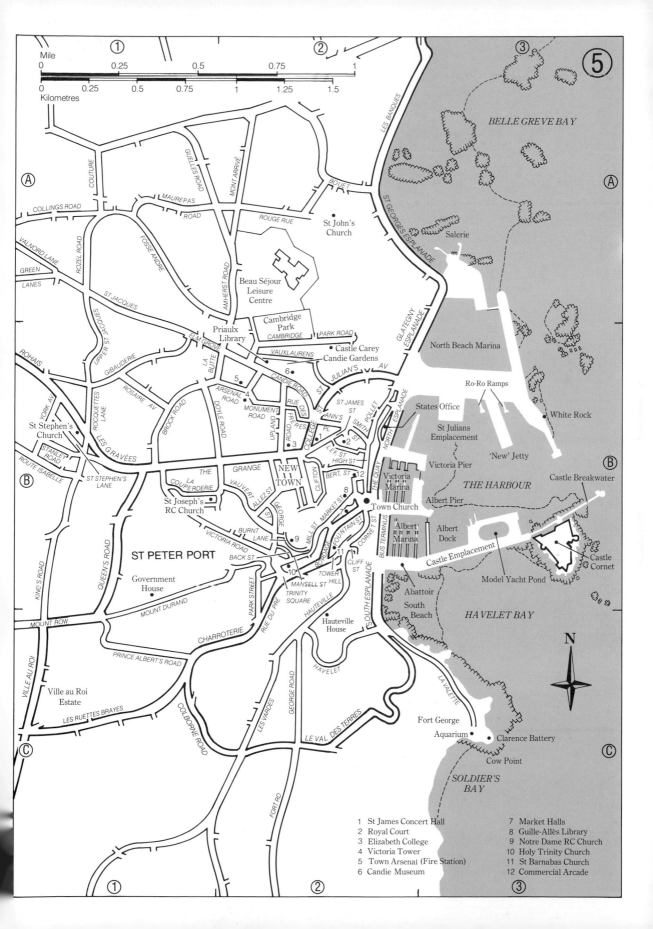

Mile
0   0.25   0.5   0.75   1

Kilometres
0   0.25   0.5   0.75   1   1.25   1.5

① ② ③ ⑤

BELLE GREVE BAY

COLLINGS ROAD
VALNORD LANE
GREEN LANES
COUTURE
MAUREPAS ROAD
GUELLES ROAD
MONT ARRIVÉ
ROUGE RUE
BOUET
LES BANQUES
ST GEORGES ESPLANADE

St John's Church

Salerie

ROZEL ROAD
FOSSE ANDRE
AMHERST ROAD

Beau Séjour Leisure Centre

Cambridge Park
CAMBRIDGE
PARK ROAD

ST-JACQUES
UPPER ST JACQUES
GIBAUDERIE
Priaulx Library
ELM GROVE
LA BUTTE

GLATEGNY ESPLANADE

North Beach Marina

VAUXLAURENS
Castle Carey
Candie Gardens

ROHAIS
ROSAIRE AV
ROQUETTES LANE
LES GRAVÉES
BROCK ROAD
DOYLE ROAD
ARSENAL ROAD
MONUMENT ROAD
UPLAND
CANDIE ROAD
RUE DES FRÈRES
COLLEGE ST
JULIAN'S AV

Ro-Ro Ramps

States Office
St Julians Emplacement

York AV
St Stephen's Church
STANLEY ROAD
ROUTE ISABELLE
ST STEPHEN'S LANE

5
4
3
6
ANN'S PL
ST JAMES ST
SMITH ST
POLLET
LEE ST
HIGH ST
BERT. ST.
THE QUAY
NORTH ESPLANADE

Victoria Pier
'New' Jetty
White Rock

2

THE HARBOUR

Castle Breakwater

Victoria Marina

THE HARBOUR

Albert Pier

THE
GRANGE
LA COUPERDERIE
VAUVERT
ALLEZ ST
GEORGE
NEW TOWN
CLIFTON

St Joseph's RC Church

12
8
Town Church

Albert Marina
Albert Dock

Castle Emplacement

Castle Cornet

Model Yacht Pond

ST PETER PORT

Government House

QUEEN'S ROAD
KING'S ROAD
MOUNT ROW
MOUNT DURAND
VICTORIA ROAD
BURNT LANE
BACK ST
MILL ST
MARKET ST
BORDAGE
FOUNTAIN ST
CORNET ST
BUS TERMINUS

9
11
10
TOWER HILL
MANSELL ST
TRINITY SQUARE
PARK STREET
RUE DU PRÉ
HAUTEVILLE
CLIFF ST
SOUTH ESPLANADE

Hauteville House

Abattoir
South Beach

HAVELET BAY

CHARROTERIE
PRINCE ALBERT'S ROAD

Ville au Roi Estate

VILLE AU ROI
LES RUETTES BRAYES
COLBORNE ROAD
LES VARDES
GEORGE ROAD
HAVELET
LE VAL DES TERRES
LA VALETTE

Fort George
Aquarium
Clarence Battery

Cow Point

SOLDIER'S BAY

FORT RD

N

1 St James Concert Hall
2 Royal Court
3 Elizabeth College
4 Victoria Tower
5 Town Arsenal (Fire Station)
6 Candie Museum
7 Market Halls
8 Guille-Allès Library
9 Notre Dame RC Church
10 Holy Trinity Church
11 St Barnabas Church
12 Commercial Arcade

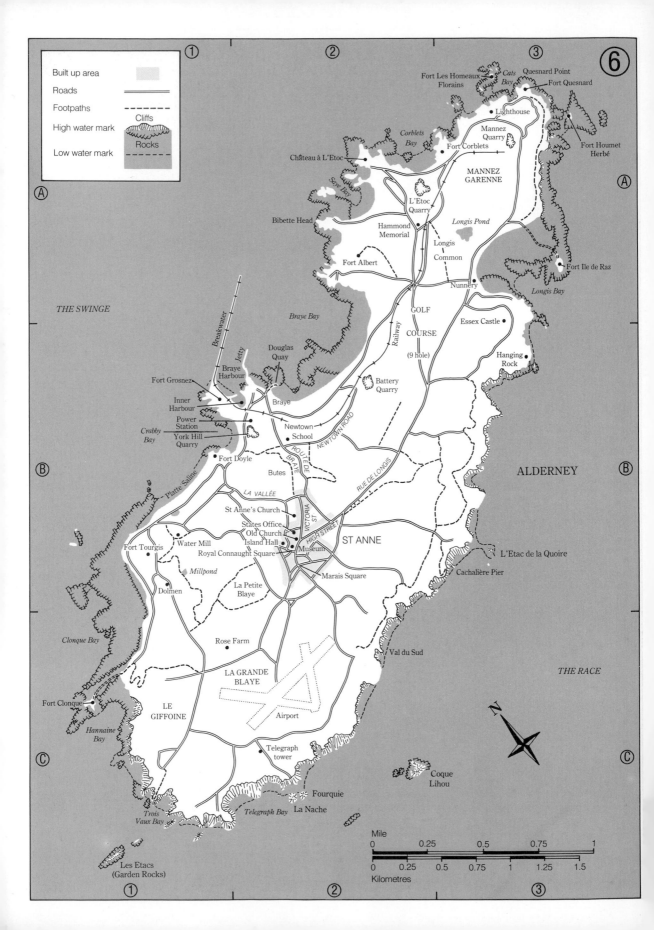

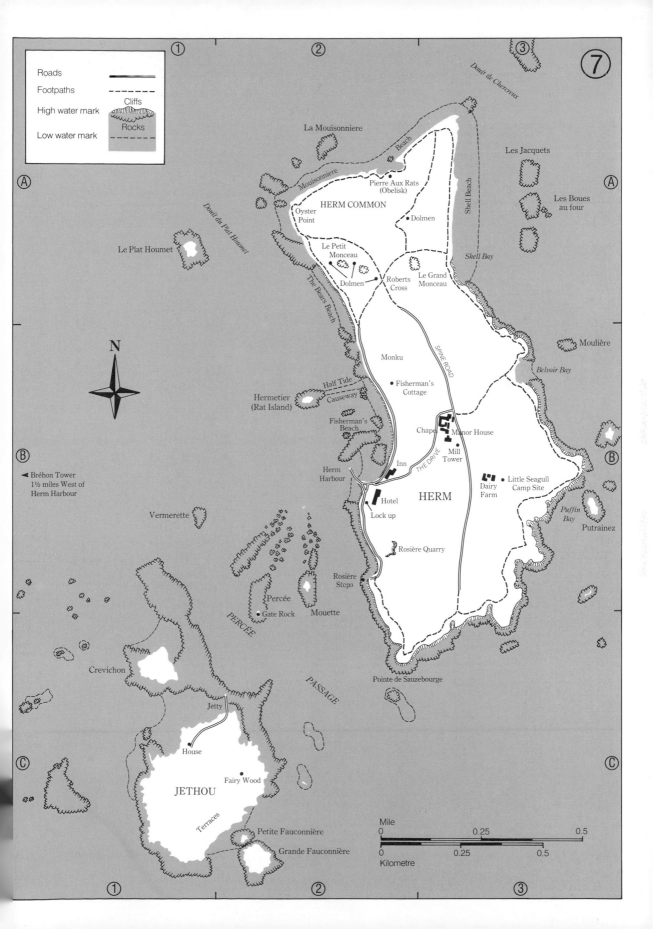

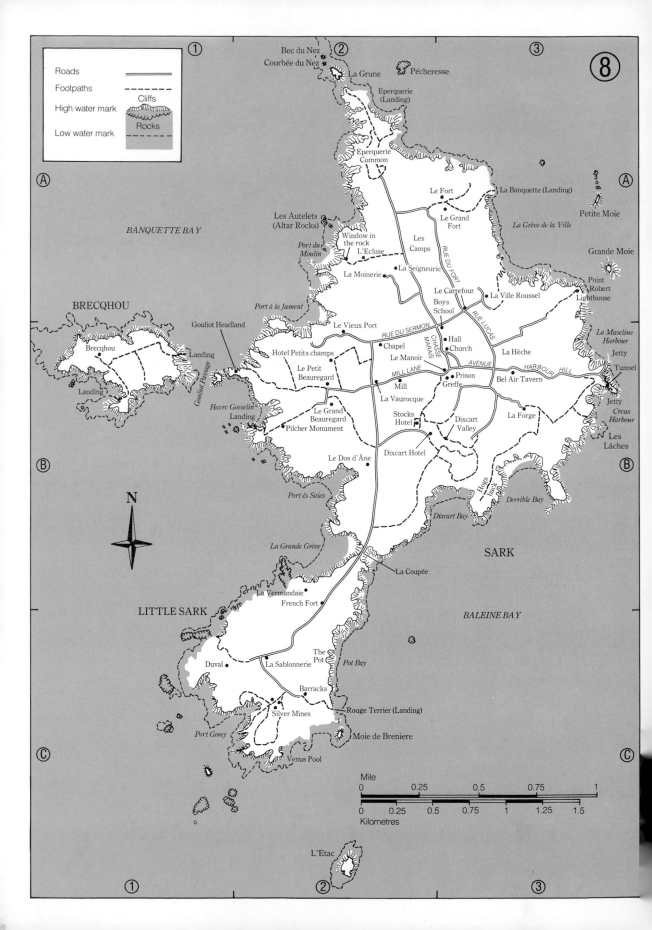

Index

Numbers in *italics* refer to illustrations